HIGHEST PRAISE FOR JOVE HOMESPUN ROMANCES:

"In all of the Homespuns I've read and reviewed I've been very taken with the loving rendering of colorful small-town people doing small-town things and bringing 5 STAR and GOLD 5 STAR rankings to the readers. This series should be selling off the bookshelves within hours! Never have I given a series an overall review, but I feel this one, thus far, deserves it! Continue the excellent choices in authors and editors! It's working for this reviewer!"

—*Heartland Critiques*

We at Jove Books are thrilled by the enthusiastic critical acclaim that the Homespun Romances are receiving. We would like to thank you, the readers and fans of this wonderful series, for making it the success that it is. It is our pleasure to bring you the highest quality of romance writing in these breathtaking tales of love and family in the heartland of America.

And now, sit back and enjoy this delightful new Homespun Romance . . .

HEART'S FOLLY
by Mary Lou Rich

"*Heart's Folly* is another fine example of the spirited heroines and lovable heroes Ms. Rich does so well. Hats off to this talented writer."

—Sue Rich, author of *Aim for the Heart*

HEART'S FOLLY

MARY LOU RICH

JOVE BOOKS, NEW YORK

HEART'S FOLLY

A Jove Book / published by arrangement with
the author

PRINTING HISTORY
Jove edition / May 1996

The Putnam Berkley World Wide Web site address is
http://www.berkley.com

ISBN: 0-515-11846-X

A JOVE BOOK®
Jove Books are published by The Berkley Publishing Group,
200 Madison Avenue, New York, New York 10016.
JOVE and the "J" design are trademarks
belonging to Jove Publications, Inc.

PRINTED IN THE UNITED STATES OF AMERICA

10 9 8 7 6 5 4 3 2 1

This book is dedicated to my mother, Eunice,
and my mother-in-law, Agnes,
both of whom know full well the joys—
and the trials—of raising children.

And, as always,
to Raymond and Johnny.

Love is like the measles—all the worse when it comes late in life.

—DOUGLAS WILLIAM JERROLD

❦ ONE ❧

The wind moaned around the eaves of the weather-beaten building, and the rain from the blustery spring storm continued to turn Main Street into a smelly sea of knee-deep manure and mud.

The widow McFearson placed the OPEN sign in the window of her millinery shop, then wondered why she bothered. She hadn't sold a hat in two months, and even if the sun were shining brightly it was unlikely that any patrons would arrive at her door. She had Jake Turnbull to thank for that.

She peered through the rain-dotted panes and shot a look of intense dislike toward the saloon and brothel across the street. *They* weren't suffering from a lack of patrons. In spite of the early hour—if she could judge from the raucous noise and music—they seemed to be busier than ever.

You'd think the town would have shown *her* a little bit of loyalty since she'd lived in Sweetheart all her life. You'd think they would have sided with one of their own. But, no. *They'd* backed that brash, loudmouthed Texan. She angrily tucked a stray lock of hair behind her ear, then whirled away from the window and strode past the curtain separating her shop from her small living quarters.

1

When she entered the room, her calico cat jumped from the needlepoint cushion of the rocking chair and trotted ahead of her to the large, nickel-plated cookstove.

"Hungry, Bridget, old puss?" Her own stomach growling, Mattie took two golden-crusted loaves of bread from the oven and set them on her kitchen table to cool. She sniffed the delicious aroma and tried not to think of the weevils she'd had to pick from the flour before she'd made them. Reflecting on her desperately strained finances, she lifted the lid from a cast-iron kettle and added a small piece of salt pork to the pot of beans that simmered on the rear of the stove.

The cat let out a plaintive meow.

Mattie knelt, extending the sliver of meat she'd saved, only to see Bridget sniff the tidbit and then stalk haughtily away.

"Picky, old girl? By next week, you'll be grateful for salt pork, even if it is a bit rancid. I'm afraid we both will be," she added softly, getting to her feet.

Ordinarily they wouldn't have had this much to eat, but she'd hoped a slight celebration might raise her spirits. Not that she had anything to celebrate. Today she was twenty-nine years old and had nothing to show for it except a dingy room behind a business that couldn't make enough money to even pay the rent.

Adding to her melancholy was the memory that today would also have been her tenth wedding anniversary, if a drunken cowboy's stray bullet had not made her a widow before she'd known what it was to be a wife. She'd buried her young husband and never married again.

Some folks said she'd been afraid to tempt fate a second time. Others said she was being too persnickety in her choice of a mate.

Actually, neither was true. The fact was, nobody else had ever asked her.

Most men found her too outspoken and stubborn for their tastes, preferring instead a simpering, obedient type of female. But as far as Mattie was concerned they could either accept her as she was or forget it, as she had no intention of pretending to be something she wasn't. She thought her upbringing had a lot to do with her attitude. She'd been eight when her mother died, and although her father had done the best he could, he hadn't found it easy to raise a girl child in a rough mining camp. Since he had to be in the diggings a lot, Angus McFearson had taught his daughter to be wary. He'd also taught her how to shoot.

Shaking his finger to emphasize his words, he'd lectured her in his Scottish brogue. "Always trust your instincts, lassie. And never trust a man that won't look you in the eye."

Mattie had taken her father's words for the gospel truth, and for sure they'd served her well after a half-broken horse had trampled him to death. Her forthright manner had earned her respect from honest men, and a grudging awareness of her ability to see through those who had less than honorable intentions.

To this day, she had met very few men—honest or otherwise—who could meet her steady gaze without becoming so uneasy they soon made an excuse to leave her presence.

Outside of her dearly departed husband, the only exception to that rule had been Jake Turnbull.

Mattie considered that more of an irritation than anything to be said in his favor. The fact that Jake Turnbull could meet her eye without backing away didn't mean he was trustworthy—only so pigheaded and ornery that he'd face down the devil himself rather than admit he was wrong.

And he had been wrong. He claimed he was bringing prosperity to the town by attracting cattle drovers and miners from the scattered diggings—that had been his excuse when he'd installed a building full of fallen women on Main Street. He hadn't put the brothel somewhere out of the way, somewhere inconspicuous. No. He had the audacity to put it smack dab in the middle of town—and directly across from her shop.

Since there were other sites available, she knew Jake had picked that particular spot out of pure spite. It was his way of getting even for her leading the town's womenfolk against him.

Mattie considered her temperance rally successful, in spite of the fact that her actions had landed her in jail. But her ladies' protests hadn't counted for much. In Colorado women had not yet been granted the right to vote as they had in Wyoming—a matter Mattie intended to rectify as soon as she could summon enough support. And because they didn't frequent either the bordello or the saloon, the wishes of the female population of the town had been ignored.

After the march, the men of the town considered Mattie an undesirable influence, a troublemaker, and had forbidden the women under their domination from entering her establishment. As a result her millinery business, for all intents and purposes, had ceased to exist. And now that her savings were gone, what before had been a skimpy existence at best had now become a fight for survival. One she was rapidly losing.

Mattie smoothed her apron over her middle and made herself a cup of weak tea. She had just raised the cup to her lips when her shop bell tinkled. She wasn't prone to having visitors. It must be someone wanting a hat. Her hopes soaring, she set down her cup. She hurried into the main room, only to stop abruptly.

Bob Jamison, the teller from the Rocky Mountain Bank, stood just inside her doorway.

Damnation! Drawing in a breath, she forced a smile. "Hello, Mr. Jamison."

"Sorry, Miss Mattie." Noticing the water he had dripped on her floor, the young man gave her a shamefaced look. "Mr. Satterfield asked me to deliver this." He held out a soggy white envelope.

"Another demand for the rent, I suppose." She shoved

the paper into her apron pocket. "Would you care for some t—"

He bolted from the shop before she could finish.

"Well, for goodness' sake." Staring after him, Mattie frowned, then, in weary resignation, took the sodden letter from her pocket and opened it. "An eviction notice!"

What was the matter with Satterfield? He knew she would pay. Eventually. Shaken, she folded the order and put it back in her pocket. "Things have to get better soon." But a sinking feeling in her middle told her things didn't have to get better and probably wouldn't.

"Two weeks?" She envisioned herself and Bridget being put out on the street, forced to live on the charity of others. The picture wasn't a pretty one.

There has to be something I can do, Mattie thought as she donned her serviceable blue wool cloak, then anchored her felt hat into place.

Determined to make the bank president, Ben Satterfield, change his mind, she stuck the CLOSED sign in her window and went out into the pouring rain.

Two hours later, seated in the lobby of the bank, Mattie knew that no matter how long she waited, Satterfield intended to wait even longer. She glared at the closed door. *Enough of this!* She rose and crossed the floor.

"Mrs. McFearson, you can't go in there," Bob Jamison called out, hurrying to head her off.

"We'll just see if I can't," she muttered under her breath. She turned the knob. "Mr. Satterfield," she began, only to find the room empty. She whirled toward the teller. "Where is he?"

Bob looked stunned. "I don't know. He was in there earlier. I told him you were here."

"Well, he isn't here now." She stepped inside the banker's office. One door—and one window. The coward had apparently crawled out the window rather than face her. "Will he be back?"

"Well—he does have to close the bank."

"Then I'll wait." She waved a warning finger under Bob's nose. "This time, *don't* tell him I'm here."

Bob swallowed, his bobbing Adam's apple betraying his indecision. "But what will I say?"

"Don't say anything." Before he could protest, Mattie pushed him out and closed the office door. Leaning against the wood, she scanned the wildlife paintings on the paneled oak walls, the colorful pattern on the carpeted floor, the welcome heat that enveloped her sodden clothing. She stripped off her hat and cloak and hung them on the clothes tree to dry. She noted the hour on the elegant banjo wall clock. It was a long time until closing.

After pouring herself a cup of coffee from the pot she'd discovered on top of a small, ornate heating stove, she settled into the banker's own plush leather chair rather than the straight-backed wooden one that was obviously meant to intimidate visitors. Then, her feet propped on a footstool she'd found hidden beneath the desk, she sipped the strong brew and planned her strategy.

"Miss Mattie."

"Hmm?" Curled up in the chair, Mattie yawned and opened her eyes to see Bob Jamison standing before her. Embarrassed to be caught in such a position, she immediately straightened and looked him in the eye. "Is he here?"

"Uh—no. Not exactly." The young man gave her a sickly grin. "He was—then he left."

"You told him I was here?"

Bob shook his head. "No, ma'am. I didn't say a word. Mr. Satterfield opened the office door and saw you asleep."

"He didn't try to wake me?"

"No. He just shut the door. Then he closed the bank and hightailed it for home. He told me to wake you after he was gone."

"Damnation!" Taking note of the teller's startled look, Mattie let out an exasperated sigh. "I don't suppose you expect him back before tomorrow."

"Tomorrow's Sunday. The bank's closed. Mr. Satterfield won't be back until Monday."

"Monday!" Now that he knew she had gone so far as to hide in his office to waylay him, she doubted the man would give her the opportunity to do it a second time. After everything she'd planned to say to him, she ruined her chances by falling asleep. That, too, she blamed on Jake Turnbull. If it wasn't for him and his noisy patrons, she wouldn't have had so many sleepless nights.

Outside on the boardwalk, she noticed that while the rain had slackened, it still showed no sign of stopping. Her mood as gloomy as the murky twilight sky overhead, Mattie picked her way down the slippery, mud-caked sidewalk and wondered what she would do about the rain when she had no roof over her head.

"Fire!" someone shouted. A man raced past her, yelling to another. "I think it's the Miner's Delight."

"Good," she muttered. "I hope it burns to the ground." But in spite of her anger, she prayed no one was hurt.

The large bell beside the mercantile clanged out the alarm. Men with sacks, mops, and more buckets gathered on Main Street, then ran in the direction of the brothel.

She hurried after them, then came to a skidding halt. They weren't in front of the whorehouse, they were . . . "No! It can't be!" She broke into a run.

A thick cloud of smoke belched from her broken front window. A large, fair-haired man in a yellow slicker kicked at the front door. She heard the hinges groan and the wood split, then the man charged inside. Other men with pails of water followed. As soon as one bucket was emptied, it was passed to the fire brigade outside and a full one was handed forward to take its place.

A few minutes later, one by one, the men came back outside.

The large man was the last to exit. Emerging from the billowing smoke, choking and waving one hand in front of him, he carried a bailed kettle that he deposited on the sidewalk. "Ain't no fire, boys. It's just Mattie, cooking beans," he bellowed in a voice she couldn't fail to recognize.

Jake Turnbull! She lifted her skirts and hurried toward the crowd of gaping onlookers.

"Cooking beans?" a man said. "That blamed woman could have burned down the whole town."

"Old Satterfield's gonna have a fit when he sees the inside of his building," another added.

My shop! Mattie fought tears. Everything she owned was probably scorched and ruined.

"If she stayed home like a decent woman ought to, 'stead of sticking her nose into everybody else's business, nothing like this would have happened," Hiram Gibbons, the mercantile owner, chimed in.

A murmured assent rose from the men.

Elbowing her way through the throng, she peered inside the building.

"There she is," cried a man who spotted her.

"She's a menace, and it's time we did something about it," shouted another.

Noting the angry tone of their voices, Mattie took a hesitant step backward. Her eyes widened. She'd seen lynch mobs in a better mood than this.

Jake Turnbull moved between her and the men and held up a staying hand. "No harm done, gentlemen." His soot-blackened face split in a grin. "At least nothing a little soap and a lot of water won't take care of. Now y'all just go on back to the saloon and let the little lady examine the damage," he drawled, daring to wink at her.

Mattie drew herself up and shot him a look that would have shattered stone. He didn't even notice.

"I want to thank you boys," he went on. "We'll all sleep easier in our beds knowing such fine firefighters are on the job."

"Fine firefighters my foot," she muttered, thinking of her broken window.

While the men milled restlessly, they showed no sign of leaving. She saw Jake frown, then glance from her to the crowd.

"By the way," he said, "tell Charlie I said drinks are on the house."

A shout rose from the firefighters and they hurried across the muddy street and pushed through the swinging doors of the saloon.

When the last of them disappeared inside, Mattie released the breath she wasn't aware she'd been holding. She had no doubt that if anyone had shown up with the tar, somebody else would have gleefully supplied the feathers.

"You ought to be more careful, Mattie," Jake said in a stern voice.

"There wasn't any fire," she said through gritted teeth. "It was only a pot of beans. If you had minded your own business I wouldn't have this mess."

"If you stayed home and tended to yours, your cat wouldn't have been yowling loud enough to wake the dead. If it wasn't for that blamed cat, the whole town might have gone up in flames."

"Is Bridget all right?"

"Bridget?"

"My cat. You said something about my cat."

Jake stared down at her. "Don't worry, the varmint's just fine." He hooked a finger toward the saloon. "It showed up at the kitchen door, yammering for something to eat." His blue eyes twinkling, he gave her a crooked grin. "Considering the critter's options, I can't say that I blame it." He pointed at the still smoking pot. "Looks like your supper's ruined. The rest of the place is a sight."

Hoping he was making it sound worse than it was, Mattie edged around him and entered her shop.

Ribbons of all colors that had once waved in gay banners from spools near the ceiling now hung in blackened strings like soggy spiderwebs. Airy bolts of tulle had been dragged from the shelves and now lay in sodden heaps of gray and black, mixed with the mud from the men's boots as they had tramped across the floor. Her beautiful hats. All were ruined!

She clamped a hand over her mouth to muffle her cry of dismay. Had they been trying to put out the fire—or destroy everything she owned? Whichever, they had accomplished their purpose. Overwhelmed by the damage, she swayed on her feet, blinking back tears.

Jake put a steadying hand around her waist.

In a burst of anger, she shoved it away.

Wisps of smoke still hung in air thick with the stench of burned beans, wet wood, and fabric. Waving her hand in front of her stinging eyes, she made her way into the kitchen. Most of her furniture had been reduced to kindling. The only thing they hadn't destroyed was the iron stove.

Expecting the worse, she opened the door that led to her bedroom. At least the furnishings were still intact, but she noted that while it had fared better than the other rooms, it, too, was a smoke-blackened mess.

Jake gripped her shoulders and turned her to face him. "Look, you can't stay here. I've got a perfectly good room for you across the street. It has a comfortable bed, and we've got plenty to eat. Then tomorrow I'll get somebody to help you clean this up."

"What?" Mattie gasped. *He expected her to stay across the street? At the whorehouse*? "Why, you no-account scalawag!" Spying her skillet on the floor, she retrieved it. Waving it in front of her, she stalked toward him. "You get out of here." Her voice shook with rage.

"All right," Jake said, retreating. "But you're acting like a fool. The offer still stands if you change your mind."

Mattie let the skillet fly.

Cursing, he dodged and bolted for the door.

"And don't come back!" she shouted, following him onto the sidewalk and into the rain.

When he reached his side of the street, Jake cupped his hands to make himself heard over the rowdy merrymakers and tinkling piano music. "You're crazy! You know that, Mattie McFearson. Crazy!" Mumbling something else she couldn't hear, he shoved through the door and entered the saloon.

The heavy spring mist had become a winter night's rain, cold, black, and dismal. Left alone in the darkness, Mattie shivered and glanced up the street where occasional beams of yellowish light streamed from the residing shopkeepers' windows. She imagined them all, warm and dry, their stomachs full, as they made ready for bed.

Her own stomach cramped with hunger, the little food she had was sitting in a burned kettle in the middle of the sidewalk. She hadn't seen her freshly baked loaves of bread, but knew even if she did find them, they would be inedible.

A strong gust of wind sent her hurrying back inside, but when she attempted to close the door to shut out the gale, it fell off the hinges and toppled to rest on the weather-bleached planks of the sidewalk beside the blackened pot. Mattie stared at it, then around her at the rest of the shop. "Some celebration," she murmured, thinking of her earlier intention. A tear slipped down her cheek and she turned to go back inside.

A burst of laughter erupted from the Miner's Delight. In the darkness, the scores of lights and the gleaming gold and scarlet trim decorating the house gave the white building the cheerful appearance of a large Christmas tree.

Mattie thought of Jake's promise of food and a warm bed and for the barest moment she was tempted to take him up on his offer. She immediately rejected the notion. Maybe she was crazy, as Jake claimed, but however desperate her circumstances she was far too sensible to ever allow herself to be found in a house of ill repute.

But as she groped her way through the shop's murky darkness she couldn't help but indulge in the fantasy.

Did the women sleep in feather beds topped with silk

sheets? Did they wear sheer night rails, feather-decorated wrappers—or nothing at all?

Mattie imagined herself reclining in some exotic pose and waving a feathered fan as she gave the come-hither look to some cowboy. The image was so ridiculous, she chuckled.

Running her hand down her own ample curves, she remembered the warmth of Jake's hand on her waist and wondered what it would be like to have a man make love to her. Her own dear Jaime had been struck down before he'd had the chance. How would it feel to be married, protected, loved by one man? She tried to envision it, but somehow she didn't fit in that picture either.

Standing in the kitchen, she felt the silence and noticed the rain had stopped. A pale watery moon made faint veins of light against the blackness of her soot-streaked kitchen window. When a gleam showed her enameled coffeepot among the rubble, she picked it up and set it on top of the stove. Then, hands on her hips, she surveyed the room and thought of the chore she had to face tomorrow.

But when she compared it to what else had happened to her today, she thought the job of cleaning up would seem like a picnic.

✦ T W O ✦

After a restless night, Mattie opened her eyes to find she'd overslept. She quickly rose from the only dry spot on her mattress and parted the soot-streaked bedroom curtains. The sun beamed brightly down on the alley behind her house, its heat sending wisps of steam into the air as it dried the muddy streets.

A noise startled her. She froze. There it was again. Somebody was inside her millinery shop. Her eyes narrowed. *Jake Turnbull, no doubt.*

Not wanting to be caught half dressed, she rushed to her closet and scrambled into her chemise and underdrawers, then yanked on her oldest petticoat and dress. Unable to take the time to locate her stockings, she slid bare feet into her shoes, then hastily ran a brush through her hair, twisting it into a knot and anchoring it in place with pins.

Determined to oust the saloon keeper, she yanked aside the curtain to her shop. "Get—" It wasn't Jake.

A small foreign man dressed in a short robe and pajamalike pants was on his hands and knees in the middle of her floor. She didn't know his name, but she'd seen him before—with Jake Turnbull. She was sure the man lived at the Golden Nugget Saloon.

"Who are you?" she demanded. "And what do you think you're doing?"

The elderly man lifted his graying head and gave her an

13

inscrutable look, then went back to his cleaning.

"Stop that at once," she insisted. "I want you to leave."

"Bock Gee help."

"I don't need your help."

The man's almond eyes met her own. "Jake say big mess. Bock Gee stay."

"Damn Jake!" She stared down at the wiry little man who continued to scrub her floor. Apparently Bock Gee understood very little English. She couldn't bodily remove him. Besides, the man was only obeying his employer's wishes. But she didn't want to be beholden to anybody—especially Jake Turnbull.

Radiating with fury, Mattie hoisted her skirts and waded through the ankle-deep mud to the opposite side of the street, and shoved through the swinging doors.

The piano player stopped midkey. Necks craned and a hushed silence came over the room.

Blushing furiously, she walked around a table of gaping cardplayers and wrinkled her nose at the stench of rotgut whiskey and unwashed bodies. She approached the polished cherry-wood bar and addressed the balding man behind it. "I want to see Jake Turnbull."

The bartender put down the glass he was wiping and motioned toward the stairs. "First door to the right—but you can't go up there."

Tired of being told what she could or could not do, Mattie headed toward the staircase.

"Miss, come back!"

Reaching the top of the landing, she hesitated, then approached the door on the right and knocked.

"What?" a gruff voice asked.

She turned the knob. "Mr. Turnbull, I—" Meeting the shocked gaze of the couple in the large wooden bed, her eyes widened. "Oh!"

"What the hell are you doing here?" Jake bellowed, bolting to a sitting position.

"Who is she, Jake?" The redhead next to him shot Mattie an astonished look, then jerked the sheet up to her chin.

"Mat-tie Mc-Fearson. I'll—I'll come back—later," she stammered, backing through the doorway.

"Like hell you will!" Clad only in his underdrawers, the saloon owner leapt from the bed and stalked forward.

Mortified, Mattie slammed the door shut in such haste that she caught her skirt in the process. Before she could free herself, the entry shot open and Jake Turnbull, his face livid with anger, stormed toward her.

"I'm leaving." She backed toward the stairwell.

"It's a mite late for that." He grabbed her arm and dragged her into an office. Once there, he prevented her escape by slamming the door and leaning back against it. He crossed his arms. "You wanted to see me. Well, here I am." His eyes locked on hers, angry, bold, penetrating.

For the first time in her life, Mattie found herself speechless. She could do nothing but stare.

Tall as a barn door, bare-chested and barefooted, Jake Turnbull seemed larger than life—and twice as intimidating. "Well?" he demanded in a voice that made her think of gravel rolling off a tin roof.

His blond hair, tousled from sleep, bore traces of silver as did the curling, golden hair that ran in a wide vee from his chest and disappeared into the low-slung tops of his drawers.

She hadn't thought he would be so tan, but then she never thought she'd be viewing him almost naked either.

"If you're through gawkin' . . ."

Gawking! She yanked her gaze back to his face, noting the lines that fanned out from his flashing blue eyes. Dear Lord, why had she ever come here? Riveted, Mattie felt confusion roil within her, turning her insides to mush. Her pulse pounded so fiercely she thought she might swoon.

"I think we both could use a drink," he said tersely, breaking the spell. He opened the door. "Coffee, Charlie," he yelled down the staircase in a voice that could be heard two blocks away.

Immediately footsteps sounded and the apron-clad bartender carried a tray into the room. "I tried to stop her," the man called Charlie said apologetically.

"You didn't try hard enough." Jake ushered him out and closed the door. He hoisted the pot and poured two crockery mugs half full, then took a dark glass bottle from his desk drawer and added a jolt of amber liquid to each. He handed one to her. "Here."

Mattie started to protest, but watching his eyes darken, she decided under the circumstances that wasn't the wisest thing to do. She took the cup.

"Don't just hold it. Drink it," he ordered.

She took a swallow. Scalding hot, it burned a trail all the way from her tongue to her toes, and the liquor in it made her cough and gasp for breath.

"Mattie, I didn't think you'd be such a sissy." He raised a hamlike hand and swatted her on the back.

"Sis-sy?" she said when she was able. "I am no sissy. I'm just not accustomed to drinking whiskey before breakfast."

"What time of the day do you drink it?" He stretched, sending the muscles rippling and dancing across his hair-dusted chest. The movement made the rest of his anatomy only too apparent beneath the form-fitting underdrawers.

"I-I—" she began, then forgot the rest of what she was saying. Broad-shouldered and thick of body, there was not an ounce of fat on him that she could see—and this morning she'd managed to see quite a bit. He reminded her of a tall, sturdy tree, and with his widespread stance, he seemed just about as immovable.

"Ten o'clock?"

"Wh-at?" she asked, then noted the time on the Regulator clock that hung on the paneled wall behind him. "No, nine."

He grinned and motioned toward her cup.

"What?"

"You said you started drinking at nine, so bottoms up."

"Why, I said no such thing." She set the cup down with such force that its contents sloshed over the edge and puddled on the oak desk. "I should have known there's no talking to you."

Ignoring his chuckle, she dodged around him and jerked the door open, then slammed it behind her with such force that it jiggled the bawdy pictures decorating the hall wall.

It was only when she was halfway across the street that she remembered why she had gone there in the first place.

Jake padded barefoot to the window and watched the swish of Mattie's petticoats as she waded to the other side of the muddy street. *Mad as a rain-soaked hen.* Remembering the comment Bock Gee had made about her, he grinned. *He's right. She is a firecracker.*

He wondered how she would react if she knew the Chinaman not only understood but spoke perfect English? Angry as she was, it should make for some interesting conversation between himself and Bock Gee later when the old man returned to the saloon for dinner.

Working for Mattie had been Bock Gee's idea. For some strange reason the old coot seemed fascinated by the curvy little widow. *Maybe he has designs on her virtue.*

In spite of the fact that she had a bit more meat on her bones than Jake personally preferred, Mattie wasn't bad-looking. *Wonder why she never remarried? Probably because no man with any sense would put up with her.*

Reminded of her temper, Jake's jovial mood vanished. He downed his coffee and the remains of the feisty widow's as well. Her march on his saloon had put a dent in his business, the loss of which he could ill afford. A man was entitled to a little comfort. He considered it a God-given right, and no sharp-tongued female should have the liberty to interfere.

He thought of the miners who frequented his establishment in search of a body-warming drink, a word of cheer, or a woman to pass the time with on a cold winter night.

The men certainly had little else to look forward to.

Jake knew that to be the gospel truth, for his own father had been a miner. From the time he was big enough to carry a shovel he had followed the tall solemn man who had sired him into the black hole in the ground. Even now the thought of the mine made him shiver. Nine years old and skinny as a stick, he'd been terrified of the inky darkness and the things with claws that had scuttled over his bare feet.

Heaven help him, he'd almost been glad when his father had gotten hurt and been forced to leave the mine and move into town. His mother had taken in laundry, and Jake had done every odd job he could to help her put food on the table. Unable to work anymore, his crippled father had spent most of his time in the saloon—much to his mother's despair. At night their shack had rung with bitter arguments. The only laughter in the house had come from Elizabeth, his baby sister, and she'd been too young to know better.

Maybe that's why he'd been so fascinated by the saloon. Even though the mere mention of the place had riled his mother something fierce, Jake thought it wondrous. The noisy frivolity, the bright lights, the beautiful painted ladies—all had been a balm for his young soul.

When Jake was fourteen, his father had died after being struck down by a brewery wagon. Unable to live with the dour, nagging woman that his mother had become, Jake left home. He'd sent money when he could, but he'd never seen his mother or sister again. Although he'd felt guilty about not going back, he had never been able to make himself do it. And he wouldn't—until he had something better to offer.

That was the main reason he'd bought the run-down ranch outside of town. The land had grass aplenty for horses and cattle. A band of renegade Utes had torched the house, making most of it uninhabitable, but someday he planned to rebuild it. Then he would find his family. He'd discovered the pleasure of owning the saloon had paled after a while, and now that he was getting older, he found he enjoyed the peace and quiet of the range.

He gazed through the window and watched Mattie carry a bucketful of dark water from the shop and dump it into the street. He unconsciously compared his mother to the widow McFearson, both of whom had been dealt a raw deal by fate.

As if sensing his scrutiny, Mattie raised her soot-streaked face and glared at him.

He gave her a toothy grin in return.

Her body rigid with anger, Mattie whirled and stalked back inside her shop.

Unlike his Ma, though, Mattie McFearson would never take life lying down. That little widow would put starch in a man's spine if she had to strap a broomstick to his backside to do it.

He chuckled, remembering her outrage when she'd caught him in bed with Jolene. Even he had to give the devil his due, the widow did have spunk.

Knowing Jolene would be curious about Mattie's visit, Jake went back into the bedroom and was surprised to find it empty, the bed neatly made. In the light of day, Jolene, his partner in the saloon and owner of the whorehouse, had retreated to her own quarters down the hall.

He opened his closet and took out a clean suit of clothes, wondering what the widow would say if he told her that nothing had happened between him and Jolene. *She'd think I was a bald-faced liar.*

Jake slipped on and buttoned his shirt. Mattie would really be amazed if she knew the true situation between them. While Jolene had shared his bed more nights than he could count, they had never made love. And they never would.

He thought of the nightmares that brought Jolene running to his bed in the middle of the night. The dreams that made her sob and cry out in her sleep. Like a frightened child, she'd cuddle close, seeking shelter from her tormented past—a past that she had never revealed, even though he knew some of it and could guess at the rest.

She'd been fourteen when he'd found her in that cat-house on the border, all bones, wild red hair, and big eyes. Even though she'd experienced things no young girl should have, she had reminded him of a lost kitten. He'd had to kill a man to get her out of there, but he had never regretted it, not one bit. A while after that she'd disappeared. He'd searched, but never found her.

Ten years later Jolene found him. She'd grown older, wiser, her eyes hard beyond her years. Somewhere along the line she'd picked up a pocketful of money.

Together they enlarged the ramshackle affair that had housed his saloon, and she had personally overseen the building of the Miner's Delight. After her background, Jake had been surprised that she wanted to operate a whore-house, even though her establishment was unlike any he'd ever seen.

For one thing, Jolene insisted that the Miner's Delight be closed on Sundays—that day to be used for rest and reflection. And, unlike other houses, she insisted that the men patronizing her establishment treat her girls with kind-ness and respect. Those who didn't obey the rules were tossed out on their ear and were denied future admittance. Her girls did not have to entertain any man that repulsed them—no matter how much they offered to pay.

After several of the women left to get married, Jake teas-ingly accused Jolene of running a matchmaking parlor.

"No woman really wants to be a whore, Jake," she'd said. "I'm glad if they've found a better life."

A lusty man himself, Jake had found the Miner's Delight aptly named, for the place was not only kept spanking clean but its ladies were a joy to behold. Young, lovely, with enough experience to bring a man back again and again. Yet, each of them surprisingly had an air of genteel inno-cence.

He didn't know where Jolene found her young beauties, and he didn't care. To his way of thinking, that would be like looking a gift horse in the mouth.

As Jake lifted his pants from a chair and pulled them on, he remembered the shocked look on the widow's face and wondered what she'd have done if she had really caught him in action. Probably split her corset. Just finding him in bed with a woman had rendered Mattie speechless. Didn't take her long to recover though, he thought ruefully. The woman had a tongue like an asp.

The brilliant sun shining through his window made Jake long for a change of scenery. Now that the storm was over, he decided it might be a good time to check up on things at the ranch. He finished dressing and went downstairs to give the bartender some instructions. A few minutes later he saw Mattie peeking at him through her window as he rode out of town.

"It's just like him to run away," Mattie said furiously. She whirled toward the Chinaman. "Jake's gone. Now you can go, too."

"Bock Gee stay." In the severe lines of his thin dark face, the deep eyes he fixed on hers shone like burnished bronze. A thin, drooping mustache flowed into the man's long silver beard, almost, but not quite, hiding the hint of a smile.

"All right, stay. But don't say I didn't warn you." Mattie went into the kitchen to get her own pan of water and a brush. When she returned she saw that another visitor had entered the shop.

"Well, Mattie, I see you've really done it this time," the elusive Mr. Satterfield said, carefully stepping over a bolt of sodden cloth to inspect the premises.

Afraid she might yield to temptation and toss the water she carried in the banker's smug face, Mattie gritted her teeth and set the bucket on the floor. "I intend to clean it up. And as soon as I am able, I also intend to pay the back rent."

Ben Satterfield stared at Bock Gee, then gave her a cold

look. "We both know *I'll* be growing a pigtail and a long gray beard before that happens. You have two weeks." He picked his way across the floor and left the building.

Mattie sighed and joined Bock Gee on the floor. While she'd had only a slight chance to change the banker's mind before, now, after the fire, he'd made it clear that she had none.

She was amazed when he returned a few hours later with two gallons of white paint.

"A man from the hardware store will be here this afternoon to fix the door and replace the panes in the windows," the banker stated. "If there is anything else you need repaired, have him take care of it while he is here."

"No. That will be fine." Stunned, Mattie turned to thank him, but he had already gone. "If wonders won't cease," she said, gazing at the paint. She'd never known Ben Satterfield to be overly generous. There must be a reason. But whatever it was she had no time to think about it now.

Three days later Bock Gee and Mattie stood in the midst of their freshly painted surroundings and admired their efforts. "Thank you, Bock Gee." Mattie extended her hand to the elderly Chinaman. "I couldn't have done it without you."

The little man gave her a look of surprise, then clasped her palm in his. He narrowed his long eyes and regarded her with amusement. "No thanks needed, Mattie McFearson. After all, you did most of the work," he said in crisp, precise English. His hands folded, he bent his head in a respectful bow, then left before she could recover her voice.

"Why that wily little rascal!"

After he left, Mattie took stock of her remaining inventory. Even though she had scrubbed the fabric thoroughly, the bolts of filmy tulle still bore traces of black and smelled of smoke. There was no way to salvage any of it. The only hat remaining that she could sell was one she had intended for herself. Needing money far worse than the hat, she removed the large floral bandbox from the shelf in her chifforobe and carried it into the shop. There she took off the lid and parted the tissue paper, then carefully lifted the creation and proudly displayed it on a papier-mâché stand in the center of her newly paned display window.

It was a beautiful hat, a pale, finely woven leghorn straw swathed in soft lavender tulle. A cluster of deep-velvet violets and tiny white flowers decorated a spot just off center. "If that doesn't draw the ladies in, then nothing ever will."

Because it was her one and only item of merchandise, she filled out a tag and marked it twice her usual price. It wouldn't be enough to pay the rent, but it might keep her from starving.

Reminded of food, she thought of her cat and frowned. She hadn't seen Bridget since the day of the fire when the animal had gone begging to the Golden Nugget Saloon. Even if she dared enter that place again, she couldn't ask Jake about her roving feline. As far as she knew, the man was still out of town. Mattie glanced at the Miner's Delight and noticed it was shuttered and quiet, closed until the sun set for the day. She shook her head. She could hardly go knocking at the front door of the brothel.

A vision of the redhead she'd seen in Jake's bed flashed into her mind. Unlike her expectations of filmy see-through garments with spangles and beads, the woman had been clad in a flannel nightgown, long-sleeved and high-necked, such as any respectable female might have worn. Curious, she thought. Considering the little she knew about Jake Turnbull, she would have thought he preferred his women to wear little—or nothing at all.

"Good grief," she said as heat rose to her cheeks. "Surely you have something better to do than stare out the window and wonder about Jake Turnbull's love life." Her footsteps echoing hollowly in the emptiness of the shop, she retreated into the rear room.

*   *   *

Mattie thought her prayers had been answered when the tinkling bell announced a customer. "May I help you?" she said brightly, coming forward to greet an elegantly gowned young woman.

"Hello, Mrs. McFearson." The voice was low, cultured. "I'm Jolene Lassiter—from across the street. I've come to return your cat." She nodded toward the basket she carried.

The redhead from Jake's bed. Although if the woman hadn't identified herself, Mattie wouldn't have recognized her. Not knowing what to say, she blushed furiously and remained silent.

In spite of the heat outside, Mattie noted that the mauve silk dress the woman wore had a close-fitting stand-up collar edged with lace. Other lace edged the long sleeves. Tall, regal, the woman carried herself with dignity. If Mattie hadn't known she was the madam, she never would have guessed. The woman looked that respectable. She scarcely wore any makeup, just a faint outlining of kohl that made her green eyes appear even larger. Her complexion was flawless, smooth, and white as cream.

In spite of the woman's distasteful profession, Mattie had to admit this person, Jolene, was strikingly beautiful.

The woman's pink lips tilted in a faint smile, and she held out the purring cat. "I wanted to bring her back sooner, but I thought you might be busy—cleaning up after the mishap and all."

"It's all right," Mattie said, taking the squirming animal. "She certainly looks well fed. You must have taken good care of her."

"She's a darling. I've never owned a cat. She must be a lot of company." Watching the animal, a sad look shadowed the woman's eyes, and Mattie sensed that she, too, was lonely.

"She is, when she stays home."

"She's gotten used to the basket, and I have no use for it. If you don't mind, I'd like for her to have it." Jolene Lassiter set the golden straw container on the floor.

Bridget immediately leapt from Mattie's arms and ran to the basket. Curled up on the large, down-filled, blue velvet pillow, the cat yawned and gave Mattie a smug look, as if to say she'd had better sense than to sleep on a smoky, wet bed.

"It doesn't appear like I have much say in the matter," Mattie said wryly. "Thank you for taking care of her—and for the basket." Mattie didn't understand the impulse that made her wish she could offer the young woman some refreshment, but having nothing to offer, instead she held out her hand.

A wary look crossed Miss Lassiter's face, then after a moment's hesitation, she shook Mattie's hand. "Well, I guess I'd better be going." She turned to leave and her gaze touched upon the hat Mattie had placed in the window. "Oh, it's beautiful," she said, moving to examine it. "Did you make it?"

"Yes. I did."

"Would—would you mind if I tried it on?"

"Not at all." Mattie removed the hat from the stand and placed it on Miss Lassiter's perfectly coiffured head. The filmy tulle set off the woman's delicate, heart-shaped face to perfection. It was as though the hat had been created especially for her.

"I want you to have it," Mattie said suddenly. When the woman started to protest, she held out a staying hand. "It's the least I can do to repay you for taking care of Bridget."

"I'll take the hat, but only if you let me pay you for it." Miss Lassiter lifted the price tag and frowned.

"If it's too much—"

"It's not near enough. It's no wonder you can't make a living." Suddenly aware of what she'd said, the young woman raised a manicured hand to her mouth. "I'm sorry."

"Don't apologize for saying what everyone knows is true." Mattie gave her a lopsided smile. "Miss Lassiter, I do want you to have the hat, though.''

She grinned. ''Good, even if I do feel as if I'm stealing it. And, please, do call me Jolene.''

Mattie wrapped her creation with tissue and placed it into a hat box. ''Here you go—Jolene.''

The young woman dipped into her reticule and handed Mattie the correct amount of money, then holding the box by its strings, she bent and gave the cat one last pat. ''Bridget, you can come and see me anytime.''

She straightened, her face dimpling with mischief. ''But as for you, Mrs. McFearson, it might be better if you didn't come to visit.'' One green eye closed in a saucy wink, then the redhead turned with a swish of silken skirts and drifted out the door.

After spending part of her hoard on a few food staples at the general store, Mattie returned to her shop to discover she had more visitors.

She instantly recognized Mr. Satterfield. The other two, a man and woman, were unfamiliar.

Resplendent in a new three-button sack coat, piped vest, and well-cut trousers, the banker interrupted his conversation with the rosy-cheeked young couple and turned to greet her.

''Here is Mrs. McFearson now,'' Satterfield said smoothly. ''Mattie, I'd like you to meet the Grubers—the new tenants.''

''Pleased to make acquaintance with you,'' the young man said in broken English. His young, flaxen-haired wife gave Mattie a shy smile.

Too shocked to return their greeting, Mattie stared at her landlord. ''New tenants?'' She opened her reticule. ''If it's the rent, I can pay part of it now.''

''It's too late for that, Mattie,'' Satterfield said smugly. ''Mr. Gruber has already paid me three months in advance. He plans to open a boot shop.''

''A boot shop.'' Now it all made sense why the banker

had been so nice to her. The new paint. The door. The windows. The new shelves he'd ordered built, even though she hadn't asked for them. Satterfield must have rented out the building even before the fire.

"This will be our first home," the shoemaker said, gazing fondly down at his blushing wife.

"You can take possession at the end of the week," the banker said. "You can be out by then, can't you, Mattie?" The look on his face told her that he would personally see to it that she was.

Mattie sighed with defeat and nodded, even though she had no idea of what she would do—or where she would go.

"Good." The banker drew his watch from his vest pocket and checked the time. "Now that everything is settled, I want you folks to join me for dinner." His eyes cold, Satterfield gave her a stiff nod. "Good night, Mrs. Mc-Fearson."

"Good grief," she said when they had left the shop. She gazed around her, all her hopes and dreams vanishing like smoke.

How could she have been so gullible as to think the banker had been acting out of kindness? She realized that he had probably intended to paint the building anyway and had used the fire as an excuse to get her to do the labor. She had to admit the mishap had caused a mess, but it wasn't all her doing. Most of it had been caused by Jake Turnbull and the firemen. But Ben Satterfield certainly wasted no time in seizing the opportunity to kick her out. Probably thought he was justified.

And she couldn't fault the Grubers for being so anxious to move in. She wished the young couple well. The town needed a shoemaker, and they wouldn't care if *his* shop sat across from a whorehouse and saloon.

But it still didn't solve *her* problem.

❧ THREE ❧

After tripping over the cat for the third time that morning, Mattie gave an exasperated sigh, scooped Bridget up, and deposited her on the sidewalk outside her shop door. "All right, run along, you ungrateful creature."

Without giving Mattie a backward glance, the cat dashed across the pothole-puddled street to the Miner's Delight, unerringly drawn by the delightful smell of fried bacon and freshly brewed coffee that drifted on the morning air.

"Can't say as I blame you." Mattie grimaced as she considered her own breakfast of unsweetened, lumpy mush. At least the bread she'd baked that morning had been good, and insect-free, thanks to the new flour she'd purchased with money from the sale of the hat.

After taking her broom from the hook by the door, she carried it to the sidewalk and briskly swept away debris the wind had deposited the night before. Although it wouldn't be her shop for long, she intended to keep it tidy just the same.

She still hadn't found a place to live; everything habitable was occupied. And she hadn't found employment, even though she'd asked almost everywhere.

Shoving such dreary thoughts aside, she gazed at the rain-drenched hills surrounding the settlement; hills stripped of trees, dotted with yellow mine tailings and rotting timbers. Mere traces of the glory from the time when

29

the town had been in its heyday.

Her father had christened the town Sweetheart, in honor of the obstinate mule who had led him to the first gold discovery in the area. His claim, like that of so many others, had petered out. But Mattie was determined that the town he'd been so proud of would not wither away like so many others that had bloomed, then died and been blown away leaving scarcely a trace that they had ever existed.

While some of the more prosperous mines remained, the gold was deeper, more difficult to remove, and expensive to haul and process. A few determined old-timers insisted the mother lode was still there, close to the surface, waiting for one of them to find it. Mattie wished them well, but doubted there was anything left to find. She believed the future of Sweetheart lay in its citizens, not in some mythical treasure.

The area had so much potential. No place could offer a healthier climate. And timber, where it hadn't been removed for the diggings, was abundant, more than enough for houses. Water was sweet-tasting and plentiful. The lower valleys had grass aplenty for cattle. She could see nothing to stand in the way of the town's progress. But for Sweetheart to grow, it needed people, families, children. It needed a school and a church. She glared at the buildings across the street. It definitely did not need places like that.

She finished her sweeping, then paused to gaze at the cloud-laden sky before going back inside. The sporadic rain that had begun just before dawn brought back memories of the last storm. She'd thought her situation was bad then, but since that time, it had grown steadily worse. Only five days remained until her time was up, then she and her belongings would be put out in the street.

She might be forced to accept Jake Turnbull's offer of a room after all, she thought ruefully, but after she'd barged in on his amorous escapade, she doubted if that offer still held good. She heard the rattle of an approaching wagon and turned. "Speak of the devil."

The blond man pulled the buckboard up in front of the saloon, then he got out and tied the team to the hitching rail. "Mornin', Mattie," Jake called out, bringing her to the attention of everyone within earshot.

"Good grief," she uttered as a rush of crimson washed over her. Afraid he might cross the street and attempt to engage her in conversation, she quickly went inside her shop and shut the door. But curiosity drew her back to the edge of the window where she could watch without being seen.

Eyeing her shop, Jake hesitated. She let out a sigh of relief when he shrugged his broad shoulders and went into the saloon.

The rain continued in earnest. About midafternoon, finding herself at loose ends, Mattie pulled a chair close to the shop window and stared across the street at the Miner's Delight. Her thoughts drifted to Jolene and how different she'd been from what Mattie had expected. Instead of hard and coarse, the girl had seemed gentle, sad, and almost shy. Only her eyes, old beyond her years, had betrayed the life she led.

How would Jolene be spending the day? she wondered. Even though Mattie herself considered Jake Turnbull a pompous jackass, it was apparent that if Jolene shared his bed, she must bear the man some affection. Maybe her feelings were not returned. Was that the reason for her sadness?

She was shocked by her thoughts. She never thought she'd be concerned about the feelings of a madam. *You'd do better to worry about your own problems, Mattie.*

She had started toward her living quarters, but the jingling of harness bells drew her back to the window.

The stagecoach had drawn up by the corner across the street. Unusual, she thought, considering that wasn't his customary stop. The driver jumped down and opened the door. *Must be somebody important, or he wouldn't bother.* A few moments later the coach drove away.

Mattie's brow wrinkled in a frown when she spied the five small children left standing on the sidewalk. *Would you look at that? Poor little tykes.*

The oldest, a little girl, who couldn't be more than eight, balanced a crying baby on her hip. Next to her, struggling to maintain her hold on an obviously heavy carpetbag, stood a younger girl who also looked ready to burst into tears. Two little boys, as much alike as two peas in a pod, crumpled to a sitting position next to the building.

Wondering where their parents were, Mattie went to the door and looked up and down the street, but there wasn't another soul in sight. *Wherever they went they should be horsewhipped for leaving those babies to stand out in the rain.*

When her conscience wouldn't allow her to wait any longer, she put on her wool cloak and bonnet and crossed the muddy thoroughfare.

"Hello, there," she said, approaching the wide-eyed children. "I'm Mattie McFearson, and I live across the street."

"Hello," the oldest little girl said, giving her a faint smile. "I'm Faith Kinsington and the baby's Joshua. Sh-h, it's all right," she crooned to the sobbing infant. "My sister's name is Hope and the boys are Lory and Hal. That's short for Glory and Hallelujah," she confided in a softer voice, "because that's what Pa said when he first saw them."

Mattie smiled. "I'm very glad to meet all of you. Where are your parents?" she asked, kneeling on the sidewalk beside them.

"We're orphans," Hope volunteered.

"Orphans?"

Faith added, "Our pa was taken to the Promised Land by a sinner's bullet, and our ma died of consumption. Since we didn't have any more family, the town took up a collection to send us to our uncle."

"Your uncle? Was he supposed to meet you?" Mattie

asked, ready to give the man a piece of her mind.

"Oh, no, ma'am. We just got on the stagecoach and came."

"Well, the first thing we have to do is get you out of the rain, then we'll see if we can locate your uncle. Do you know where he lives?"

"The stage driver said he lives down here somewhere," Hope said, swinging the bag back and forth.

"In Sweetheart, you mean."

"Yeah. Said one of these is his house," one of the twins chimed in.

Mattie looked at the buildings behind them. "But, children, that can't be right. See." She pointed to the sign. "That place is—uh—" she stammered, hoping they wouldn't know what the place was. "That other building is the Golden Nugget Saloon."

The second twin got to his feet and wiped his runny nose on his jacket sleeve. "One of 'em must be Uncle B. J.'s."

"Uncle B. J.'s?" Mattie looked at the saloon, then at the children. All blonds with deep blue eyes. It couldn't be— but the resemblance was striking. "What is your uncle's name?"

"Burton Jacob Turnbull. Mama called him B. J., but she said everyone else calls him Big Jake."

"Big Jake?" Mattie clutched the porch post. "Your uncle is Jake Turnbull?"

"Yeah, that's him all right," the twins said in unison. One of the little boys put his hands up to his face and bent to peer through the gilt-edged windows.

"Oh, no, no," Mattie cried, reaching out to pull him back. Not only was she having trouble picturing Jake as a parent, but under no circumstances could she allow those innocent children to go anywhere near that saloon—especially after what she had witnessed the one time she'd dared enter.

"Set the bag down there by the door, sweetheart," she instructed Hope. Then knowing there was no time to lose, she lifted the chunky infant into her own arms. "Come along, children. We must get you out of the weather."

Moving as rapidly as she could and still allow the children to keep up, Mattie stepped into the muddy street and led the way to her shop. After herding the bedraggled brood up the steps, she shoved her door open and ushered them inside.

"Let me have your wet coats, then I'll dish you up a nice bowl of soup."

The "soup" was little more than boiled jerky, with a few vegetables added, but it was hot and the children quickly devoured it.

They're hungry, she noted. Thinking they might need something with a bit more substance, she checked the bread dough she'd left rising, then placed it in the oven to bake.

Only when the youngsters were warm and fed did she dare think of the problem at hand. Whether she wanted to or not, she had to tell their uncle. She couldn't let them walk in without being expected. Knowing firsthand of Jake's temper, there was no telling what he might say or do.

"I have to go out for a little while," Mattie said to the oldest. "Will you be all right here alone?"

"We've been alone lots of times lately," Faith confided.

Her heart filled with compassion for what these little ones must have endured as Mattie slipped on her cloak and crossed the street.

When she entered the Golden Nugget, a sheet of rain and an accompanying gust of wind blew a flurry of leaves across the mud-caked saloon floor before she managed to slam the double doors shut.

Startled by the commotion, an instant hush came over the participants, and there was a rustle of cloth as all craned their necks in order to focus their eyes on her.

"What's she doin' here?" one cardplayer asked another.

The apron-clad bartender peered disapprovingly over his wire-rimmed spectacles. "Mrs. McFearson, is there some reason for this intrusion?"

"There is a very good reason," Mattie assured him, as primly as she could under the circumstances.

"There damn well better be," Jake rumbled from where he sat on the top step of the stairs. "What the hell are you doing here, Mattie? This isn't another of your temperance marches, is it?"

"No, it isn't."

"Well, at least I've got my pants on this time," he said dryly.

He would have to bring that up. Her face crimson, she approached the foot of the staircase. "Mr. Turnbull, I want you to accompany me across the street."

"What for?" Jake gave her a suspicious look. "You burn more beans?"

"No, I didn't burn more beans," she returned, trying to hold her temper amid all the snickers and guffaws.

"Why should I go across the street? It's raining out there. You made it over here by yourself, can't you make it back?"

"Of course I can. That's not the point," Mattie snapped. "Are you coming, or not?"

He arched a brow, then he got to his feet and ambled down the steps toward her. A lazy grin twisted his mouth. "I think I get the idea."

"What idea?" Mattie asked, certain that the conversation had taken a turn she wasn't aware of.

"You'd better get a move on, Jake, before she changes her mind," chimed one of the men. Another made a lewd remark.

"Might be worth getting wet for after all," Jake said, giving her the eye.

"Oh, good grief!" Too flustered to explain, she grabbed his hand and towed him toward the door. "It's not what you think," she hissed. "I'll explain across the street."

"It had better be good," he grumbled. "Hang on a minute, no sense in drownin'." He grabbed a slicker from a peg by the door and draped it over both their heads. Sweeping her right along with him, he left the saloon and stepped into the rain.

Mattie felt like a chick tucked beneath the wing of a very large rooster. She sucked in a nervous breath and inhaled the masculine aroma of bay rum, cigars, and brandy. His size, the heat radiating from his body, and the clean, all-too-male scent combined to bombard her senses, making her feel weak in the knees and all too aware of the fact that she was a woman. Unnerved, she tried to shove the rain gear aside. "I'm already wet. You keep the slicker."

"Don't be silly." Before she could step off the walk, he looped a brawny arm around her waist, and half dragged, half carried her across the muck-filled street.

"There," he said, depositing her on the sidewalk. "Now, what's so all-fired important?"

"I have something that belongs to you," she began somewhat breathlessly, only too conscious of the fact that he still had her captured in his arms.

"What's that, Mattie?" he asked softly.

"In there," she squeaked, feeling like a mouse about to be eaten by a very large cat. When he relaxed his grip, she bolted for the door.

Chuckling, he followed.

This wasn't at all the way she'd planned to tell him, but now she had no choice.

"Miss Mattie, is that you?" Faith called out.

"Yes, dear. It's me."

Five sets of wide blue eyes focused on the man at her side. "Is that him?" asked a small boy.

"Where in hell did you get all these kids?" Jake boomed.

"Mr. Turnbull, please, don't shout. You're frightening them," Mattie admonished, moving forward. "They are the reason I came to the saloon."

With the children gathered in front of her, Mattie turned to face him. "This is Faith—and Hope," she said, touching each on the shoulder. "The twins prefer to be known as

Lory—and Hal.'' She smiled down at the babbling baby. "And this darling little boy is Joshua.'' She held up the grinning toddler for Jake to admire.

"That's all well and good, Mattie, but did you need to drag me out in the rain to introduce them?''

"I really thought I should—especially since they all belong to you.'' She raised her head and met Jake's astounded gaze.

"To me? The hell you say.''

"I'm sorry to tell you like this, Jake, but your sister passed on recently, and—''

"Bitsy's dead?'' A look of pain washed over Jake's face.

Hal nodded solemnly. " 'Sumption got her.''

"What about your grandma?'' Jake asked, dropping down on one knee.

"She died a long time ago,'' Lory said.

Jake was silent for a moment, then, his eyes suspiciously bright, he glanced up at Mattie. "Don't they have a pa?''

"He's dead, too. They're orphans, Jake, and since the children had nowhere else to go, the town sent them to you.''

"To me?'' He eyed the bunch, then swallowed and rose to his feet.

When he looked as though he might bolt for the door, Mattie unwound the toddler's arms from around her neck, then plopped the little boy into Jake's arms. "There, delivered all safe and sound.'' She drew the rest of the group toward him. "Children, meet your Uncle Jake.''

"Are you gonna be our new pa?'' one of the twins asked, tilting his head back to gaze up at Jake, who upon hearing the question uttered a very audible gasp.

"He cain't be our pa. He's our uncle,'' said the other.

"We ain't got a pa, so why can't he?'' Hal argued.

" 'Cause he probably don't want to, that's why.''

"He ain't got no choice. We don't have nobody else.''

A faint smile on her face, Mattie looked first at the children, then at Jake who had turned a pasty shade of gray. "Jake Turnbull, a daddy. Interesting idea," she said.

He glared at her but made no comment.

Joshua, on the other hand, gazed up at the scowling face above him. Then the baby's lips drew into a quivering pout and he let out a loud wail.

"Can we have some more hot chocolate?" Hope asked, making herself heard over the din.

"Of course." Mattie sniffed the fragrant air. "I think we might manage a bit of freshly baked bread and butter, too." She turned to the white-faced saloon owner and retrieved the squalling toddler. "Come along, Jake. You look like you could use some, too."

"I don't need hot chocolate. I need a real drink." He looked longingly at the door.

"Jake," she hissed, "remember the children." She took him by the arm and led him into the kitchen where his nieces and nephews were already lined up on benches at the kitchen table.

After getting Jake and the baby settled in the rocking chair off to one side, she helped the older children to servings of watered-down hot chocolate and butter-laden bread. Then she prepared two additional slices on a plate and carried it and a cup to Jake.

She watched the way the big man almost fearfully dangled the chortling youngster on his knee, and her mouth lifted in amusement. He was clearly out of his element. From the awkward way he held the one-year-old, she could tell he had no experience whatsoever with children.

Remembering all the times she had condemned him to perdition, she couldn't help but enjoy his misery. Unfortunately, the fate of the orphaned children rested in his hands. Concern filled her.

"Here we go, boys. Try some of this." She set the plate on a small stool in front of Jake and the baby. "Be careful, it's hot," she warned, handing Jake the cup.

Before she could intervene, Joshua immediately helped himself to a slice of buttered bread. His lips smacking, the baby took a few messy bites. Then, talking in a language only he could understand, he whirled and slapped the bread against his uncle's cheek, depositing a large wad of butter.

"Damn!" Jake caught the wad before it dripped onto his shirt. "Does he always eat like this?"

"I imagine so. Most babies do." Mattie took the corner of her apron and wiped Jake's hand and square jaw in an attempt to remove most of the mess. "Hold still."

"It's not me that's wiggling. What the—?" He sucked in a breath, then closed his eyes. "Oh—piss!"

"You really should watch your language around the children. They aren't your saloon patrons, you know."

"I'm not cussin'." He held up a dripping hand. Then he stared down at the wet stain that was rapidly spreading across the front of his pants.

Covering her mouth to keep from bursting into laughter, Mattie hurried to a kitchen drawer and removed a large, white dishcloth. "This should do."

He took the cloth and immediately began dabbing at his pants.

Mattie shook her head. "That was supposed to be for the baby."

"Well, why didn't you say so?" He handed the cloth to the child, who clutched it in one chubby fist and gaily waved it in the air.

"Good grief!" Mattie sighed. "Don't you know anything about babies?"

"Hell no! And what makes you such an authority? You never had any, did you?"

"No. But any fool would know that when they are wet you have to change their britches."

"Oh." He eyed Joshua as if the youngster had just grown horns. "How?"

"First I have to get another dry napkin," she said, heading back for the drawer.

Mattie returned with the cloth and instructed Jake in the fine rudiments of changing a diaper. Although she had never done the job before either, she'd learned enough from the wet one she'd removed to bluff her way through.

"There." She handed the child back to Jake.

"What am I going to do about these?" Jake pointed to his own wet pants. The sodden cloth clung to his bulky frame, leaving no detail to the imagination.

Blushing, Mattie averted her eyes. "I'm afraid I can't help you."

"I could go across the street and change," he suggested.

"You *are not* taking those children into a saloon."

"Then what *am* I going to do with them?" He gazed at her with a hopeful expression. "Could you——?"

"Only until you get your pants changed." She held out her arms for the baby. "And if you are not back in ten minutes, I'm coming after you."

"You're a hard woman, Mattie McFearson. A hard, hard woman." Muttering to himself, he left.

After depositing Joshua on the bench beside his sister, Mattie sliced the remainder of the bread and slathered it with butter, then poured the rest of the chocolate into the children's cups. Watching the twins wolf it down, she wondered how she would entertain the boisterous youngsters when she ran out of food.

She didn't have to worry long, for exactly ten minutes later, Jake strode through the door.

"Henry's bringing the wagon around, then we'll be going out to the ranch."

She hadn't known he had a ranch. So that's where he went all those times she'd seen him leaving town.

He glanced at the kids, then shot her a disturbed look. "You sure you can't——?"

"I'm sure," Mattie said firmly, now that she knew they wouldn't be living in a saloon. "Where would I put them? I have to move by the end of the week. Besides, they're your responsibility." She couldn't resist a grin. "Having children might be good for you."

"Yeah, like a dose of the plague."

"Hey, guess what?" a twin shouted from the doorway. "It's stopped rainin'."

"Here comes the wagon," Hope called from her spot in front of the window.

"Uncle Jake, I think Lory ate too much bread and butter," Faith said, leading the pasty-faced boy forward.

"Uh, maybe some fresh air would help." Mattie took the groaning child by the hand. Just as they reached the sun-swept porch, Lory broke free and headed for the alley.

"I don't feel so good either," Hal confessed.

Dodging around Jake, who she noticed had turned as green as his nephews, Mattie rushed back inside and grabbed up several washcloths and dampened them. When she returned to the porch, Jake, too, had disappeared.

"Here," she said, thrusting the bundle of cloths at Jake's foreman, Henry Hobbs, who had just pulled the team to a stop. "I think you're going to need these."

"I was afraid you'd say that." After glancing toward the alley, the tall, sandy-haired man flashed her an anemic smile.

"If you're about done, Jake, we'd better get going," he yelled. "We need to get these kids indoors before dark."

After their meager luggage was loaded, Mattie gave the girls and the baby a hug, then she helped the pathetic-looking little boys into the wagon.

Jake managed to climb in by himself. Barely.

Murmuring a quiet prayer for all of them, Mattie stood in the middle of the muddy street and waved as the wagon rolled noisily out of sight.

❧ FOUR ❧

Jake woke before dawn and carefully eased out of the bed he'd been sharing with the twins. He cast an apprehensive glance toward the boys, whose faces in sleep bore a cherublike innocence, their limbs tangled in the quilts, half in, half out of the covers.

He then peered over the edge of the whiskey crate at the baby, who slept, one thumb stuck in his mouth, the other fist tightly clutching a tattered rag doll. The same doll Jake had spent half the night trying to find. Once he'd recovered the toy, the baby had quit crying and gone to sleep.

He, on the other hand, had spent the remainder of the night dodging bony arms and flailing legs that had seemed determined to put out his eye, puncture a lung, or disman him. Praying they would all stay asleep long enough for him to down a cup of coffee in peace, he carefully lifted his clothes from the seat of a ladder-backed chair, snatched his boots from beneath the edge of the bed, and tiptoed from the room.

Four days they had been there, and that four days had been the most exhausting in his life. Taking care of the kids made the back-breaking work of a roundup seem like a Sunday school picnic. Four days—and a lifetime to go. Just the idea of it was enough to make a grown man cry.

It wasn't that he didn't like the kids, because he did. They were blood kin. He sadly thought of his mother and

43

sister. The kids were the only kin he had left. But damned if he knew how to cope with them.

Once he made it to the kitchen, he raised bloodshot eyes to stare at the counter littered with dirty plates and bits of food. The stove was caked with boiled-over, burned mush he'd attempted to prepare the morning before. He'd intended to clean it up, but with one thing and another, he hadn't had time.

The room looked like it had been hit with a white tornado as a result of the flour sack he'd dropped when the baby had crawled over and bit him on the leg. He rubbed the still tender spot just below the back of his knee. For such a little fella, Joshua sure had sharp teeth.

A thick black trail of ants snaked their way across the floor and up one leg of the table. After the sugar the twins had spilled, no doubt.

He'd never been overly neat and felt uncomfortable around anyone who was, but neither had he been slovenly. He could go for six months without lifting a finger and the place wouldn't look half as bad as it did now. He knew he had to get it cleaned up, but he didn't know where to start. He'd seen cleaner pigsties. His stomach rumbled but casting another glance around the room robbed him of his appetite.

He slumped down on a straight-backed chair and ran his hand over a three-day growth of whiskers that covered his chin, then letting out a groan of pure misery, he buried his face in his hands.

He needed help. He had to have help. He couldn't handle it by himself—the last four days had proved that. But who?

After meeting the kids, the cowboys, those who hadn't quit, had decided the spring on the far side of the range needed a fence around it. In their eyes, even digging post holes, a hand's most hated job, was preferable to staying around the ranch yard where they might be pressed into corralling younguns.

Even Henry had abandoned him. The foreman had left

on a cattle-buying trip two weeks before he was scheduled to go. Claimed he wanted to have time to pick out the best stock, but Jake knew that wasn't the reason.

Bock Gee had suddenly come down with a dozen different ailments, even though Jake knew the old man was three times healthier than any individual half his age.

"Some friends, deserting a man in his hour of need," he muttered. He pried his foot loose from the sticky floor and shoved it into a sock that seemed to have suddenly developed more holes than not. He poked his protruding toe into his boot.

Fur wriggled against his bare flesh.

"Hellfire!" Jake yanked his foot out, then carefully reached inside the boot. His thumb and forefinger grasped a long thin tail. He pulled out the twins' pet mouse. "Solomon, you came near to being toe-jam this morning." Jake shuddered as he released the creature and watched it scamper across the floor.

Most boys had a natural curiosity, he knew that from being a boy himself, but Lory and Hal—he shook his head. Those two latched on to everything that couldn't move fast enough to get away. He'd never seen the like. In the short time they'd been there, they'd gotten into more mischief than a whole tribe of liquored-up Comanches.

He still couldn't tell them apart—a fact they took full advantage of. Not that it mattered. If one of them was into something, the other was bound to be into it, too.

But the baby was the one that kept him worn down to a nubbin. When he'd finally managed to get some food in one end of that youngun, it was coming out the other. And by the time he'd gotten that end cleaned and changed, Joshua was yowling for something to eat again.

And the girls—while they weren't prone to get into as much trouble as the boys—were just as worrisome. He'd never seen either of those little gals laugh or smile. Course they hadn't had much to smile about, losing both their ma and pa the way they had. They sat around, stared at him, their faces long as a cowhand's rope, and quoted Bible verses.

Knowing their missionary upbringing, he tried not to cuss around them, but every time he slipped and let off a little steam, they clamped their hands over their ears and ran from the room like the devil had ahold of their coattails. It was plain to see they didn't approve of him at all.

He shook out the other boot, felt inside to make sure it wasn't harboring any varmints, then pulled it on. He brushed his hair out of his eyes, shoved himself to a standing position, and started toward the stove.

Now, for that cup of coffee.

He gingerly tiptoed across the sticky floor and examined the contents of the sink, then the stack of pots that littered the top of the cabinet. Finally, he knelt and peeked into the oven. Coffee? Fat chance. Hell, he couldn't even find the pot.

"It's Uncle Jake," a small blond boy shouted. He and his brother exploded from the cookshack and raced toward the wagon Jake had pulled to a stop in front of the ranch house. Jake's red-bone hound, Rusty, trailed after them.

Jake groaned.

Their eyes full of curiosity, the boys and dog lined up and stared at the hefty Norwegian woman that sat beside Jake on the wagon seat.

"Is she the lady that's gonna take care of us?" one of the twins asked.

"She's awful big. I'll bet she eats a lot," the other boy said soberly.

Damn it. He'd hoped to get the woman settled first, then break it to her about the children a little bit at a time. "Why don't you boys go help the hands feed the horses or somethin'?" he suggested, hoping to waylay any more unwanted observations.

"We can't. They ain't found the horses yet."

"What?" Jake asked, before he could stop himself, certain he'd be better off not knowing.

"We didn't mean to let 'em out."

"We only wanted to swing on the gate."

"What this?" The blond woman waved a chubby arm toward the twins, then turned her little piggy eyes on Jake.

Jake managed a weak grin. She didn't look amused. "Boys, uh, why don't you two go help Mooney?"

The twins looked at each other and shook their heads. "Don't think we'd better."

"Jake, 'bout time you got back." Mooney, the ranch cook, jumped off the porch and hobbled toward him. "You know what them younguns been up to?"

"Yeah, they told me." Jake shot a warning glance toward the man. "Help me unload Helga's trunk. I'll get her settled, and you can put the team away." Grabbing one end of the luggage, Jake leaned close to Mooney and hissed. "Shut your dammed mouth. I didn't tell her about the kids yet."

Mooney rolled his eyes, and gave Jake an *I-hope-you-know-what-you're-doing* look. Then he latched on to the other end of the heavy trunk and helped Jake lower it to the ground.

Jake went back to the wagon and flashed his most charming smile. "Now, Helga, let me help you down. You can go on inside, freshen up a bit, and take a look around. Mooney and I have some business to take care of."

The wagon groaned, then leveled itself out as the woman heaved her bulk to the ground. She snorted, lifted her skirts from the dirt, and plowed toward the house.

"Now, what about the kids?" Jake asked, knowing the man was flat busting to tell him.

"It's a good thing you hired that woman. One more day of *them*, and she can have my job, too," Mooney declared, his round face red with indignation.

"That bad, huh?"

"Them boys dumped the pickle barrel—and the molasses. Trying to catch a mouse, they said. The girls won't eat my cookin', and the baby's got the dribbles."

"The what?"

Mooney pointed toward his rear end.

"Oh." Just what he needed. "Well, things ought to be better now that Helga's here." Jake motioned toward the trunk. "Let's get this inside . . ."

"Uh-oh. Here she comes," the cook moaned.

Helga stalked across the yard toward them. "I quit!" she announced, crossing her arms over her ample breasts.

"You can't quit," Jake argued. "Hell, you just got here!"

"You tell me you need woman to cook. You not tell me you have children." She pointed toward the girls and the baby who had joined the twins behind Jake. "You not tell me you live in barn. No, not barn—peegsty. I quit!" she said with a sharp nod of her blond head.

"I'll pay more money," Jake promised, hoping that would make her change her mind.

"Humph! You not have that much money." She bent from the waist and grabbed the handles of her trunk and set it back on the tailgate of the wagon. Then she turned toward Jake and held out a pudgy hand. "You owe me one day."

"What for? You didn't do nothin'." He watched her eyes narrow, then recalling the ease with which she had lifted the heavy trunk, he dug in his pocket, took out several coins and deposited them in her palm.

She lumbered to the front of the wagon and climbed up onto the seat. "We go now."

Jake looked from the woman to Mooney. "I guess I'd better take her back." He started toward the front of the wagon.

"No, you don't." Mooney grabbed Jake by the shirt-sleeve. "You ain't leaving me here with *them* again. *I'll* be the one going to town." The crippled cook clambered onto the wagon seat with the agility of a monkey. He lifted the reins, then gave Jake a wry smile. "Good luck."

"Do you suppose one of the hands . . ." Jake began desperately.

"I don't think so. I don't think I'd even mention it if I was you—especially since two of them already quit." The cook wheeled the team, then pointed the wagon back up the road.

"I'm sorry, Mattie. You know I feel the same as you do about that evil place," the gray-haired woman behind the counter said in a hushed voice as she busily refolded a stack of chambray work shirts. "Even if we could afford to hire you, Hiram wouldn't hear of it. He's still mad enough to spit about me taking part in that temperance march you organized. And after you took an ax to that barrel of whiskey he had in the storeroom—" Sara cast a surreptitious glance toward the curtained-off back room. "He'd probably pop a gusset if he even knew you were here. Jake Turnbull is one of his best customers, you know."

"All right, Sara. I can see my being here is making you uncomfortable." Mattie forced a smile, then turned toward the back room. "You can come out now, Hiram. I'm leaving." Her skirts swishing, Mattie marched out, slamming the mercantile door behind her.

That had just ended her last hope, her last chance to obtain employment. The only place she hadn't tried was the saloon—and the Miner's Delight. She'd set herself down on the nearest street corner and starve rather than submit to that.

Even if she could bring herself to sink so low, she wouldn't be hired. Jolene's girls were young and pretty. Mattie was nearing thirty, her nose a trifle too sharp, her mouth a tad too wide, her figure a bit too ample. Never in her wildest dreams would she ever think herself pretty.

As she strode past the bank, she saw Mr. Satterfield gazing out the gold-lettered window. When he spied her, he lifted his lips in a smug smile. Squashing the urge to go inside and smack him, Mattie straightened to an almost re-

gal position and sailed on by. The banker might take away
her home, her livelihood, but he could never take her respectability, nor could he break her spirit. No man alive,
she vowed, would ever do that.

Mattie cuddled her restive cat and wondered if she might
have to eat her words.

"Hurry up, men. Get that stuff out of here," Ben Satterfield ordered, impatiently glancing at his watch.

Two men grasped each side of Mattie's domed trunk and
carried it through the shop and then on down the boardwalk, depositing it with the rest of her possessions a short
ways down the street.

"Are you going to stand there and let them do this?"
Mattie demanded of the silver-haired man standing next to
her.

The sheriff sighed. "Mattie, I don't have a choice."

"You have a choice. You just don't want to take it."

"Anything else here belong to you?" the banker asked
coldly.

Too furious to speak, she shook her head.

Satterfield gestured toward the door.

When she made no attempt to move, the sheriff took her
arm and firmly escorted her outside. She stood helplessly
while the banker padlocked the shop door. Then he, the
lawman, and the two miners left her and headed down the
street.

Mattie stared after them. Somehow she never thought it
would come to this. Never thought it would really happen.
It had been easy to be brave with a roof over her head, but
faced with the grim reality of being set bag and baggage
onto the sidewalk, she found it hard not to be afraid. She
gazed down the dusty main street. People who'd known her
all her life glanced in her direction, then just as quickly
looked away, as if she had suddenly become invisible, had
ceased to exist.

Knowing she'd get no help from any of them, she turned

her back and walked to the very end of the narrow planked walk where the men had placed her pitiful pile of belongings. They could have left them in front of the shop, she thought bitterly. At least there with the small porch overhang she might have had some shelter in case it rained.

She told herself that it wasn't the miners' fault. They had only followed the banker's orders. She should be grateful they hadn't walked another two feet and dumped the whole mess into the street.

Cradling the cat in one arm, she bent and lifted her overturned oak rocker and set it upright. Then she sat down and tried to think. What in the world was she going to do?

If her trunk wasn't so heavy she might have been able to drag it to the grove of cottonwoods down by the river. Once there, she could have set up a makeshift camp. Being a miner's daughter herself, it wouldn't be the first time she'd been forced to live outdoors. But the trunk was too unwieldy for her to move by herself, and she was too proud to ask any of them for help. Neither could she risk leaving it. While the contents were not exactly valuable—books, a few quilts, linens, and her clothes—they were all she had left in the world.

A brisk wind ruffled the hair on her bonnetless head, and flattened her skirts against her legs. When she shifted positions and put her back to the wind, the cat, disturbed from its sleep, let out a plaintive meow. Mattie sighed and absently rubbed its head.

She lifted her head to gaze at the mountains beyond the town, at the snow glinting on their white-capped peaks. Today it was warm, almost hot, but tonight when the sun went down, it would be cold, maybe even freezing.

What would she do then?

❧ FIVE ❧

"All right, you two, into the kitchen," Jake bellowed. His stance wide, his arms crossed, he stared down into the children's faces.

Eyes narrowed, mouths set in a mutinous pout, the twins glared back.

"We ain't takin' no bath."

"We had one last month."

"You smell like you haven't had one in a year." Jake refused to let them get the best of him.

"We ain't gonna."

"And you cain't make us."

"Oh, I can't?" he asked in a deceptively soft tone.

A flicker of fear danced in their eyes, but they held their ground.

He stalked forward, then, before they had a chance to run, grasped each of the defiant youngsters by the shirt collar and deposited them kicking and squealing in front of the washtub. "Are you going to take your clothes off?"

Two heads shook from left to right.

"Suit yourselves." He hooked an arm around the first child's waist, swung him over the tub, and released him.

"Why you—"

Jake cupped a hand over a mass of tangled blond hair and pushed. A moment later he allowed the boy to splutter to the surface. "You were saying," he growled.

53

Mud ran in streaks down a freckled face, but the blue eyes blazed. "You got soap in my eyes."

"There's no soap in there—but now that you mentioned it—" He whirled and snatched up the bar of coarse lye soap from a rusty dish on the kitchen counter. He rubbed it between his dripping hands and stalked forward.

The wet child eyed him warily. "I kin do my own washin'."

"Yeah, we ain't babies. We know how to take a bath," the one that was still dry added.

"Oh?" Jake tossed the bar into the tub, then followed it with a tattered washcloth. "If you know how—then do it." He whirled toward the boy standing beside the tub. "When I come back, I'd better see both of you clean and in dry clothes." The look he gave them would have made most men quake in their boots.

The twins merely peered at each other, then back at him. Finally one and then the other nodded.

Trying to contain a satisfied grin, Jake strode to the door. There he sneaked a peek and saw the one in the tub grab the soap and begin to scrub himself vigorously along with the clothes he still wore. "And don't forget you got ears," he said sternly, then before they had a chance to comment, he shut the door and escaped outside to draw a breath of air. The grin he'd fought so hard to suppress now spread across his face. While they were a handful, they also reminded him of himself at that age. Stubborn as a pair of Missouri mules, but they had guts, he'd give them that.

A while later, their hair in staggered parts and plastered to the sides of their heads, and wearing wrinkled but clean clothes, the twins took their places in the back of the wagon.

The girls, their mouths as thin and unyielding as the braids that sprouted from each side of their heads, sat stiffly on the front seat beside Jake.

The baby Joshua, his lower half double-wrapped for the trip to town, sat in a crate at Jake's feet.

Due to his unsteady nerves, Jake's own face was scraped and bleeding from a good half-dozen razor nicks, and while he had managed to find one clean shirt, the rest of his clothes looked like he'd slept in them. He stared down at his charges. "I have to go into town to tend to some business, and while we are there I want y'all to mind your manners. That understood?" He met each pair of eyes. Detecting the mischief dancing in the deceptively innocent gaze of the twins, he sighed and held out his hand. "Give me the damned mouse."

A somewhat deflated little boy placed the wriggling creature in his palm.

Jake turned to the other one. "Now you. Empty your pockets." After taking possession of two squashed worms, a bug, and a fuzzy caterpillar, he deposited the rodent back in the house and the rest of the menagerie on the ground. "Anything else?"

"I need a drink of water," Hope said.

"I have to go pee," Lory stated.

"Me, too," Hal echoed.

"Do it. Then park your butts back in the wagon. And no collecting varmints on the way," he called after the two who had scrambled over the tailgate and raced toward the outhouse. Hope disappeared into the house in search of a drink.

"And what do you two need?" he said, glaring down at the remaining girl and baby.

Faith looked thoughtful, then she smiled. "My Bible?"

"I think you know enough verses to get you to town and back," he said, remembering how she spouted chastisement at him morning, noon, and night. Hell, he knew he was a sinner. No doubt about that, but it was going to take more than one big-eyed, eight-year-old girl to make him change his ways.

Her dress soaked down the front, Hope returned to join her sister on the wagon seat. The twins, their hair standing on end, their shirttails flapping and covered with dirt, climbed into the back.

"How did you get so dirty just going to the privy?" Jake asked in despair.

"He pushed me."

"He pushed me first."

"Never mind!" He bent to release the wagon brake. A peculiar smell drifted toward his nose. He sniffed suspiciously and glanced down at Joshua who returned his look with a broad smile. "You didn't."

"He didn't," Faith said indignantly. "Lory let a poot."

The towheaded youngster gave him a snug smile.

A second telltale sound rumbled from the rear of the wagon, and the boys erupted in a fit of giggles.

"Aren't you going to do something?" Faith asked, plainly outraged.

His hands trembling, Jake picked up the reins. Do what? What could he do?

The twins were already engrossed in another argument. He tried to shut his ears to the din.

The girls were vying to see who knew the longest Bible verse.

Joshua grunted and grew red in the face. This time the smell didn't come from the back of the wagon.

Jake shot a desperate gaze toward the sage-dotted prairie. He couldn't take it anymore. Somehow—somewhere he had to find some help.

By the time the wagon had rolled into Sweetheart, Jake had retreated so far into himself it was as if he were in a drunken stupor. The worst of it was, as bad as he needed it, he hadn't had a drop to drink.

He shook himself back to reality and peered over his shoulder. The twins, after pummeling each other into exhaustion, had fallen asleep. The girls were engaged in a game of cat's cradle with a piece of string. He glanced at

the baby. Joshua, though he smelled to high heaven, had
fallen asleep, too.

Jake halted the wagon in front of the mercantile and quietly instructed the girls to keep an eye on things while he
went inside. Sara Gibbons, the owner, knew everybody and
everything that went on in town. He figured, if anybody
could help him, it would be Sara.

A while later, cursing the idea that he ever thought of
Sara, he strode out of the mercantile and climbed back onto
the wagon seat.

Mattie McFearson?

He wouldn't do it.

He couldn't do it.

"Joshua's stinky," Faith announced calmly.

"Why didn't you change him?"

"You didn't bring any nappies."

"Nappies." Hell, he'd had enough to do just getting the
kids in the wagon. "Stay put." He went back into the mercantile. A moment later, a large package under his arm, he
returned to the wagon.

"What's that?" a sleepy voice from the back asked.

"Nappies," Jake growled.

"Heck. I hoped it was somethin' to eat. I'm hongry, ain't
you, Lory?"

"Hongry as can be."

Jake was hungry, too, but he wouldn't admit it. He
thought about the pancakes, burnt on one side and raw on
the other. The eggs with flecks of shell he hadn't been able
to remove. He hadn't had time to clean up the mess. It had
taken him all morning to get the kids ready to go to town.
Now it was the middle of the afternoon. If he didn't find
someone soon—

He cast a wistful eye toward the Miner's Delight, then
he remembered how outraged Sara had been when he had
mentioned he might ask Jolene to take care of the kids. The
woman had practically threatened him with tar and feathers.
Said the ladies of the town would never stand for it. And

he had no doubt that bunch of old biddies would descend on him like the wrath of God, if he attempted it—even if Jolene would agree to it. She'd never had any truck with kids that he knew of and somehow he doubted that she'd be willing to start now.

But Mattie? Recalling Sara's suggestion, he shuddered. Of all the women in the town why did Mattie have to be the only one available? Even if there was anybody else, he doubted if they could get along with the little hellions.

At least Mattie liked them. He remembered the day the kids had arrived and how the widow had taken them under her wing. They liked her, too. That, in itself, was half the battle. It didn't matter if he and the outspoken woman detested each other.

Hell, he reasoned, they wouldn't even have to see each other that often. Once he had talked her into moving out to the ranch, he could spend most of his time in town. Of course, he'd go out from time to time and check on the kids. They were his responsibility after all. Suddenly he felt as if a great weight had been lifted from his shoulders.

For the first time since their arrival, Jake looked at his unruly brood and smiled.

Hearing the rumble of wagon wheels against the hard-packed earth, Mattie peered toward the wagon making its way down the pothole-filled street. *Jake Turnbull.* She scowled and returned her attention to the tent she was trying to make, using four sticks she had driven at strategic positions between the planks of the boardwalk, and a blanket.

Instead of stopping at the Golden Nugget, the blond man guided the horses down the street and came to a stop beside her. "Good morning, Mattie."

Come to gloat, no doubt. Determined not to give up a shred of her dignity, she released the corner of the quilt she'd been tying, tucked a stray lock of hair into place, then head high she turned to face him. "Something I can do for you, Mr. Turnbull?'' Her tone was as cold and un-friendly as she could make it.

Then seeing the children, her voice softened. "Hello, my dears."

"Hello, Miss Mattie," they echoed.

"You kids stay put!" Jake shook a warning finger to-ward the squirming youngsters.

"I gotta go," one of the twins said, dancing in the back of the wagon, first on one foot, then the other.

"Me, too," the other added.

"Go find a bush, then get back in the wagon—and no collecting . . ."

The identical duo flashed impish smiles, then raced around the edge of a building and out of sight.

"My leg has gone to sleep," Faith complained.

"I'm thirsty," Hope said.

Mattie found it hard not to grin when Jake closed his eyes and let out a weary sigh.

"Take a walk," he told his niece. "That'll wake your leg up. There's a well over yonder, maybe you can help your sister get a drink."

As if expecting the worst, he eyed the baby, but Joshua appeared to be asleep.

"He looks like a little angel," Mattie said softly, gently touching Joshua's cheek.

Jake climbed down to stand beside her. "Mattie, we need to talk. Could we go into your shop?"

"It's no longer my shop, or haven't you noticed," she said bitterly, motioning toward her belongings.

"Would you—?" He pointed toward the saloon.

"Not on your life. Anything you have to say to me can be said right here." While she might like the children, her opinion of him hadn't changed one bit.

Jake glanced from her to her pile of possessions stacked on the board sidewalk and noticed the quilt tent flapping in the wind. He had no doubt that she intended to spend the night camped right there on the street. The idea that he was partly responsible for her plight grated on his conscience. On the other hand, he found himself hoping it might make her more willing to listen to his proposition.

"Mattie, it appears like you have a problem, and since I feel partly to blame, I'd like to make amends."

"Amends?" Was he planning to offer her a one-way ticket out of town?

"Why don't we load up all your stuff in the wagon, and you can move on out to the ranch with me."

"Wh-what?" she spat, giving him an outraged look. "Jake Turnbull, if you think I'm—"

He held up a hand. "Now, hold on. Don't get your drawers in an uproar. I'm offering you a job and a roof over your head."

"A job?" she asked suspiciously. "What kind of a job?"

"I need a housekeeper, and someone to help with the kids."

So that's why he offered me employment. He can't handle the children. She could tell by his confident manner that he expected her to say yes. After all, in his eyes, what other choice did she have?

"No."

"No?" Plainly taken back, he stared at her. "Why not?"

"It wouldn't be seemly."

"Seemly? What the hell does that mean?"

"It wouldn't do at all. I have my reputation to consider. What would people think if I, an unattached female, were to move in with you?"

His brows drew together in a scowl. "I don't have any designs on your virtue, if that's what you're worried about. I only want you to cook, clean, and take care of the kids."

"Oh, is that all?" she replied dryly. She could see it now. Her at the ranch taking care of his responsibilities, while he spent all his time in town doing no telling what. It would be easy to care for the kids, too easy. And in six months or a year, after she'd grown to love them, what would she do if he decided to replace her with somebody else? Knowing his temper and the way they grated on each other's nerves, she had no doubt that would be exactly what would happen.

"No, I'm sorry, but I can't do it," she said firmly. "Besides, it wouldn't be proper for me to live there without benefit of clergy."

"Clergy?" Jake took a step backward, eyeing her like she had just turned into a deadly rattler. "Are—are you talkin' about gettin' married?"

She glared back. "Don't be absurd. Even if I were in the marriage market, you would certainly be at the bottom of the list."

He was relieved she didn't want to get married, but bottom of the list? "What's wrong with me?" he asked, feeling a bit insulted. He wasn't bad-looking. He had a cheerful disposition. And he had a successful business. Most women would consider him a prime catch.

She studied him for a moment. "For one thing, you're too big. For another, you're too loud. You own a saloon— and—and frequent a whorehouse."

"Hell, I never claimed to be a saint."

"Well, that's a relief. At least you aren't a hypocrite."

He grinned in spite of himself. He noticed the way her eyes shot sparks, and the way the sunlight danced through her hair. She was so lively, a man almost forgot how plain she was. A firecracker. That's what Bock Gee had called her. Yeah, she was that all right. He wondered if she'd be that feisty in bed.

A sharp blast of wind flattened her skirts and made her shiver. The sun had dipped even lower in the sky. She glanced at Jake. No. She'd have to be crazy to even consider such a thing. "It's out of the question," she muttered.

On the other hand, it would solve both their problems. At least she would have a place to live without fear of being ejected the moment he got his tail feathers ruffled. Then there were the children . . .

She'd lifted a ringlet from Joshua's hair and twisted it

around her finger. So precious. So adorable. She'd always wanted children. It wasn't fair that Jake had so many, especially when he didn't even want them. She would have given her soul for just one.

"Mattie, be reasonable. You can't stay out on the street. Besides, I know you like the kids. They like you, too. They need a woman around. The poor little tykes miss their mama something awful," he said, playing on her sympathy. He saw the indecision in her face. She was weakening, he could tell. "The ranch house needs some fixin', but it isn't such a bad place. There's some apple trees, and you could plant a garden. With that and some beef, you'd have plenty to eat." He saw her glance at the sidewalk. "Why I'd even throw in a dollar or two every now and then," he said magnanimously.

Mattie thought about all he'd said. It was his fault she was out here. And while she was in dire straits, she would survive. She always had.

On the other hand, the children did need a mama. They needed someone who would love them, wipe their noses, fix their skinned knees, and teach them right from wrong. They needed her. And she needed them.

She squared her shoulders and looked him right in the eye.

He gave her a hopeful smile.

If she had to take Jake Turnbull along with them, then so be it. "Since you brought the subject up—" she said thoughtfully, "marriage sounds like a good idea."

His smile vanished. "Now hold on—I thought you said you didn't want to get married."

"I changed my mind."

Jake's jaw dropped. He tried to protest but could only utter a hoarse croak.

"It would be a purely platonic relationship, of course."

He swallowed and tried again. "What does that mean?" he asked warily.

"You know—a business proposition. You provide me

with a roof over my head and the respectability of marriage, and I, in turn, agree to take care of the house and children.''

''A business relationship, you say.'' He rubbed his chin. It wasn't exactly what he had in mind, but . . . He trailed his gaze over her figure. A wee bit plump, but curved in all the right places. Might be nice to have something besides the dog to curl up with on a cold winter night.

She waited for that to sink in, then she added, ''I would expect a separate bedroom, of course.'' She narrowed her eyes and raised a finger at him. ''And I need to warn you up front, the first time you tried anything funny, I'd be out the door.''

Taken back, he crossed his arms and looked at her. ''If it is a business proposition, then why do we have to get married at all?''

''Because that's the only way I'll agree to it.'' She waited a minute, then she said, ''The circuit judge is in town for a trial. I heard he is leaving on the morning stage. He could marry us tonight.''

''Tonight?'' He hadn't even agreed to this marriage thing yet, and even if he might consider it, he'd envisioned an engagement first—a long engagement.

''Uncle Jake, we're hungry and Hope needs to go to the bathroom,'' Faith said, running breathlessly toward them.

Jake shot a desperate look toward Mattie. She stood there calmly, resolutely, waiting for his answer.

He shifted from one foot to the other.

A high-pitched shriek echoed from up the street. Mattie traced the sound to the mercantile and saw the twins burst through the door. The shopkeeper, hot on their heels, grabbed the pair by their shirttails and marched them down the street.

''Now what?'' Jake muttered.

''Joshua needs to be changed,'' Faith said matter-of-factly, holding the squirming infant toward him.

Jake shot another beseeching look toward Mattie.

''Well?'' she said, trying to keep the laughter out of her

tone. She could wait—but he couldn't. He looked to be at the end of his rope.

"All right!" he croaked. "We'll get married."

"You needn't sound so overjoyed about it," she said wryly. "And before you agree, there is one thing more."

"What?" he growled, trying to balance the infant without getting saturated himself.

"After we are married, you will not visit the Miner's Delight, nor any other place of ill repute. Once you are my husband, I will expect you to be loyal and faithful."

"Loyal and faithful?" She made him sound like a dog. His eyes narrowed. "Let me see if I've got this straight. This marriage is to be a business proposition. You want a separate bedroom—and I'm not to come near it."

"That's right."

"And I'm not to go near the Miner's Delight. That will be a little difficult considering Jolene and I are partners," he said sarcastically.

"That wasn't what I meant, and you know it."

"I'm a man," he bellowed. "A healthy man. What you want is not natural." He shook his head. "No, I won't do it."

Mattie shrugged. "Suit yourself." She turned and stepped back up onto the boardwalk.

"Jake, do these belong to you?" Hiram Gibbons, almost purple with fury, led the wriggling boys forward.

Startled by all the commotion, Joshua let out a loud wail.

"Uncle Jake, we couldn't find the privy, and Hope had an accident."

Jake glanced from the outraged shopkeeper, to the mutinous twins, to the crying baby, to the tear-stained cheeks of his youngest niece. His stomach knotted. He shot a look toward the widow.

She glanced at the children, then back at him, but she didn't say a word.

She had him by the short hairs and she knew it. "Mattie," he said through gritted teeth.

"Yes, Jake?"

"You win," he said, sagging in defeat.

Mattie looked up from the children to the big blustery man who, too, appeared on the verge of tears. This morning she had no one but herself and her cat. By tonight, she would have a family. Her gaze rested a moment on each of them. She squared her shoulders and smiled. "It's settled then." Whether they knew it or not, they needed her—all of them.

❧ SIX ❧

After cleaning the kids up as best he could, Jake marched the kids to Mama Maria's Kitchen, that being the only respectable eating place in Sweetheart, and ordered them supper. Once his own steaming plate was set in front of him, he found he couldn't swallow a morsel.

He found it hard to believe that after managing to avoid marriage for some thirty-five years, he would now be tying the knot. Especially to Mattie McFearson. The very woman who had been a thorn in his side ever since he'd set foot in town.

He didn't love Mattie. He didn't even like her. But then loving or liking had nothing to do with it. Besides, he'd never been in love in his life and didn't expect to start now.

The widow could hardly abide him at all. Maybe in a way that was better. At least that way with no expectations, there would be no hurt feelings or illusions.

He thought about Mattie herself. A woman of definite opinions, and not shy about expressing them. They'd probably have one battle after another, but then he never cared for a namby-pamby-type woman either. He had to admit life with Mattie would be interesting. More like downright aggravating, he amended with a scowl.

He filled a spoon with mashed potatoes and shoved it into Joshua's open mouth. The baby swallowed, then opened again. Like feeding a little bird, he thought, filling the spoon again.

Mattie did seem real taken with the kids. Too bad she never had any of her own. Life didn't seem fair sometimes, especially since he had five he didn't know what to do with.

"You boys eat those potatoes and stop throwing them at each other. No, Hope, you can't have pie until you eat your supper."

The children did need a mama. Sometimes they still cried themselves to sleep at nights, especially the baby. He'd tried to comfort them, but most of the time it hadn't helped. Sometimes his helping had even made it worse. Women were better at that sort of thing, he guessed.

"Joshua's wet again," Faith said, pointing to the trail of yellow liquid that ran off the seat of the chair and onto the floor.

Jake mentally counted the remaining diapers.

With Mattie around, he wouldn't have to change any more dirty diapers. He wouldn't have to wash them either. He smiled.

He thought about the kitchen and the mess he'd left it in. She'd clean it up.

Could she cook? After the episode with the beans he had his doubts. But then, she couldn't do worse than he had.

The more he thought about it, the more getting Mattie moved to the ranch sounded like a good idea.

But damn it, he still didn't see why they had to get married!

In the anteroom of the sheriff's office where the ceremony would be held, Mattie nervously twisted the ties to her reticule and waited for the rest of the wedding participants to arrive.

The sparsely furnished courtroom contained only a few rough benches and a cot in one corner where an occasional drunk was allowed to sleep it off. A plank over two whiskey barrels made do as a desk, behind which during trials, the judge sat and resided over his court. A lone chair sat to the right of that.

Not the most auspicious place to begin a life together, she thought, but nothing about her union to the saloon keeper was ordinary. A marriage of convenience, pure and simple.

Mattie bent toward the basket she'd set on one end of the bench and absently stroked the back of her sleeping cat. The rest of her things had already been loaded into Jake's wagon, so that immediately after the ceremony they could head for the ranch. Since she had never been there, she had no notion of what the place was like, or what she'd be getting into. Just the idea of moving into Jake's home, sleeping under the same roof, filled her with trepidation.

Hearing voices, she straightened and hastily adjusted the lace collar on her navy-blue marino dress. Then, not wanting to fidget, she clenched her hands in her lap to hide her nervousness.

The sheriff and judge entered first and greeted her politely. The sheriff, a bored look on his face, took the only chair. He sat down and leaned back, balancing it on its rear legs, its ladder back propped against the wall.

The judge lifted his broad-brimmed felt hat by the crown and placed it on a rack next to the door. He opened a black cowhide satchel and took out a Bible and some papers and placed them on the makeshift desk.

With a banging of the door and mischievous giggles, the twins bounced into the room. Faith and Hope sedately followed. Jake, carrying the baby, entered a few seconds later.

Mattie got to her feet. When she gazed at the muscular blond man who would soon be her husband, it was all she could do to keep from bolting out the door. Only the sight of the children kept her rooted where she stood.

"Sit—and be still," Jake ordered the twins who began squirming the moment their small bottoms touched the bench. Jake handed Joshua to Faith who let out a very audible sigh of resignation. Next to her, Hope removed the calico cat from the basket. Bridget, cuddled in the little girl's lap, purred in contentment.

Hope tilted her blond head toward Mattie and smiled. Then as if remembering something, the little girl reached into her dress pocket and pulled out a handful of wilted violets that Mattie knew the child must have filched from Sara Gibbons's yard. "We picked these for you," she said, holding the bedraggled bouquet toward Mattie.

"You can't give her those," Faith scolded. "They look awful."

Hope's face crumpled.

Mattie knelt beside her and took the flowers from her hand. "I think they are lovely. And they smell wonderful. See?" She held the crushed petals out for them to sniff.

"You really like them?" Hope asked anxiously.

"I love them. Thank you very much." Mattie gave the child a smile.

Behind her the judge cleared his throat. "If you all are ready . . ." he said in a brusque voice tinged with weariness.

Catching sight of a stranger, the baby's eyes widened, then he opened his mouth and began to squall.

"What's the matter with him?" The judge bent close and peered over his spectacles at the child.

"You scared him," Faith answered.

"Well, shush him," Jake ordered.

"He won't!" Faith said indignantly. "If you want him shushed, you'll have to hold him."

"Shall we get on with it?" the judge asked impatiently.

Jiggling the sobbing child in his arms, Jake shot a hopeful glance toward Mattie, who ignored him, even though it broke her heart to do so. She didn't dare give in—not yet.

"You two stand here." The judge pointed to a spot directly in front of him.

Mattie moved forward. Jake took a position by her side.

The sheriff, who was acting as a witness, rocked the chair forward, the bored look gone from his face. He looked from the kids, to Jake, to Mattie, then his face split in an ear-to-ear grin. "Well, I be danged. I never thought it would be you two getting hitched. I thought one of Jolene's girls was getting married." The sheriff got up from his seat. "Wait till I tell—"

"You git back here," Jake ordered the lawman. "This is a private ceremony. The only reason we got you was to make it legal. I damned sure don't want it turned into a circus."

"Dearly beloved," the judge shouted to make himself heard over the din.

Lory left his seat and came to tug on Jake's coat sleeve. "I gotta go," he whispered loudly.

"Me, too," Hal said, dancing behind him.

"Sit!" Jake yelled. "You can hold it for a minute."

"I can't hold it!" Lory cried, hopping up and down.

"Me neither. I gotta go now!"

"Oh, hell!" The judge slammed the Bible shut.

"Judge, please. Remember the children," Mattie admonished.

"How could I forget them?" the balding man growled.

"Go, then get back here, pronto!" Jake told the boys, who immediately sprinted from the room.

Jake looked at Mattie and rolled his eyes. She found it difficult to repress a hysterical giggle.

The sheriff erupted in laughter.

The judge pulled his watch from his vest pocket and checked the time. "I hope this doesn't take all night," he said dourly.

"We're back," the twins announced, bursting into the room.

"Now, if you are ready . . ." the judge said.

The boys raced to their bench and immediately began to argue about who was supposed to sit where.

Jake stalked over and grabbed the nearest one by the ear. "Sit! Anywhere! The bench. The floor. Just sit!" he yelled.

Upset by the commotion, Bridget let out a frantic yowl,

then the cat leapt from Hope's lap and cowered, hissing and growling, in the corner. Hope followed, trying to console her.

The judge, apparently deciding things weren't about to get any better, opened the Bible and began to read. After a minute or two, he paused and stared at Jake.

Jake, who obviously hadn't the vaguest idea of what was expected of him, looked at Mattie.

Mattie shrugged and shook her head. She couldn't help him; she hadn't heard a word the man said.

"Just say, 'I do,' " the judge snarled.

"I do?" Jake said.

His forehead beaded with perspiration, the judge turned to Mattie. "Do you, Matilda, promise to love, honor, and obey this man?"

"Ha, that'll be the day," Jake said.

Since she wasn't about to promise any of those things, Mattie glared at Jake but remained silent.

"Do you want to marry this fool or not?" the judge demanded.

Mattie looked at Jake, who appeared to be daring her to say the words. Her eyes narrowed. If it weren't for the children she'd walk right out the door. But as she took in the weariness, the expectancy on each small face, a rush of determination filled her very being. She straightened and stared straight into Jake's eyes. "I will," she said, all the time wondering if she was doing the right thing, especially since the big man standing next to her looked like she had just condemned him to a hanging.

"So be it," Jake said softly, the words more of a threat than a promise.

What other choice did she have? Mattie had prevaricated when she'd told him she had to consider her reputation. Truth be known, she could care less what any of the town thought. She could have gone to the ranch without marriage, cooked, cleaned, cared for the children.

Cared for the children.

That was why she had to do what she did, she argued with herself. For the children. God help her, she loved them already. They deserved better than an old-maid house-keeper, for even though she'd been married all of five minutes before her dear Jaime had been murdered, that was the way she had always thought of herself.

They also deserved better than a part-time uncle-father. Probably very part-time once she had taken over his re-sponsibilities.

Engrossed in her thoughts, she hardly knew when Jake lifted her hand and slipped a heavy gold band on her finger. But when he bent and brushed his lips against her cheek, she jumped and let out a startled gasp.

"I'm not going to eat you, Mattie," he hissed next to her ear. "The judge told me to kiss the bride."

"Bride?" She blinked in surprise. "It's over?"

Jake gave her a humorless smile. "Yeah, it's over."

"Well, Mr. and Mrs. Turnbull, I guess that's that." The judge closed the Bible with a snap.

Mrs. Turnbull. Stunned, Mattie realized she and Jake were truly married. Somehow she thought there would be more—that she would feel different—something . . .

"You two, sign these papers, then maybe I can go have some supper." The judge shoved a document toward them.

Mattie quickly signed her name, then peered up at Jake. "I think Joshua's wet." She motioned toward the dark spot that was rapidly spreading across Jake's chest and inching downward toward his pants.

Jake glanced down and groaned. "Not again."

"Let me take him." She held out her arms.

Jake quickly relinquished the baby, then turned to affix his signature to the paper.

Grinning broadly, the sheriff stepped forward and signed his name as witness, then he slapped Jake on the back. "Well, Jake, I never thought I'd live to see the day, but looks like you've finally gone and done it."

"Congratulations, Mattie." The sheriff grabbed her

shoulders and gave her a swift but thorough kiss. "Good luck, you two," he called on his way out of the room.

The judge finished the document and gave them a copy. He looked from Jake to Mattie, then he shook his head. "Good luck is right. You're going to need it," he added, stepping around the twins as he made his way out the door.

Mattie, having changed Joshua's britches, gathered up the rest of her brood and gave each of them a hug. She looked up to see Jake standing by her side.

"Well, *Mrs. Turnbull*, you got what you wanted. *Now* can we go home?" Jake's blue eyes were as flinty and cold as his tone.

Mattie swallowed. For better or worse, it was too late to back out now. "Yes, Mr. Turnbull, now we can go home."

❧ SEVEN ❧

After a fitful night, Mattie woke to a cold gray dawn and for a moment, gazing around the tiny room with the peeling paint and patched plaster, she wondered just where she was. Then she remembered. She was at Jake's ranch. Her new home, she amended. It hadn't been a dream. For better or worse—probably worse—she was Mrs. Burton Jacob Turnbull.

"Shh!" warned a small voice.

"Don't shh me. Uncle Jake said to wake her up."

Mattie twisted toward the door and saw two pairs of blue eyes peering down at her bed. "Good morning, girls. Aren't you up awfully early?"

"It's pert near eight o'clock," Faith said solemnly.

"Eight o'clock?" Her first morning as a wife and mother and she'd overslept. She, who'd never slept beyond six o'clock in her life.

"And we're awful hungry," Hope added.

"I'll bet you are. Give me a minute, and I'll get dressed."

"We'll tell Uncle Jake you're awake." They went out and closed the door.

Jake! Mattie bolted from her bed. He'd make sure she never heard the end of this. She pulled on her clothes, then hastily yanked the brush through her hair and twisted the mass into a tight knot.

75

It being so late last night, she'd been too busy getting
the children to bed to take note of her surroundings. When
they had entered the house Jake hadn't even lit a lantern;
he showed her to the bedroom with a candle, which she
thought was a little odd at the time. But maybe he'd been
afraid it would rouse the children.

Jake had said that he had given her and the girls the best
bedroom; he and the boys were sharing a room in another
part of the house.

Glancing around her, she noticed there was no water, nor
any facilities for washing. The room contained only the
barest necessities, but being the home of a bachelor, she
could hardly expect any of the niceties. She and the girls
shared the rustic wooden-framed bed. A rickety shelf hung
from one wall. On another, a few scattered pegs held var-
ious items of Jake's clothing.

The girls apparently had yet to unpack, as their clothes
peeked from the edges of their battered old carpetbag.
Bridget's basket, with the snoozing calico still inside, sat
next to it.

She felt among the dustballs under the bed and retrieved
her shoes, then put them on. "The place could certainly
use a woman's hand," she muttered grimly.

When she reached the kitchen she found Jake and the
children gathered around the table, apparently waiting for
her to fix something to eat. A grizzled red-boned hound
dog peered hopefully up at her from his spot next to the
stove.

"Good morning, I'm sorry—" She scanned the rest of
the room and her eyes widened. Good grief, no wonder he
hadn't been able to find any help. No wonder he'd agreed
to get married. No one in their right mind would ever vol-
unteer to clean this up. Pots and pans of every size and
shape littered the lone countertop and floor. The stove—
her stomach rolled. She certainly couldn't cook on that.

She sucked in a breath and turned to Jake. "I need hot

water and lots of it. I can't cook until I clean up this mess.''

"I guess things did get a little dirty," he admitted, not bothering to rise from his place. "Me being so busy and all.''

Busy? You just think you've seen busy. Wait till I get through with you. Mattie crossed her arms and drilled him with a look that would have made any army sergeant proud. "Water," she barked. "Now!"

Jake blanched, then grabbed a bucket and headed out the door.

Three hours later, Mattie set their breakfast on the table. The pan of biscuits and the platter of steak and eggs disappeared before she'd taken her seat.

"I'm still hungry," Lory complained.

"Me, too," his counterpart answered.

Mattie wrinkled her brow in despair. She'd been used to cooking for only herself. Even with the extra food she'd allowed, it apparently hadn't been enough. "I'll fix some more.''

"Don't bother, Mattie," Jake said, rubbing his chest. "That should be enough to hold us until lunch."

"What time is lunch?"

Jake took his watch out of his pocket and checked the time. "Usually about noon, but since it's already after eleven, we'll wait till one to eat today."

Less than two hours, then she had the whole thing to do over again. "I'll try to prepare enough next time."

"Good. That first batch just whetted my appetite." Grinning, Jake gave her a slap on the back and headed toward the door. "Come on, kids, let's get at the chores."

Mattie sank into her chair and studied the greasy streak floating on top of her coffee. The pot must still be dirty. She'd been in such a hurry to prepare the meal that the kitchen looked almost as bad now as when she'd started.

She'd envisioned their first breakfast together, the children bowing their heads as she said grace, then she and Jake conversing as they ate their meal. Instead they had devoured the meal like a pack of hungry dogs. A muffled sound drew her attention to the floor on the other side of the table. "Bridget?" She got to her feet and went to investigate.

Peering through the bars of a wooden box, Joshua gave her a toothy grin.

"Oh, sweetheart," she murmured, bending to lift him into her arms. She'd been so steeped in her own misery, she'd forgotten about the baby. She drew a finger down his chubby cheek and wiped away some crumbs. "Well, I see they gave you a biscuit at least." But they hadn't changed his diaper or washed his face.

After a hastily concocted lunch of thick slices of beef between freshly baked bread, Mattie once again cleaned the kitchen and hung up the towels to dry. She rinsed the beans she'd put to soak earlier and set the cast-iron kettle on the stove to simmer. She took a quick peek at the napping baby, then went to examine the rest of the house.

The main ranch building had been designed like a fortress, square and with a courtyard in the middle. But due to a raid by the Utes who had set fire to the ranch about ten years previous, the only undamaged part was the kitchen and pantry, which she decided was now the bedroom she shared with the girls.

Jake had stated that before the children had arrived, he'd rarely stayed in the house, and usually had bunked in the long house with the rest of the hands.

By the looks of the place, she could well believe it. She discovered the cooking area was separated from the rest of the house by a narrow corridor. Leaving the kitchen door ajar so that she could hear Joshua if he awakened, she crossed the hall and opened the door of what was apparently the main room.

While large enough, it had apparently not been used since the fire. Its walls were smoked to a dismal gray and grimy black cobwebs swung from the beams that supported the ceiling. Faded blankets hung over the windows shutting out most of the light. It smelled of horse and mice and other things she didn't care to put a name to. But the room was large, and the huge rock fireplace centering the back wall would make the room cozy on the coldest winter nights.

Behind another door she found the bedroom that Jake had been sharing with the boys. It, too, barely accommodated the bed and a narrow dresser. From what she had seen on the outside, the house appeared much larger than it actually was.

Thoughtful, she went back into the larger room, then walked to one of the blankets on the back wall and pulled it to one side. Not a window as she had thought, but a passageway. She took a few steps, then a scurrying of something in the darkness sent her rushing back the way she came.

Dusting her hands together to remove the dirt, she left the house and strolled into the sunlight. Under a trio of gnarled cottonwoods, a trickling spring overflowed a circle of moss-covered boulders and made a verdant green trail across a stone-flagged courtyard. A drinking cup, green with age, hung from a chain. She filled it from the bubbling spring and took a sip, finding the water ice-cold and sweet. She rinsed the cup and paused to gaze at the remainder of the house. One side was in ruin, with only the adobe walls and rotting timbers remaining. The far end had apparently been used for storage or horse stalls as there were no doors on any of the rooms. The side she had been trying to explore . . .

She walked beneath the sway-backed porch and tried to peek between pieces of boards that covered the paneless windows. Dark as a tomb, wet and dank, like a musty old barn long vacant. But from the outside, at least, it seemed to be intact.

She smiled, envisioning what the place could look like—with some structural repairs and a lot of hard labor.

A high thin wail told her Joshua had awakened and

needed her attention. She brushed the cobwebs off her skirt and headed for the kitchen. For now, she had enough to do with the part they were occupying to keep her busy for the next few days. But soon, she promised herself. Soon.

Jake groaned and then attempted to stretch out the kinks in his legs and back. He'd thought when Mattie arrived that things would be a lot easier. He'd thought *she'd* be doing most of the work. She soon disavowed him of that notion.

Ever since the woman arrived she'd been like a tornado whipping everything in her path into a frenzy. She'd made dust fly that hadn't been stirred in a hundred years.

And she wasn't through yet. Nor was he—he gritted his teeth—if she had anything to do with it.

"Jake, I need for you to beat these rugs, then after I get the room swept down and mopped you can start white-washing the walls." Mattie, her head swathed in one of Joshua's diapers, the rest of her covered by a soot-streaked apron, pointed toward a stack of woven Mexican rugs she had unearthed in one of the back rooms.

"Mattie, we don't have to do the whole thing in one day," Jake protested.

"It's only ten o'clock. My goodness, we can get a lot of it done before dark."

"Yeah, if I live that long," he grumbled under his breath. He lugged the rugs into the yard, then he grinned. "Hey, kids, how would you like to have some more fun?"

"I don't think so," Lory said, eyeing the stack of rugs with suspicion.

"I'm plumb tuckered from all the fun we had yester-day," Hal added.

"Traitors," Jake said under his breath when the boys disappeared around the side of the house. Yesterday, Mattie decided they needed to do all the bedding. Mattresses had to be turned and fluffed. The rooms scrubbed from top to bottom. The boys' job had been to put the blankets in a washtub and poke them until they were clean. Then Mattie lifted them from there into the hot water and finished the chore. Jake's job had been to hang them. All of them. He never knew a wet quilt could be so danged heavy. Then last night after everything was dry, she'd made him help her make the beds.

He didn't know where she got so much energy. In the last three days he'd eaten so much dirt he felt like he'd been caught in a dust storm. He'd carted, brushed, and beaten till he was worn to a frazzle, and that didn't account for the scrubbing and whitewashing she'd made him do.

One thing he could say for the woman, she would have made a damn fine general. With her giving orders, the other side wouldn't have had a chance.

"Jake, have you got those rugs done yet?"

He closed his eyes, longing for the good old days when he and dirt led a peaceful coexistence. The days before Mattie McFearson—Turnbull, he amended ruefully—came into his life.

"There, now doesn't that look better?" Mattie stood hands on hips and admired the living room. The stone floor gleamed and smelled of beeswax, and the freshly white-washed walls reflected the sunshine streaming in the sparkling windows. Plump calico pillows rested on each end of the lumpy, old horsehair couch and a long brightly colored Mexican rug ran in front of it on the floor. Mattie's rocker with a table beside it sat to one side of the fireplace and Jake's rawhide chair sat at the other.

"Yeah, Mattie. It looks damned fine," Jake agreed. "I doubt it looked that good when it was new." It did look nice—and comfortable. He sank down in his chair and just started to close his eyes when he saw her tilt her head sideways and thoughtfully gaze toward the other wall. He knew that look—too well.

"I've got some horses on the north range to see to," he said, bolting to his feet. "But I'll be back in time for supper." He snatched his hat from the deer-antler rack and sprinted toward the door.

❧ EIGHT ❧

"Danged ol' cat!"

"Get 'er outta here!"

"Not again," Mattie said, recognizing the twins' voices. She propped the broom she'd been using against the wall, then making certain that Joshua was still in his pen and out of mischief, she gathered her skirts and hurried toward the commotion.

"Oww! It bit me."

Bridget let out an outraged yowl, then shot from the room, a bolt of yellow and black crashing into Mattie's legs, then disappeared out the door.

Entering the bedroom, Mattie placed her hands on her hips and gazed down at the little boys. "All right. What happened now?"

"You and that mean old cat. Don't know why you had to come here in the first place," Lory cried, wiping a tear from his cheek.

"I came here because I married your uncle," Mattie said softly.

"Uncle Jake didn't want to get hitched. He told me so," Hal said.

"I also came here to take care of you."

"Hope says you're our new mama. Well you ain't. Our mama's dead."

Mattie looked from one small angry face to the other.

Her eyes filled with tears, but determined not to let them see how much their words hurt, she blinked them away. "No, I'm not your mama, and I would never presume to take her place. I know you must miss her dreadfully."

Mattie sat down on the edge of the bed. "You know, I lost my own mother when I was only eight. I was lucky enough to have my father to take care of me." She was the one who had taken care of the both of them, but she couldn't tell the children that. "I didn't have any brothers or sisters, and many times I would have liked to have had someone to talk to. You know, like a friend."

"Don't need no friend," Lory mumbled.

" 'Sides, we already have a friend." Hal patted the bulge in his shirt pocket. "Solomon."

So that's it, Mattie thought. "Was Bridget bothering Solomon?"

"Yeah. Scairt him pert near to death."

"Mean old cat."

"How did she get in here?" Mattie had put the feline outside early that morning, and had been careful to see that the cat hadn't crept back in.

"She came in the window."

"Jumped right in."

Mattie gazed down at their solemn little faces. She lifted a hand to brush a lock of blond hair from Lory's eyes, then thinking better of the notion, dropped her hand back to her side. Would she ever be able to break down the boys' resistance? The more she tried, the more withdrawn they became. Why? What was it about her that made them so wary?

Part of it she knew was due to Jake. He seemed as adverse to change as the boys, even though everything she had done was for all of them, for his well-being and comfort as well as that of the children. Jake behaved as if she were a tyrant, a shrew. With their uncle as a role model, how could she expect the boys to behave any differently?

"I'm sorry about the cat," she said sympathetically.

"Maybe you should keep the window shut—at least until Bridget learns she is not supposed to be in this room."

"Couldn't you tell her to stay out?" Lory asked.

"I could, but I doubt if it would do much good. I'm afraid Bridget has a mind of her own."

"Stubborn, huh?" Lory asked, taking a seat beside her.

" 'Fraid so."

"Solomon's like that sometimes," Hal said, taking up a position on her other side.

"He is?"

"Yeah. I tell him not to eat my socks, but he does it anyway."

All those little holes— Mattie fought to hide her smile. "Well, maybe he's hungry. I've got an idea. How would you boys and Solomon like a cookie?"

"You ain't mad 'cause Lory bit the cat?"

"B-bit the cat?" Mattie asked in a strangled voice.

"I didn't bite her hard. 'Sides, she bit me first," Lory declared. "Are you still gonna give me a cookie?"

"Well, since she started it, I guess she had it coming. But please, don't do it again."

"I won't," the little boy assured her. "Got my mouth plumb full of cat hair."

Not daring to comment on that, Mattie got to her feet, then motioning for them to follow, led the way to the kitchen.

While she could understand the twins' anxiety over their pet, Bridget had her sympathy, too. The poor thing had been bodily removed from the only home she had even known and now was forced to live in a place where Jake's dog, Rusty, reigned supreme. Right now the cat was probably hiding in the barn. But Bridget had survived the town dogs, and Mattie was confident her pet would adjust to this situation as well.

While the boys were washing their hands, Mattie took Joshua from his play pen and put him in his high chair, and handed him a cookie. Then she prepared cookies and milk and placed equal portions in front of the boys. "Here you go."

"What about Solomon?" Lory asked, holding out the mouse.

"I haven't forgotten." She placed the rodent on the floor, next to a cookie she'd crumbled into a pan, and watched as Solomon began to eat.

After the battle she'd fought to keep the mice out of her millinery, she never dreamed she'd be feeding one of the creatures in her own kitchen. But she had to admit, with his overlarge ears and soft gray fur and twitching nose, Solomon was an engaging little fellow, and it was quite clear the twins doted on him.

Lory finished first, then he squatted on the floor beside the mouse and waited for him to eat his fill. When the mouse stopped eating, Lory picked him up and gave him a pat. "He's too full to run very fast, so guess I'd better put him back in our room."

"Indeed, he does seem to be putting on weight," Mattie said, stroking Solomon's fat little tummy.

"About that friend business—" Lory began, gazing up at her.

"Yes?" she said hopefully.

"Hal's my best friend. And I guess Solomon is second best."

"Aren't you lucky?" Mattie declared. "Must be nice to have so many friends."

The boys looked from one to another, then Lory, his blue eyes narrowed, stared up at her. "Maybe you could be a third best friend—if'n you were of a mind to."

A third best friend. Not a mother or anywhere near, but a definite start at least. "I would like that very much," she said, smiling.

"Guess we'd better put Solomon up." Hal slipped the rodent back into his pocket, then together he and his brother headed toward the bedroom.

A few minutes later Mattie watched them leave the house

and race across the yard toward the corral where Jake and two of the hands were working with some horses.

She cleaned the table and washed the baby's face and hands. She held him close, cuddling him, breathing in his baby smell, talking softly to him until he began to squirm, then she sat him on the floor and gave him a tin pot and spoon.

No, she wasn't their mother, but that didn't mean she didn't want to be. No mother could love them more. But she was a third best friend and that was a definite beginning.

Now if she could just get Jake to relent, if even a little. She was beginning to wonder if he would ever see her as anything but an intruder into his life. He never ceased to grumble and complain, but she noticed he certainly had no qualms about being the first to the table. He ate enough for two and while he never offered to either clean the table or do the dishes, he did make certain she had enough kindling to operate the cookstove, especially after that first day when she'd told him she wouldn't cook if he didn't. She'd said it out of desperation, but he had apparently taken her at her word.

She had made some progress. He now brushed the dirt from his clothes and wiped his boots before he entered the house. Probably because he feared she'd make him haul water to clean the floors and beat the rugs if he didn't.

She peered through the window, her gaze taking in the trio perched on the top rail of the corral fence—the large blond man, a towheaded child on each side.

Even though they'd been married only a short time, she grudgingly admitted there was more to Jake than his gruff demeanor. Through all his blustering, she'd seen a sensitive side, especially with the children. He had a keen, if somewhat odd, sense of humor, and he was kind to animals. The orphaned calf was proof of that.

After its mother had died of snakebite, most ranchers would have disposed of it, considering such a young animal more trouble than it was worth, but Jake had bundled it in his coat and carried it back to the ranch. He'd spent the rest of the day trying to teach the calf to drink from a bucket, after the milk cow they kept at the ranch refused to allow the baby to suck.

After two days of watching, Faith and Hope had pleaded to take over the chore. And now the gangling bull calf followed the girls everywhere they went. Mattie only hoped the children wouldn't grow too fond of the calf as later on it would most certainly either have to be sold or butchered.

Mattie glanced toward the pile of ironing she'd dampened, then cast a wistful gaze toward the doorway where the bright sunshine beckoned. "Too nice a day to spend inside, isn't it, little one?"

The baby babbled something and grinned up at her.

Mattie cast off her apron, then scooped Joshua up and placed him on one hip. Without a care for the work she'd left undone, she strode purposefully out the door.

A squeal of excitement made Jake turn toward the house. He smiled when he saw Mattie and Joshua playing "ring around the rosy" on the only spot of green in the yard. The woman and the baby tumbled onto the grass and their laughter, caught by the sage-scented wind, drifted toward him. Mattie's hair, never overly neat, had come undone, and a waterfall of sun-touched, brown curls danced around her shoulders.

Motherhood became her, he thought. She didn't look like the stiff-necked widow who had blackmailed him into marriage, then turned his house—and his life—upside down. She'd changed, grown softer, more womanly. But she still had a tongue that could flay the hide off a man at ten paces. She seemed younger. From here she almost looked pretty. He snorted at the notion.

Suddenly aware that the noise around him had ceased, Jake looked back at the corral to see that the cowboys had stopped work. They each stood, one booted heel hooked on the lower rail, their arms draped over the top of the fence. Both of them eyed Mattie like they were starving and she was a fresh-cooked steak.

Jake noisily cleared his throat, and the hands gave him a guilty look, then returned their attention to the horse they had been attempting to break.

"Think I'll go join *my wife*, if you fellers think you can handle that cayuse by yourselves," he said pointedly.

"Shore, boss, you go right ahead," a tall cowboy named Slim said quickly.

"If you're nice, she might give you a cookie," Lory suggested.

"They're awful good," Hal added.

"De-licious," Slim said.

"How would you know?" Jake's eyes narrowed.

"Your missus brought a platterful down to the cook-shack this morning," the hand said.

"She did?"

"She even gave one to Solomon," Hal told him.

"That so?" Jake got down from his perch. Since Mattie was having so much fun, he wouldn't bother her. He could just help himself to the cookies, that way he could sneak a second helping. His mouth watering in anticipation, he strode toward the house and into the kitchen.

The cookies weren't on the table, like he'd expected. And they weren't in the tin. He peered into the pie safe. Empty. He scratched his head, then lifted the curtain covering the lower half of the cupboard. Not there either. "Well, damn it!"

"Jake, what are you doing?" Mattie asked from behind him.

He whirled, feeling as guilty as if he'd already eaten them. "Kids said you made cookies," he growled.

"Yes. I did."

"Where did you put them?"

"I guess they're all gone."

"Gone?" She'd baked cookies. She'd given them to the

hired hands, the kids, even the damned mouse got one. Everybody but him. She hadn't saved a one for him.

"I'm sorry," Mattie said softly. "I didn't know you liked cookies."

"Where did you get that idea?" He didn't know anybody who didn't like cookies.

"The bunkhouse cook said you never ate any of his."

"I had good reason. Mooney's cookies are hard as horseshoes and taste like a cross between cow dung and sawdust." Just thinking of the cook's baked goods made him shudder.

"Oh."

He stared down at her. "I *like* cookies. Just never get any," he grumbled. Never got anything else either, thanks to that damned agreement she made him swear to.

"I'm sorry," she said, placing her hand on his arm.

She sure didn't look sorry. Her eyes fairly danced with laughter.

He gave an indignant sniff, then he slowly inhaled again. She smelled like flowers, and green grass and sunshine. He sucked in another whiff. She also smelled like woman. The scent inflamed his body. Afraid she would notice, he abruptly turned away.

"If you are that hungry for cookies, I could make some more tomorrow," she promised brightly.

He was hungry for cookies. He was also hungry for something else. Something she'd forbidden him to have. Something he was starting to crave as much as air.

"Tomorrow?" she said, picking a piece of hay off his sleeve.

Jake twitched like she'd touched him with a hot branding iron. The fresh air had done her good, he noticed. Her skin was clear and golden and a sprinkling of freckles like tiny gold nuggets were scattered across the bridge of her nose. Her hair caught the sunlight that streamed through the open doorway, making it the color of spun honey shot with bronze, the texture of silk. He clenched his hands at his sides before he yielded to the urge to tangle his fingers in it.

"Jake, are you all right?"

He didn't answer. He couldn't. He had to get out of there before he did something he'd be sorry for. He stepped around her and strode out the door.

"Hey, Jake," Romero yelled.

Too furious to answer, he lengthened his stride, then when the cowboy called again, Jake cursed and whirled toward the corral. "What do you want?"

"Thought you might want to finish riding this cayuse out while we start on another," Romero shouted back.

"Why not?" He sure had nothing better to do. Besides, the way things were going, the horse might be the only thing he'd be astraddle for a while.

"Did you like the cookies?" Lory asked.

"Didn't get any," Jake mumbled.

"What?" Hal said, leaning closer.

"They were all gone," Jake bellowed, glaring toward the cowboys.

The hands gave him a startled look, then they began to laugh.

"Am I payin' you two to work or act the fool?"

"I think we had better go get that horse," Romero said, hastily exiting the corral.

"I agree, amigo," Slim said, chaps flapping as he followed. The men disappeared around the side of the barn, but the distance didn't quell their laughter.

Jake scowled as he checked the cinch on the gelding. The hands weren't the only ones playing the fool. Mattie was making a fool of *him* and there wasn't a thing he could do about it.

His stomach rumbled. Disgruntled, he opened the corral gate and swung into the saddle. Before nightfall the whole ranch would know *he* hadn't gotten any cookies.

As he rode across an open field, he also thought about the cowboys and the way they had looked at Mattie. That rankled worse than not getting the cookies. It also made him wonder if they knew what else he wasn't getting.

❧ NINE ❧

Sighing wearily, Mattie paused to gaze through the window before she stripped off her soiled dress. Outside, the rain splattered against the windowpanes, much the same as it had all through the night. Inside, the day so far had been one disaster after another, what with Joshua dumping his porridge in her lap, and the twins spilling theirs on the floor. She had fixed them each another bowl and cleaned the floor as best she could. Leaving the remainder of the mess to clean up later, she'd retreated to her room to change.

Jake had gone to the barn before breakfast to feed the calf. This task ordinarily belonged to the girls but since both of them had colds, Mattie didn't want them out in the wet. Joshua was teething, and with the weather being so bad, both of the twins would be confined to the house as well.

Not knowing if Jake had returned yet, and reluctant to leave the brood on their own, she hurriedly yanked a clean dress over her head and buttoned it. Then, not even pausing to check her appearance, she headed back toward the kitchen.

Bridget, knowing it was time for her breakfast as well, padded along behind her.

"Pass the biscuits," boomed a voice.

Mattie grinned. Obviously Jake was back. Not much could make him late for a meal. It was only after she rounded the table to take her own seat that she noticed Rusty, Jake's red-bone hound, had come up from the barn and taken up residence at the end of the cookstove.

"Hello, boy," she said.

The old dog thumped his tail and gave her a hopeful look. Then the hair on his back rose, and he let out a low growl.

"Meow."

"Bridget!" Mattie whirled to capture the cat but it was too late.

The dog sprang to his feet, his toenails scrapping the floor as he fought for traction.

In seconds, the never quiet morning meal exploded into a riot with Mattie caught right in the middle. Trying to separate the snarling dog and yowling, spitting cat, Mattie twisted toward Jake who calmly sat at the table buttering a biscuit. "Do something!"

"What?" He took a bite, his gaze never leaving his plate. "Too much racket, can't hear you."

"Get Rusty out of here!" she screamed.

"You get the cat out." Jake waved his fork toward Bridget. "She's the one who started all the ruckus."

The cat, trapped in the corner, shot toward the window—only to discover it closed. A mass of hissing, spitting, yellow-eyed fury, she whirled to face the snarling dog. Bridget got in one good swipe before Rusty attacked. One leap ahead of the bared teeth and snapping jaws, the cat headed up the curtain. Reaching the top, Bridget yowled her outrage as she struggled to maintain her precarious perch atop the wooden curtain rod.

The dog lunged, hurling himself against the swaying fabric, baying for all he was worth.

The curtain drooped under the dog's assault, and then began to fall. Determined to save her cat, Mattie grabbed the broom and swung it toward the dog—and missed.

"Uncle Jake, help Bridget," Faith screamed.

"Rusty will hurt her," Hope cried.

"Oh, all right." Grumbling, Jake rose from the table and bellowed for the hound to get outside.

The dog redoubled his effort, seeing his quarry sag within reach.

Frightened by all the noise, Joshua let out a piercing shriek.

Hal, frantically clamping both hands over his shirt pocket, turned and yelled at his baby brother. "Shut up! You're scaring Solomon."

"Oh, dang it! There he goes!" Lory shot up from the table after the mouse who darted straight into the middle of the cornered cat and the snapping dog.

"Get out of there before you get bit," Jake yelled, reaching into the melee to grab the youngster by his shirttail.

"No, I have to get Solomon," wailed Lory, struggling furiously to get free.

The wide-eyed mouse froze, then with a flurry of scratching claws and squeaking for all he was worth, he ran toward the only sanctuary he could find—Jake's boot.

The dog caught a glimpse of movement and whirled, teeth flashing.

Taking advantage of the dog's distraction, Bridget leapt to the kitchen tabletop and safety.

The mouse squealed in fright, then ran straight up Jake's pant leg.

"Holy hell!" He jumped on one foot, shaking his pants with one hand while he strove to keep Lory away from the dog with the other.

"Take this one," Jake yelled. He all but threw the little boy toward Mattie.

She wrapped her arms around him and held on tight.

"Don't you hurt Solomon," Lory screeched.

"Hurt him, hell! He's trying to ruin me for life." Jake whooped and jumped and beat at his leg trying to dislodge the persistent mouse inside his pants.

The dishes rattled and danced, then one by one they shimmied off the shelf and crashed to the floor.

Her ears ringing with the children's cries, Joshua's screams, the raging battle between the dog and cat, and Jake's curses, Mattie stared at them all, her eyes wide with horror, and wondered how on earth she had ever gotten herself into such a mess.

She had no time to ponder the matter, because at that moment the mouse skittered down Jake's leg and onto the floor.

Solomon lay there a moment, then, still dazed, he fled in a drunken line toward the leg of the table. Urged along by the boys, and the dog who had spotted their pet, Solomon clawed his way up the table leg. Then the mouse careened along the tabletop, like an inebriated sailor, upsetting a glass of milk and the sugar bowl in the process.

"Rusty, get out!" Jake opened the door and waved his arms at the dog.

Rusty, who already had a corner of the tablecloth in his mouth, headed toward the threshold, taking food, dishes, the cat, and the mouse along with him.

The girls screamed as glasses and plates tinkled and crashed. Utensils and tin cups clanked and rolled across the floor. Food splattered everything in sight.

Mattie grabbed one end of the table covering and yanked it away from the dog. The mouse, getting his second wind, untangled himself and disappeared into the other room.

The cat shot off in the opposite direction.

Just when Mattie thought the commotion was finally over, three of the ranch hands—guns drawn—burst through the open doorway. They came to a halt and stared around the room.

"What the hell are you gawkin' at?" Jake picked up his chair from the floor and set it next to the table.

Mattie lifted the sobbing baby into her arms, then she collapsed onto her own chair.

"We thought you was being attacked by Indians or somethin'," Slim said, sheathing his Colt.

"Well, as you can see, that's not the case," Jake said.

"We were just having a little family breakfast. It's over now, so you can go on back to work."

"Breakfast?" Dutch, a burly blond cowboy, whispered as they turned to leave.

Romero rolled his dark eyes and grinned.

Slim laughed out loud. "If that's a family breakfast, I'd shore hate to see what they do for supper."

Mattie glanced from the wide-eyed children to the destruction of the kitchen. Then she looked at Jake.

Pale beneath his tan, he gazed from the room to her, then he ran a shaking hand through his hair. His eyes looked wild, almost desperate. He attempted to speak, but only a croak came out. He picked up his hat and shoved it on his head.

"Jake? Where are you going?"

"I've got to get out of here. I have to see if everybody's gone insane, or if it's just me that's crazy."

"But it's storming."

"Hell, after this a tornado would be a picnic."

"You can't leave me," she cried. "Not with all this." But it was too late, he had already gone.

It was late that afternoon when the rain finally stopped and Jake had downed enough courage to return to the ranch. Bock Gee rode on the wagon beside him.

"I don't know what I'm gonna do." Jake ran a trembling hand over his cheek.

"Count your blessings," the old man said sagely.

"What blessings? I've got kids I didn't want. A wife I didn't want. Plus a cat, a mouse, a calf, and a damned hound dog. And the lot of them are driving me berserk. My nerves are so bad that I'm shaking in my boots when I haven't had a drop to drink."

"Yet, when I saw you last week, you were a happy man, is that not so?"

"That was last week."

"What changed?"

What had changed? Jake pondered the question. The ranch was the same; he still had horses to break and stock to tend. The kids were wild and rowdy, but that was normal. Mattie—? Naw, she'd been there last week, too. "Nothing's changed."

"Mattie not cook good?"

"She's a good cook. She even makes cookies." Not that he ever got any.

"She not keep house clean?"

"No. It's neat as a pin. You know she makes me clean my boots before she lets me inside?"

"That makes you angry?"

"No. Keeping a house is hard work." He'd found that out the week she had turned everything inside out—and made him help.

"She not wash your clothes?"

"No. My clothes are clean—and ironed."

"Sounds like Mattie make you a good wife."

Now that he thought about it, she was a good wife. She cooked, she cleaned, she washed clothes, and she took good care of the kids. A damned good wife—in every way but one. He scowled.

"You not like the way she looks?"

"That isn't it either. She still looks the same." Then he shook his head. No, she didn't either. She did look different. Healthier, or something. Her eyes had a sparkle to them; her skin glowed. "She wears her hair down sometimes. It looks real nice."

"How she make love?"

"How should I know? She won't let me in her bedroom," Jake confessed. "We have what she calls a 'platonic relationship.' You know—like a business deal. That's the only way she would agree to come to the ranch."

"Ah-ha, and I thought it was true love," Bock Gee said wryly.

"And worst of all, she won't allow me to visit Jolene's."

"Terrible problem." The old man nodded his head, then

he peered over his spectacles at Jake. "You could visit Jolene's anyway."

"Naw. I gave my word." Truth was, he'd been in Jolene's today. Since she wasn't good at figures, she'd asked him to look over her books. The girls had been pretty and attentive as ever, but he'd felt so guilty he couldn't wait to finish his business and get out of there. That surprised him. It also irritated him. It was as if being married to Mattie had emasculated him or something.

"What is that rattle?" the old man asked curiously, eyeing the barrel in the back of the wagon.

Jake gave him a sheepish look. "I told you about what happened at breakfast. I figured if I ever wanted anything else to eat, I'd better get her some new dishes."

"Ahhh, so. You get her anything else?"

"Naw, nothing much. Just some new curtains. The cat tore the other ones up. And since I ran off and left her with all the mess, I picked her up a bottle of scent, a hand mirror, and some geegaws."

Bock Gee giggled.

"What's so funny?"

"I think you in love with Mattie."

"Love? Me? Hell, I don't even like the woman."

But even as he spoke the words Jake knew they were a bald-faced lie.

❧ TEN ❧

Although Jake hadn't stayed in town the night before as Mattie feared he might, she still hadn't forgiven him. The fact that he'd arrived late with a wagonload of things to replace the ones that were broken hadn't helped his cause one bit.

She lifted the last of the breakfast dishes and dried it, then she held the new plate at arm's length and traced the delicate blue flowers on the rim with her finger. The new pattern was awfully pretty. The dishes that had gotten broken had been chipped and ugly, odds and ends that had apparently been left on the ranch. She had to admit, she did like these much better. Finding herself softening toward Jake, she scowled, then put the plate with the others on the shelf.

The new curtains, cream-colored with yellow flowers, made the room appear more cheerful and much lighter. They made a nice addition to the kitchen. She planned to make a rag rug with the ruined draperies and put it in front of the stove.

She rinsed and hung up the dish towel, then glanced out the window toward the end of the porch where Jake and Bock Gee sat engaged in a game of checkers.

He could buy all the presents in the world and it wouldn't change a thing. She was still furious because he had run off and left her to clean up the entire mess, when it was his dog that had caused the problem in the first place.

And when Jake had returned, he'd reeked of whiskey, and he certainly knew how she felt about that. He knew she'd be mad; that was why he had brought Bock Gee with him. He'd been too much of a coward to come home by himself.

Mattie didn't care that he had brought Bock Gee. She'd been delighted to see the elderly man, since he was probably the nearest thing to a friend she'd had for some time. She'd done her best to welcome him and make him comfortable, but it rankled that because of lack of sleeping space in the house, Bock Gee had been forced to sleep in the bunkhouse with the other men.

The house was big enough. In fact it was huge, but Jake had never gotten around to repairing the rest of the bedrooms. He still slept in the room with the twins. She still shared a room with the girls and the baby. She found it ridiculous that they all had to be so uncomfortable.

She went into her bedroom and changed the linens, putting the soiled ones aside for the laundry. Her gaze rested on the crystal bottle of scent—another of Jake's offerings—then unable to resist, she lifted the glass stopper and touched it to a spot behind her ears. It did smell delightful. And the mirror was something she had needed, since her own had been broken the day of the fire. The piece of lace and the ribbons had been welcome, too, or would have been if they hadn't been bribes.

In a way she felt flattered that Jake had brought the presents. In truth, he had behaved much like any typical husband who was trying to get back in his wife's good graces might have done.

Typical husband? She arched a brow. Now where had that come from?

There was nothing typical about her relationship with Jake Turnbull. They occupied the same house and ate meals at the same table, they even discussed the children—but that was as far as it went. They certainly didn't share the same bed, and never would as far as she was concerned.

But even as she spread the sheets, smoothing out all the wrinkles, she couldn't help but wonder what it would be like if they did share a bed.

He probably snored, she decided, adding the quilts. And mumbled in his sleep. He probably hogged all the covers, too, she thought, tucking the quilts in at the foot. She would be forced to snuggle next to him to keep warm.

She picked up the pillow and hugged it to her bosom.

Jake was a lusty man—her untimely trip to the saloon could testify to that. He would most certainly insist on his husbandly rights every night. While she wasn't quite sure how she felt about that, her pulse quickened as she imagined the two of them making love, creating a child. Adding yet another little fair-haired, blue-eyed child to their family.

But that would never happen because of their agreement. She uneasily wondered how long she would be able to hold him to it—or how long he'd be content with such a thing.

Even though she hated to admit it, her husband was quite good-looking and could charm the birds out of the trees when he took a notion. She knew there had been other women, probably more than she could count. She'd noticed the way he'd turned more than one feminine head in town, even some respectable married ones who shouldn't be paying him any attention. He'd flash that smile of his and they were eager to give him anything his heart desired.

Jake was a prime specimen as far as men were concerned. The worst part was he knew it.

He was tall as a barn door and had shoulders as wide as the span of an ax handle, and his hips, instead of being skinny and spavined-looking like so many men, were well-shaped and powerful. His legs, from what she had seen, and she had seen quite a bit that day at Jolene's, were strong and sturdy. And in spite of his tremendous appetite, there wasn't an ounce of fat on him. Yet for all his intimidating size, his movements were graceful, catlike. In fact, she thought that Jake reminded her of a well-fed mountain cat—a tawny, blue-eyed cougar.

For a moment she allowed herself to indulge in fantasy. She imagined him gazing down at her, that unruly lock of hair draping his forehead. His eyes, meeting hers, would darken with passion.

She'd smile and tangle her fingers in the triangle of golden hair on his chest. Then she would embrace him, her fingertips tracing, caressing the muscles rippling across his back.

She sighed, then catching herself, she blushed and immediately tried to banish him from her thoughts. She determinedly fluffed the pillows and straightened the counterpane.

But Jake refused to be dismissed so easily. The unbidden vision crept back into her mind.

She saw him, there, in her bed, bare-chested, and the sheet riding scandalously low on his hips, revealed he was bare everywhere else as well. A lock of dark gold hair drooped over eyes still heavy-lidded from sleep. He gazed up at her, then he lifted his mouth in that devilish, one-sided smile. Blue eyes promising delights untold, he lifted the sheet and beckoned her to the warmth at his side.

Her heart pounding with anticipation, she held out her hand and took a step toward him. He clasped her fingers . . .

Bridget leapt into the middle of the bed.

"Oh!" Startled, Mattie gasped and jumped back.

The cat eyed her curiously, then curled up next to the pillow for her morning nap.

"Good grief! What in the world is the matter with me?" Mattie whispered. She yanked up the dirty linen and ran from the room. By the time she reached the kitchen, she was panting.

Furious with herself for her imaginings, and more furious with Jake for his part in them, she tackled the rest of her chores with a vengeance.

When Jake and Bock Gee came in for the noon meal, Mattie made a point of lavishing her attention on the old man and the children. Jake, she ignored completely. But, as usual, he was so busy stuffing his face he didn't even notice.

"Aaah. Mattie, you cook too good," the old man said. "Give this dishonorable person middle like Jake."

"Thank you—I think," Mattie said, smiling at the old man.

"Much to be said for estate of marriage. Is that not so, Jake?"

"What?" Jake mumbled, his mouth full.

"Bock Gee said you're lucky to be married to me," Mattie said smoothly.

"Humph!" Jake buttered another biscuit and shoved it into his mouth.

"Sometime tree need to fall on man before he feel the wind," Bock Gee said.

"Don't go quoting all that Chinese stuff," Jake growled. "You know I don't understand a word of it. Pass the taters, Mattie."

"Did you ever hear of the word please? Or don't you understand English either?" she said, leaving the bowl of potatoes right where it was.

Glaring at her, he yanked the napkin from under his chin and tossed it onto the table. "If you feel that way about it, keep your damned taters. Rest of the food's cold anyhow." He stood, sending his chair screeching backward. "Gettin' to where a man can't even eat without gettin' picked on."

"If you are so thin-skinned, then maybe you ought to eat with the hands," Mattie suggested.

"Why should I?" He bent toward her. "That's what I married you for."

Mattie tightened her grip on the bowl, tempted to give him the potatoes he'd asked for—over his thick head.

Bock Gee watched her, then Jake. Then the old man got to his feet. "I think it time this lowly one go back to town."

"That's a damn good idea." Jake snatched up his hat. "Maybe she'll be in a better mood come suppertime. She might even put it on the table when it's hot,'' he yelled, going out the door.

"Oh, that man!''

"Thank you, Mattie.'' Bock Gee bowed and spoke so low only she could hear. "Jake say like things hot. Very hot,'' he said, his almond eyes glittering with amusement. He closed one almond-shaped eye in a wink, then he followed Jake out the door.

Mattie thought about the old man's words. "Very hot?'' Then she smiled.

"Here you go, children,'' Mattie said, placing a bowl of chili in front of each of them. "Corn bread and butter are on the table.''

"Where's mine?'' Jake growled.

"I kept yours on the stove. I didn't want it to get cold.'' She placed the large steaming bowl in front of him. "I added some fresh green onions over the top. I know how much you like them.''

"That's more like it,'' Jake said, picking up his spoon.

She poured the children's milk, then dribbled the rest into the bottom of her glass. "Oh, dear, that's the last of it. I guess I used too much today making butter.'' In truth, she had another bucket of milk in the springhouse, but she wasn't about to go get it.

"That's all right. I don't really like milk that much, and I'm not that thirsty anyhow,'' Jake said, buttering a large piece of corn bread.

Mattie took her seat, then tucked her head and concentrated on her meal.

"I like chili,'' Hal said between mouthfuls.

"Me, too,'' Lory said.

"It's very good, Mama,'' Hope agreed. Faith nodded.

"Thank you, children.''

From beneath her lashes, Mattie watched Jake fill his spoon and shove it into his mouth. Not bothering to chew, he gulped the first bite, quickly following it with a second. He filled his spoon again.

Mattie watched. "And how is yours, Jake?"

"Fine." Jake swallowed, then he blinked. "Holy— hell!"

"Jacob," she admonished. "Not in front of the children!"

One hand clutching his throat, he let out a strangled, "Wa-ter."

Mattie slowly got up from her chair and went to the bucket. "Oh, dear. It seems to be empty." She turned and gave him her sweetest smile. "I do have some *hot* water, but I guess you wouldn't be interested in that."

His eyes widened in comprehension. "You did it on purpose."

"Why, whatever do you mean?"

"Aggh!" Still holding his throat, Jake rushed past her and ran outside.

She walked to the door he'd left open and closed it. Then she removed the packet of chili tepinos from her pocket and placed them with the other spices in the back of the cupboard. Grinning to herself, she returned to the table and resumed her seat.

"What's the matter with Uncle Jake?" Lory asked, his eyes wide.

"Dear me, I really don't know." She buttered another slice of corn bread. "But I think he might have burnt his tongue."

In the days following, Mattie figured she might have made her point when Jake not only waited until everyone else was seated at the table, he also made sure he wasn't the first to taste his food. He no longer ate like he was starving. In fact, the bites he took were almost minuscule— at least until he was certain there wouldn't be any unexpected aftereffects. He even said please and thank you.

While she felt a bit guilty at having resorted to such tactics, she also felt he had it coming. Yes, she thought, he was coming around quite nicely.

❧ ELEVEN ❧

"Lory, Hal, quit your grumbling," Faith said impatiently. "It won't hurt you to wear shoes one day a week. Besides, Mama promised to tell us the story of Samson today."

"Don't care," Lory mumbled. "I'd ruther go fishin'."

"And Mattie ain't our mama," Hal argued.

"Come along, children," Mattie said, trying to ignore the hurtful words. Saddling Joshua on one hip, she herded the rest of her brood toward the kitchen. Dressed in their Sunday best, the twins almost looked civilized. Not at all like the little hellions they'd been all week.

Entering the room, she smiled at Jake, and noticed that he had donned a brown broadcloth suit for the occasion. She'd convinced him to attend the Bible lesson by playing on his conscience, telling him his presence would be a positive influence on the boys, who hated anything that forced them to sit in one spot for more than five minutes.

The girls were very knowledgeable about the Good Book. She had no doubt that Faith knew more Bible verses by heart than most devout ministers. Mattie had also been using the simpler verses to teach the boys their letters and how to read.

"Well, this is wonderful," she said, eyeing her family. She took her own place at the table. "I think we shall begin by singing 'Rock of Ang—' " She head a knock, then the door opened.

"Sorry, ma'am," Henry Hobbs said from the doorway. "Jake, can I see you outside for a minute?"

Jake shrugged in answer to her unspoken question, then he went out onto the porch with his foreman. He returned a minute later. "Something's come up. I have to go into town."

"Now?" she asked, dismayed. "Can't it wait?"

"No. It can't." He grabbed his hat from the peg and started for the door.

Mattie moved in front of him, blocking his way. "You promised," she said, her temper rising.

"It's business." He stepped around her.

Determined to speak her mind, she closed the kitchen door behind her and followed him onto the porch. "I might have known you wouldn't keep your word. I wouldn't doubt that you had this planned all along. How do you expect the children to grow up to be decent when you set such a bad example?"

"Bad example?"

"Bad example," she bit out, glaring at him. "You won't take a few minutes one day a week to worship with your family. You have to run into town, to that . . . that dreadful saloon on *business*. Or is it Jolene that has the problem this time?"

His eyes narrowed. "It's damn easy for you to be so pious. All you have to do is sit around and pray and sing songs. I'm the one who puts the food on the table. And whether you like it or not, the money for that food—and the roof over your head—comes from that *dreadful saloon*."

"Are you saying I'm not keeping my end of the bargain?" Mattie asked furiously.

"You and your damned bargain, that's another thing," he hissed low, his eyes turning hard. "I wished I'd never heard of it—or you."

Mattie recoiled from his venomous words as though he had struck her.

"And as far as Jolene is concerned, at least *she*'s not afraid to be a woman." Jake shot her a look of contempt, then he stomped off the porch and strode to meet Henry who was leading the horses up from the corral.

"If it wasn't for me, the roof would be falling in and you wouldn't have a clean dish to eat out of," she cried out when she could find her voice. But the cloud of disappearing dust told her she was wasting her breath. Jake was already on his way to town.

Mattie whirled to see the children standing in the kitchen doorway. She gazed into four sets of wide blue eyes. So like his. They were his blood, his kin. Why couldn't he see they needed him? A niggling voice inside told her she needed him as well. But he didn't care. He didn't care one whit. All he cared about was that saloon—and Jolene.

"Can we go play now?" Lory asked.

"No. You may not. Back into the kitchen," she said firmly. Well, they wouldn't end up like him, she'd see to that. Bargain or no bargain, it was her Christian duty to save the children from Jake's evil ways.

The girls quickly slid onto their seats. The twins, grumbling and arguing over who was to sit where, finally took theirs. Joshua grinned and banged his spoon on the edge of his high chair.

"Open your Bibles," Mattie instructed, taking the marker from the text she'd chosen. Her gaze drifted to the opposite page to the portrayal of a large, dark-haired man chained between two columns of a temple. Jake had been promising for weeks, and still he hadn't attended, she fumed. One excuse, then another. Before her eyes, the depiction wavered, then the man's dark hair turned to blond. The muscled figure in the toga lifted his head. Mattie stared at the illustration. Jake's mocking face grinned back. She blinked and slammed the book. *He's not Samson.*

All thought of the lesson she'd intended to teach forgotten, she rapidly thumbed through the pages. *The wages of sin* . . . Quite appropriate, considering the circumstances. "Today we will study the book of Romans."

Mattie tackled the Bible lesson with a vengeance, and it was only when the baby began to cry that she murmured a hasty prayer and closed the book.

"Is the lesson finished?" Faith asked wearily.

"Yes," Mattie said, glancing at her in surprise.

The boys bolted from the room like their pants were on fire.

Mattie hoisted the sobbing baby onto her shoulder. Wet. When the Regulator clock at the end of the room bonged two o'clock, she looked up in shock. Two hours?

"Wake up, Hope," Faith said, shaking her sister by the shoulder.

When Hope raised her head from the table, her cheek bore the imprint of the embroidered cloth. "Is she finally done?" she said with a groan. "My neck's got a crick in it, and my bottom feels like it's stuck to the bench."

"Let's get out of here before she starts on something else," Faith whispered.

Hope scrambled from her seat and both girls hurried from the room.

"There, there, it's all right," Mattie crooned to the sobbing baby. She carried Joshua to the sink and dampened a cloth to wipe his tear-stained cheeks. Through the window, she saw the boys—clothes changed and barefoot—dash toward the barn. She realized they had climbed out the bedroom window to avoid her. Shortly after, the girls, too, fled the house.

It was then Mattie realized she had been overzealous. Although mischievous, they were all good children. She had intended to read them a story from the Bible and make it entertaining enough that they would want to hear more. Instead, her mind on Jake, she had preached at them like they were sinners on the threshold of hell. Why, the way she had gone on, it would be a wonder if she hadn't put them off religion for good. And them being children of missionaries at that.

It was his fault. All his fault.

In the Miner's Delight, Jake stood in the open doorway, blinking until his eyes became accustomed to the darkness in the ornately decorated bedroom. He focused on the slender woman curled into a fetal position on the brass bed, and his brow puckered in a worried frown. "How long has she been like this?"

"Two days," Bock Gee said solemnly.

"My God! What happened?"

Bock Gee shook his head. "For many nights, she have bad dreams. She no sleep, no eat."

He would have known Jolene was in trouble if it hadn't been for Mattie and that damned agreement. He would have been in town, taking care of business and watching over her. Jake took off his hat and placed it brim up on the dresser. Then he crossed the floor, sat down on the edge of the bed, and took Jolene into his arms. "Jo? Honey?" He smoothed a tangled lock of matted red hair back from her cheek.

Her eyes were wide but unseeing, her body tense, unyielding, as if she were locked in a transparent chamber of horror.

"Jolene." He cupped her chin and forced her to meet his gaze. "Jolene. Do you hear me?" He grasped her shoulders and gave her a shake. "Baby, look at me. It's Jake."

"Sing the song," the elderly man suggested.

Jake took her onto his lap, holding her as if she were no older than Faith. His voice gruff with emotion, he began to sing a lullaby, one he'd remembered from his own childhood. The same one he'd sung to Jolene that day when he'd found her and taken her from that brothel below the border so long ago.

Then, she'd been on the point of starvation, and so badly abused he hadn't been sure if the young girl would ever be all right. He didn't know what had made him sing to her that day. Maybe because she appeared to be so lost and alone. He'd thought it might comfort her. She had responded first to the song, and then to him. After that, although slowly, her mind began to heal.

Outside of the nightmares, she had seemed all right for quite a spell now. Perplexed at what could have reduced her to such a pitiful state, he continued to croon and smooth her hair until, finally, he felt her relax.

She uttered a shuddering, weary sigh, then she blinked. She gazed up at him and recognition crept into her eyes. "Jake?"

"I'm here now," he said, trembling with relief. "It's all right, darlin'." He drew her close.

"Jake," she murmured again, then she began to cry.

Her sobs shook her body and his; her tears soaked his linen shirt. Moisture trickled from his own eyes and dampened his face. God, what she must have suffered, was still suffering. She had never told him, so he could only guess. Whatever had happened had been so horrible she had never been able to speak of it, but it haunted her nights, her dreams, bringing her to screaming awareness.

Jake wished he had the power to see into the past. His desire for vengeance was so terrible, he shook with the need. Mercy would not be granted for whoever was responsible.

Finally the deluge ended, leaving her with only hiccuping sobs. She fell asleep in his arms. Even though he felt drained and his body ached with exhaustion, he could sense her pain and he continued to hold her. After a while, he, too, must have fallen asleep because when he opened his eyes, he was lying on the bed with Jolene still cradled in his arms.

He knew he must have been there for hours because the daylight had gone, and now the windows were glazed with darkness. The faint golden glow of a lamp turned down low showed Bock Gee sitting in a chair at his side.

"She all right now?" the old man asked in a whisper.

Jake nodded. He carefully untangled himself from the sleeping woman. Then, he massaged his arm from shoulder to wrist to restore the circulation. The feeling returned, along with the pain of a thousand sharp needles. Gritting his teeth, he continued, rubbing it back to normal. Hunger gnawed at his middle, and his stomach complained loudly. He twisted toward the bed, afraid the sound might wake her.

"I stay. You go eat." Bock Gee shoved him toward the door.

Uncertain, Jake hesitated, then satisfied that Jolene was finally at peace, he nodded and left the room, gently closing the door behind him. When he went through the connecting door and entered the saloon, the tinkling of the piano, harsh voices, and rowdy laughter drifted up the staircase.

Jake found himself longing for the peace, the serenity of the ranch where only the sound of the wind and the crickets disturbed his rest.

He frowned, thinking of Mattie and how mad she'd been when he'd had to leave. She'd be even more upset if he didn't return home tonight. He shouldn't have said what he did about her being afraid to be a woman. He wouldn't have if he hadn't been so worried. After Mattie had caught Jolene in his bed that morning, she'd believed the worse. And he'd let her. She had no way of knowing their true relationship.

And because he'd never tell her, Mattie would never know the truth about Jolene, who hid behind a mask of face paint and a profession she hated. Jolene, who cried out in the night, like a lost child.

Mattie met the world head-on, but underneath that steely determination he sensed that Mattie, too, battled her own demons. Demons that she, too, would not reveal.

He stared up at the moonlit sky, torn between the desire to leave and the obligation to stay. However brave a front they presented to the world, he knew that both women needed him. Right now Jolene needed him the most.

Finally he heaved a resigned sigh and went back into the saloon. He met Bock Gee coming down the staircase.

"Jolene awake."

"How is she?"

"Hungry. I go now to get her something to eat." The small man hurried away.

Jake, exhausted from the day's ordeal, trudged up the stairway and went down the hallway to Jolene's room. He found her sitting on the edge of her bed.

"Jake, you handsome devil. What are you doing here?" she asked, her green eyes mischievous.

She didn't remember. Well, he wasn't about to remind her. "I had to come in for supplies. Couldn't leave without looking in on my best girl."

"Better not let Mattie hear you say that," she warned, giving him a grin. "How is she anyway?"

"Fine. Just fine." He observed her, searching for any sign of the torment that had put her into a state of shock. He found none.

"And the kids? Are they all right?"

"The girls are fine. The boys are ornery as ever."

"Take after their uncle." She glanced toward the window. "Night already? I guess I'd better get dressed."

"Why don't you rest tonight, honey?" he suggested gently. "Let one of the other girls take over for a change."

"Rest? What for? I feel like I've been sleeping all day." She smothered a yawn, then smoothed her hair back from her face. As she touched her tangled looks, a look of surprise, then awareness came into her eyes. She gazed up at him and frowned. "I've been sick again, haven't I?"

Jake nodded.

"How long this time?" she asked, her voice tight with emotion.

"Not long." He couldn't lie to her. "A couple of days."

Her shoulders sagged. "Two days gone, and I can't even remember." She made a halfhearted attempt at a smile.

''Well, maybe that's a blessing.'' She absently twisted a coil of hair. ''Have you been here all that time?''

''No, honey. I didn't know you were sick until this morning.''

''Thank God for that. Well, I'm fine now, so I want you to go home before Mattie comes looking for you. She did that before, you know.'' She got up from the bed and went to look in the mirror. ''What a mess. Maybe I will let Myrtle take over tonight. I sure don't want anybody to see me like this.'' She walked toward him. ''Not even you.''

''I can stay if you need me.''

''I'm fine.'' She saw the doubt on his face. ''Really.'' She took his hand and brought it to her cheek. ''Thank you for being here, even if I don't remember.

''Go, now,'' she said, giving him a push toward the door. ''And on your way out, ask Delilah if she would send up some hot water.'' Jake held up his hands in surrender. ''All right. I'm gone. If you need me . . .''

''I won't.'' She grinned at him. ''But if those kids are the handful you claim they are, I'm sure Mattie will.''

Chuckling, Jake shut the door behind him and headed down the stairs. After asking the aging black woman to send up water for Jolene's bath, he bid Bock Gee goodbye and headed for the livery.

The moon was high in the sky when he rode into the ranch yard. Although the bunkhouse was dark, the soft glow of a lamp shone through the kitchen window. Mattie stood staring out at the dark.

Jake rode on by. Drained from the ordeal with Jolene, he had neither the time nor inclination to engage in another confrontation with Mattie. Tomorrow would be soon enough for that.

He unsaddled his horse and turned it loose in the corral. Then he went into the barn and climbed the ladder to the loft. His thoughts filled with the two women, so different, yet both so much a part of his life, he stretched out on the hay and closed his eyes.

❦ TWELVE ❦

Mattie was up before dawn. Truth be known, she had never gone to sleep. She knew Jake had arrived home late. She also knew he had spent the night in the barn, even though he was aware that she had waited up for him. When he didn't show up for breakfast, she knew he was deliberately avoiding her.

She had started for the bedrooms to wake the children for breakfast when a knock sounded on the kitchen door. She opened it expecting to see her wayward husband, then she realized Jake wouldn't bother to knock on his own door.

Henry, his arms loaded with packages, gave her a hesitant smile. "Hello, Mattie. I brought the things Jake said you needed from town."

"I don't know as I needed anything, but you may as well bring whatever it is in," she said grumpily. If Jake thought presents were going to make everything all right, he had another think coming. She wasn't the kind of person who could be mollified with a few trinkets. Especially after the things he'd said.

Henry carried the armload of bundles in and placed them on the table. "There's more stuff in the wagon. Maybe you'd rather I left some of it on the porch?"

"What kind of stuff?"

"Boards, nails, paint . . ."

At last! In spite of her anger toward Jake, excitement made Mattie want to examine everything Henry had delivered. Realizing the foreman was still waiting for an answer, she said quickly, ''Yes, maybe you had better leave that outside.''

When Bock Gee had visited, Mattie had been sorry that there was no place to put the old man for a longer stay. The children adored their ''venerable grandfather'' as Bock Gee called himself and Mattie thought the children could certainly benefit from the old man's impeccable behavior and manners.

Also, as much as she loved the children, there were times when she would have given most anything for a little solitude. She had a strong suspicion that Jake felt the same.

Henry deposited the remainder of the goods on the porch, then straightened and rubbed the back of his neck. ''Is Jake around?''

''I haven't seen him this morning,'' she said, keeping to herself the fact that she had neither seen nor spoken to her bullheaded husband since yesterday when he'd left the ranch.

The sandy-haired man stepped to the ground, hesitated, then he raised his head to meet her gaze. Henry's face bore traces of exhaustion despite the early hour. ''He did come home last night, didn't he?''

''He came home—very late—and he slept in the barn,'' Mattie grudgingly admitted. ''I assume he got his *business* taken care of?''

Henry frowned. ''Don't be too hard on him, Mattie. Jake's a good man.''

''You didn't answer my question.''

The foreman shifted uneasily. ''There are things you don't know. Things it's not my place to tell.''

Before she could question him further, he climbed into the wagon and drove off toward the barn.

Perplexed by his words, she went back into the kitchen and began to open the bundles. One contained two bolts of calico; one blue with tiny pink and lavender flowers; one yellow with delicate green vines and white clusters of daisies. Enough for dresses for her and the girls, with plenty left over for curtains.

In another packet she found several lengths of sturdier cloth in blues, greens, and browns, apparently for pants for the boys. The little scamps were constantly wearing out the seats of their britches, as well as tearing holes in the knees.

In another she found an abundance of softer material perfect for Joshua's diapers, and some soft chambray for his little dresses. To Mattie's amazement, Jake had also remembered thread and buttons, as well as several lengths of bright-colored ribbons for the girls.

Overwhelmed, she sat down and stared at the pile of fabric. She was proficient with needle and thread, but where would she ever find the time? Since she arrived, just taking care of the house and children had occupied every waking moment. She heaved a deep sigh. She knew that Jake could ill afford all that he had purchased, but since he had, it was against her nature to let it go to waste. She'd have to make time. Maybe if she got up a little earlier, and went to bed a wee bit later . . .

Jake put off going to the house as long as possible, but when it was nearing suppertime, his hunger wouldn't allow him to stay away. He hoped the gewgaws he'd bought would help Mattie get over her mad spell. And if not . . . well, he reckoned in her eyes he had it coming. There was no way he could tell her the truth of the matter. For one thing Jolene would not welcome her pity—even if Mattie could understand. For another, he figured a man was entitled to a few secrets.

He gingerly made his way up the steps and opened the door, almost fearful of what he might be walking into on the other side. For a moment nobody noticed, then the girls let out a squeal and launched themselves into his arms.

"Uncle Jake, thank you for the dress goods," Faith said breathlessly.

"And the buttons and hair bows," Hope added, giving him a hug.

"Well, I reckon you're welcome," Jake said, giving them an awkward pat on the head. Their eyes shining, they danced away like miniature whirlwinds, before depositing their attention on the cat.

His gaze slid past Mattie, who was busy at the stove, and landed on Lory and Hal, who were off in one corner playing with their mouse. "Hey, boys, don't I even get a howdy?"

Lory and Hal scowled up at him and muttered, "Howdy. We don't need no pants."

"Well, I beg to differ on that score. Your hind end is hanging out of the ones you're wearing."

Hands on his hips, Hal planted his feet and stared up at his uncle. "Injuns don't wear britches. How cum we have to?"

"You ain't Injun, that's why," Jake answered.

"Aren't," Mattie corrected, setting a pan of biscuits on the table.

A little of the tension eased out of Jake. She still didn't appear too happy with him, but at least she hadn't met him with a skillet.

"We could be Injuns, if they was to kidnap us," Lory said hopefully.

"They'd soon bring you back," Mattie said in exasperation. "Now get washed up like I told you."

"Injuns don't wash, either."

"They do if they plan to eat at my table," Mattie said firmly.

"You heard the lady, now git."

Grumbling, the pair headed toward the basin of water that Mattie had fixed at one end of the cabinet.

"Thank you," Mattie said so softly the boys couldn't hear. "Those two would argue with a fence post."

"Giving you a bad time, are they? I'll have a little talk with them after supper." She not only wasn't throwing things, she didn't even seem upset. For some reason that bothered him more than if she had been mad.

The boys, their small faces contorted in fierce scowls, dipped their hands in the water and wiped them on the towel, leaving large muddy spots on the linen.

"Faces, too," Jake ordered in a no-nonsense tone.

The twins grudgingly obeyed.

"Don't be too hard on them," Mattie said at his elbow. "They are good boys, they just don't seem to have enough to do."

"Is that right?" Jake scratched his chin, then he grinned, thinking of just the thing to keep the pair out of mischief. He took his seat, then bent toward the high chair where Joshua was examining him with wide-eyed wonder. "Hi, sprout. Are you finding enough to do?"

"He's finding plenty," Mattie assured him. "And everything he discovers goes straight into his mouth."

Jake chuckled, then he leaned back in his chair and watched as Mattie carried platters of steak, potatoes, and beans to the table. She looked tired. But then, why shouldn't she? He thought about how much her life had changed. Before she only had herself and that blamed cat to look out and do for. Now in addition, she had taken on a husband and five kids as well as a house to take care of. And if the girls were as restless at night as Lory and Hal, she probably wasn't getting much sleep either.

He knew he wasn't. The twins were as active in their sleep as they were when they were awake. Last night in the hayloft was the first decent night's rest he'd had since the children had arrived.

Since he couldn't very well recommend that Mattie sleep in the hayloft—although that idea did have some merit— he vowed to see to it that she had other accommodations.

The twins, dripping wet but well washed, plopped down on their end of the bench.

And now that everyone was seated, Mattie, too, took her seat, bowed her head, and said a word of grace.

From beneath his lashes Jake watched the woman who had become the very center of his family. Contrary to what he'd thought in the beginning, he'd found a lot to admire about her. While she was danged near as stubborn as the twins, she also had shown a gentleness and sensitivity with the children and even him, even though most times he didn't deserve it. She worked harder than most men and certainly was not given to complaining. But if something was on her mind she didn't hesitate to let a body know it, not like some women he'd known who were inclined to pout.

Her prayer ended, Mattie raised her head and gazed into his eyes, then as if sensing his thoughts, she quickly looked away, diverting her attention to the needs of the children.

All through supper Jake studied her, discovering things he'd never noticed before. The way her hair gleamed in the lantern light. The flush on her cheeks when she noticed his attention. Her graceful movements when she passed the gravy. The soft melodic quality of her voice. For a moment he imagined what it would be like if she really were his wife. The children, their children. A man could certainly do worse.

He ate his fill, finding everything delicious. Sated and sleepy, he rocked back in his chair. He observed the children when they excused themselves to play a game of checkers on a rag rug they'd placed in one corner of the room.

When Joshua squirmed and wanted down, Jake lifted the baby from the high chair and dawdled him on his knee rather than set him free to disrupt the others in their play. More content than he'd been in days, he engaged Joshua in a game of patty-cake while Mattie cleared the table.

She hadn't said a word about his trip to town, or his late return. She hadn't even mentioned his spending the night in the barn. Was it because of the presents? Well, they weren't really presents, for it had dawned on him that for Mattie the things he'd brought home just represented a whole lot more work.

Somehow he didn't think the gifts had anything to do with it. If Mattie was really mad, he had an idea the grandest trinket in the world wouldn't make her change her mind. It was as though she knew it was something he couldn't talk about, but she was willing to trust him just the same. That idea made him warm all over.

The baby babbled something he didn't understand, but Jake nodded and murmured agreement with whatever it was anyway. He glanced up and caught Mattie watching him.

A becoming blush flushed her cheeks and her lips tilted in a hesitant smile. "Would you like some more coffee?"

"Thank you, but I think I've had plenty."

She turned her attention to washing the dishes.

Damn, she looked pretty. Her skin had tanned since she'd come to the ranch. Her lips reminded him of a ripe peach, full, red, and soft. He found himself wondering if they tasted as good as they looked. Suddenly he was overcome by an almost overwhelming desire to take her in his arms and find out.

He closed his eyes and imagined her in the hayloft, all soft and warm and willing. One kiss would lead to another, then . . .

Joshua, no longer content to pat his uncle's cheek, fastened a chubby hand in Jake's hair and yanked. The pain brought him back to reality.

"Oww! Let go, little fella." Jake attempted to balance the child with one hand and untangle his determined small fingers with the other. It didn't work. Finally, he called out for Mattie to help.

"Oh, dear. He does have a good grip," she said, her efforts to free him failing. "Maybe if I distract him." She hurried to the cabinet and returned with a tin. She opened it and removed a cookie. "Look here, Joshua. Umm, good." She took a bite. "Want one?"

Still maintaining a death grip on Jake's hair, the child leaned forward.

"Oww! I think he's determined to make me bald. Can't you do something?"

"Don't scare him. It'll only make things worse." She held out the sweet again. "Let go of Uncle Jake and you can have the cookie."

"Dada," Joshua said, using his other hand to pat Jake's cheek.

"Well, I'll be," he said in wonder. "Did you hear that? He called me Daddy."

"Yes, I did," she said. "Let Daddy go, baby."

Joshua grinned from ear to ear and released his hold.

"Good boy." Mattie quickly handed the child a cookie.

Jake rubbed his head and grimaced. "He is gonna be a strong one."

"Let me take a peek." Mattie leaned close and examined the sore spot.

She smelled like good food, soap—and flowers. She also smelled like woman—soft, sweet, and tempting. Her nearness made the lower part of his body snap to attention.

"It's a little red, but no blood drawn. Maybe this might help ease the pain." Smiling, she handed him a cookie.

Jake bit off a chunk. "Um, good. Ginger cookies. Was that what you made last time?"

"Some ginger. Some sugar. The children liked the ginger best."

Her hips swaying with a grace that belied her small stature, she went to the washbasin and dampened a cloth.

"I never got any of the other, so I don't know which one I like best. I'll bet they were both delicious." Something else also looked delicious, and he hadn't yet got a taste of that either. He'd never been a man to go back on his word, but somehow when it related to Mattie, he was finding it harder to hold to that damned agreement.

When she returned to wash Joshua's face and hands, she leaned close, so close he could have reached out and closed his mouth over the tip of her breast. But before he could yield to temptation, she straightened and lifted the baby out of his arms, effectively removing the succulent morsel from his reach.

He groaned in frustration. His lower region had developed a gnawing ache. Beads of perspiration dotted his brow.

"Jake? Are you all right?" She reached out and placed her palm on his forehead.

A shiver of desire shook him from head to foot.

"You must be coming down with something. You feel positively clammy." She trailed the back of her hand down his cheek.

"I think I'd better go to bed," he said through gritted teeth. "Since it might be contagious, I think I'd better sleep in the barn." *Alone. Again.* In his present condition, he didn't trust himself to sleep in the house.

"Let me get you a blanket." She handed Joshua to Hope, then disappeared into her bedroom. She returned with a quilt draped over one arm, a pillow clutched in the other. She handed them to him. "There. That at least should make you more comfortable."

"Thank you," he mumbled.

"Children, say good night to your uncle. Then I think it's time you went to bed."

She followed him to the entry. "Good night, Jake."

"Good night, Mattie." Unable to make himself leave, he stood on the porch and ogled her like he were a child and she were a jar full of candy.

Arching a brow, she drew back, then she closed the door.

Feeling like a damned fool, he strolled to the barn and climbed into the loft. He fluffed his mound of hay and arranged his bedding, then tugged off his boots and lay down, pulling the quilt over him. The minute his head touched the pillow, he knew he was in trouble. The danged thing smelled like flowers and soap—just like Mattie. He groaned, knowing it would be another night with no sleep.

*   *   *

The next morning Jake rose, determined to change the status of his marriage. To do that, he had to get Mattie off into a bedroom by herself. It was a little difficult to coax a wife into your bed when you shared it with two children. Besides, he wouldn't mind a little privacy himself.

He strode to the cookshack and picked Romero and Slim, two of the handiest cowboys, to help with the job. After giving them detailed instructions, Jake left them to finish their breakfast and headed for the house.

He found Mattie at the stove making sourdough pancakes. "Smells wonderful. I'm hungry enough to eat a bear."

"Glad to see you are feeling better, but I'm not serving bear today," she teased. "Will these do?" She waved a heaping platter of golden flapjacks under his nose.

He hurriedly took his place at the table and filled his plate. "Think I've died and gone to heaven," he said, shoving a forkful into his mouth.

"Uncle Jake, you didn't even say grace," Hope admonished, taking her own seat across from him.

"Thank you, Lord—and pass the syrup," he said between bites. Even if she happened to be homely as a mud-dabbed fence, which she wasn't, Mattie had certainly found a way to his stomach—if not to his heart.

❧ THIRTEEN ❧

All week the house had rung with the sound of hammers—and Jake shouting instructions. Mattie massaged her throbbing temples. Whatever construction they were doing had to be sturdy to stand up to the din. Although she would be glad to have the extra room, the constant noise and mess were almost more than she could endure.

Jake and the cowboys started at daylight and worked until it was too dark to see. This she didn't understand because before when she'd asked, he'd flat ignored her entreaty to do something about the house. Although the cowboys worked hard, Jake labored like a man driven, which made her wonder if there was more to this sudden desire to expand the house than met the eye. She told herself she shouldn't look a gift horse in the mouth, for when the remodeling was finished she'd finally have a room all to herself.

She tested the water she'd put on the stove to boil, then began sorting the laundry collected from the boys' room. She added to that the pile Jake had brought in from the barn. He'd continued to sleep there, even though he'd recovered from whatever had ailed him.

While Jake would go into town daily, using one excuse or another, mostly to pick up more nails or other supplies, he wasn't gone long and always returned before dark. Even though she suspected he visited Jolene, she couldn't find anything to get upset about. Not that she really had any right to complain. It wasn't like they were truly married. It was a business arrangement, and while she didn't particularly like him visiting the Miner's Delight, even on business, somehow she was certain that Jake was living up to his end of the bargain.

"Now where did that other sock go?" Certain that she'd found two, she headed back for the twins' room to collect the mate.

"Meow."

"Bridget! What are you doing in here?"

The cat growled, hovering over something captured between its paws.

"Scat, you naughty thing." Mattie flapped her apron.

Bridget lay her ears back, then jumped off the bed and ran through the doorway.

Mattie bent to see what the cat had been playing with. There on the coverlet next to a dot of blood she discovered a tiny piece of gray fur. She gingerly poked it with the tip of her finger. It wasn't just fur. It was a portion of a mouse's ear.

"Solomon?" she called, falling on her knees to look under the bed. Then she peered behind the dresser, hoping the beady-eyed little rodent would come to her call. Frantic, she searched every spot, every nook and cranny. No trace of the mouse could be found. Finally knowing she'd exhausted all other possibilities, she sat down on the bed.

Her mind filled with visions of Solomon peeking from a twin's pocket, or washing his face at the end of her sink. How cute he'd been with his cheeks stuffed with a cookie he'd daintily held between his paws. Only last night she'd discovered him asleep in her yarn box, his favorite place for napping. She had scooped his plump little body up, along with a skein of yarn, and carried him back into this very room. The yarn was still there, beside Hal's pillow. She picked it up and gently fingered the strands.

Jake found her there a few minutes later. "Mattie, what's

wrong?'' He sat down beside her. "The boys been into your yarn again?''

"Oh, Jake," she cried, turning toward him. He closed his arms around her and the warmth, the feel of his strength, was more than she could bear. She began to sob.

He awkwardly stroked her hair. "Honey, don't fret. I'll buy you some more."

"It isn't the yarn. It's—it's Solomon. Bridget a-ate him."

"Oh, damn," he breathed softly. "Are you sure?"

She pulled away, then pointed behind him. "See. There's his ear. It's all that's left." Trembling, her eyes mirroring her horror, she clutched the front of his shirt.

"Did you look anywhere else?"

"Everywhere," she wailed. "Under the bed, behind the dresser. I even searched the drawers. He's gone." She sucked in a breath, then drew back, her eyes seeking his. "The boys! What am I going to tell them?"

Jake thought about the twins and how fond they were of the pesky little varmint. He studied on it for a minute, then he gripped her shoulders and forced her to meet his eyes. "We aren't going to tell them anything."

"We can't lie. They'll know he's not here."

"We'll tell them Solomon got lonesome and went to live with some of his own kind."

She had always believed that one should tell the truth in all matters, but this time . . . "That's not exactly honest."

"It is if you believe there's mice in heaven."

"Mice don't go to heaven. They don't even have a soul."

"How do you know there's no mice in heaven?" Jake argued. "Have you ever been there?"

"Of course not, but . . ."

"Well, since you can't swear it's a lie, then it might possibly be true?"

"Highly unlikely," she said, not convinced.

"Well, then maybe you'd better go ahead and tell them."

He watched her face, seeing the war going on inside her. She bit her lip and peered up through tear-spiked lashes. ''You think it might be possible?''

''Ordinarily, no. But Solomon was pretty special.'' He extended his arm, palm out, and scanned the air before him. ''Look, you can see him now, entertaining the angels.''

''One of them might even keep him in her pocket,'' Mattie said softly.

Loath to let her go, he held Mattie in his arms until the sound of an argument brought him to his senses. ''It's the boys,'' he hissed.

''The ear,'' Mattie cried.

Jake removed a handkerchief from his pocket, then carefully picked up the tattered remains and placed them inside. He folded the cloth and placed it back in his shirt pocket. ''Anything else?''

''The coverlet. It has blood on it.''

''You're washing today, aren't you?'' When she nodded, he yanked the covering from the bed and shoved it into her arms. ''Now let's get out of here before they find us.''

A high-pitched scream sent them running into the kitchen.

Faith and Hope cowered in a corner.

The twins, grins stretching from ear to ear, stood in front of them.

''Hal's got a snake,'' Faith screeched.

''He tried to put it down my dress,'' Hope cried.

Jake heaved a sigh and strode forward. ''All right, you little devils, let me see what you've got.''

The little boy reluctantly extended his hand. A brightly colored snake wriggled in his grasp.

Jake squatted beside him. ''My, that's a fine-looking snake.'' He glanced at Mattie. ''Come here a minute.'' Even though he could tell that Mattie had rather be anywhere than near the writhing creature, she came and knelt by his side. ''Isn't that a doozy?'' he asked her.

''Oh, my, yes,'' she agreed.

"Want to pet him?" Hal poked the snake at her.

"I don't think so," she said faintly.

"Naw. We wouldn't want to scare him," Jake said. "Tell you what. Let's see if we can build him a cage or something. In the meantime, maybe Mattie can find a jar for you to put him in."

Mattie gave him a relieved smile and nodded. She went to the cupboard and returned with a large glass jar.

"You aren't going to let them keep that horrible thing?" Faith asked, her eyes wide with fear.

"It's only a little grass snake. It won't hurt you," Jake told her.

"You just say that because they haven't put it in your bed," Hope said.

"Have they put it in yours?" Jake asked.

"Not yet. But they will. I just know it," the smaller girl said.

Mattie, seeing the twins grin at each other, felt the blood leave her face. The girls' bed was her bed, too.

"All right," Jake said, giving the boys a stern look. "You can keep the snake on one condition. You keep it away from Mattie and the girls. No sticking it in the flour bin, no putting it in their bed—or any other place like that. Understood?"

"Shucks, we cain't have no fun atall," Hal grumbled.

"Sure you can," Jake said. "You can catch bugs for him to eat. I'll bet he's hungry now."

"He does look kinda lank, don't he? Come on, Lory."

"I saw some good ole juicy ants out back. I think there's some fat maggots out there, too."

"What are we waitin' for?" The two exploded from the room.

"A snake?" Mattie hissed in his ear. "Maggots?"

"Well, after what happened to Solomon, I don't think we had any alternative," Jake said softly.

"You're right, of course. Maybe I'll get used to the creature. He is a pretty color." Her lip trembled.

"Remember the angels," he said, bending close. He cupped her chin, then gently brushed her lips with his. He might have done more, but the girls giggled, making him aware that he had an audience.

Her eyes wide, Mattie gazed up at him.

Suddenly recalling that he had another chore to do, one far less pleasant, he gave her an encouraging wink, then strode out the door.

He buried the handkerchief behind the house, under a sweet-smelling lavender bush. He thought Solomon might like that. He took off his hat and used his sleeve to wipe the sweat from his forehead. He, too, would miss the furry little fellow. Moisture filled his eyes; he angrily blinked it away. "Cryin' over a damned mouse. The varmint ate my socks, peed in my bed—" And slept on his shoulder. He slammed his hat back on his head and went to see what the cowhands—turned carpenters—were doing.

Later that night, after the children had gone to bed, Jake and Mattie sat on the porch steps and listened to the crickets.

"I thought they would be more upset," she said softly. "They only said they hoped Solomon was having fun."

"Might be different if they knew the true story. To them, he just went off to play with his mouse friends. Nothing to be sad about. Besides, now they have the snake."

"I hope it doesn't get out of that jar." To be truthful the creature gave her the shivers, but since she felt responsible for what happened to the mouse, she was determined not to let her fear of the snake show.

"I'll pick up some screen wire tomorrow and make it a pen. What do you think they'll end up naming it?"

"The last I heard they'd decided on Cochise."

"A mouse named Solomon, and a snake called Cochise. Wonder what else they'll waggle home?"

"There isn't much telling." She was quiet for a minute, then she touched his sleeve. "Where did you put him?"

"Out back, under that lavender bush."

"He'd like it there."

"Yeah. That's what I thought." He closed his hand over hers and gave it a squeeze.

The sympathetic gesture brought a rush of moisture to her eyes. Determined not to cry again, she changed the subject. "How are you coming with the house?"

"It's taking more time than I thought, but it will be nice to have all that extra space. Once the whole wing is finished we could have a dozen kids and still have room."

She whipped her head around and stared at him. *A dozen kids*? Unaware of her scrutiny, Jake continued to tell her about the improvements he'd planned, but Mattie, pondering his previous statement, heard very little.

❧ FOURTEEN ❧

As the next week passed, Mattie continued to cook, clean, and care for the children. Jake divided his time between the renovations, the ranch, and his business in town. She no longer thought of it as a saloon. She found it easier to assuage her conscience that way—at least until she had received a letter from the missionary service.

She'd written a year ago, asking that they consider Sweetheart as a parish. When time passed without a reply she thought they'd probably considered the town beyond redemption. After that, with her getting married and all, she'd clean forgotten about the matter.

The letter remained in her bureau drawer—unopened. Things had been going well between herself and Jake, and she hated to complicate matters.

For the first time in her life she felt content—except for the restlessness at night. She blamed that on being so crowded—three in one bed—and on the summertime heat, and stuffiness of the room. She told herself she would sleep better when she had a bed of her own.

The house had turned into much more of a project than she had first thought. The rafters overhead had been rotten, making it necessary for the hands to go into the hills behind the house and cut trees for new ones. Then the logs had to be peeled and dried, and skidded back to the ranch. One log had torn loose and had begun to roll. If it hadn't hit a stump, they might not have had any house at all.

She'd been hard put to keep the children out of the way, especially when they were determined to help. Jake had come to her rescue with a bucket of whitewash and some brushes. Of course the children had worn more whitewash than the house, but at least it had kept them busy.

To escape the noise, Bridget had moved to the barn, which was all right with Mattie as she found it hard to feel the same way toward the cat after she had devoured Solomon.

Jake's hound had taken refuge in the bunkhouse.

Sometimes Mattie wished she, too, could escape, even for a short time. She had the feeling that Jake also longed for his former peace and quiet.

Since the evening they had sat together on the porch, he'd been too tired to do more than eat and go to bed. Some nights, like tonight, he'd been almost too tired to eat.

During supper, she'd noticed him rubbing his shoulder. After the meal, she offered to put some liniment on it for him.

"If it wouldn't be too much trouble," he said quietly.

"No trouble at all." She boiled a mixture of dried herbs and strained them through a cloth, then after the mixture had cooled, she brought it to the table. "Take off your shirt and let me have a look."

When Jake removed it, she saw a large red spot on his shoulder. "What happened?" she asked.

"One of the timbers slipped and hit me. I think I pulled a muscle putting it back."

"I didn't know it was so inflamed. A poultice might have worked better."

"I'm sure what you've got will work just fine."

Mattie dipped her hands into the mixture and rubbed it over Jake's flesh, gently massaging the muscles in his back and shoulders.

"Oh, that feels good." He closed his eyes and let his head drop forward. Her motions were soothing, comforting.

He remembered how the boys pleaded to have Mattie rub their backs each night. Now he knew why. Her touch was magic. He could have sat there all night. It was the first time she had touched him, and he savored the closeness, the intimacy. She smelled of soap and cinnamon and that flowerlike fragrance he'd come to recognize as her own. Mixed with the tangy scent of the liniment, it made a seductive combination. Her fingers drew lazy circles on his skin; her palms kneaded, then stroked, her gentle touch becoming loving, almost a caress. He scarce dared to breathe, prolonging the moment, knowing that she didn't realize what she was doing.

Mattie slathered the liquid over Jake's firm flesh, noticing how tan he was from the sun. The faint dusting of hair on his back and shoulders made her fingertips tingle, as did the contact with his body. She began to imagine what it would be like to really be married. To feel his strength next to her every night, to be held in his arms, caressed by his hands, to be kissed by his lips. Envisioning the warmth of that kiss, her motions grew slower, the vision more vivid. She closed her eyes and released a wistful sigh.

The sound jolted her back to reality. She blinked, then glanced at Jake, wondering if he had noticed. The lazy one-sided smile and the inner fire lighting his blue eyes told her he had. A rush of heat infused her, making her blush from head to foot. "I th-think that sh-should feel better now," she stammered, upset to find that she wasn't as immune to his male presence as she would have liked to have been. The discovery left her shaken.

Somehow she didn't think Jake remained untouched by the experience, either.

"It felt wonderful," he said softly. Almost too damn good.

"Would you rub my back now?" Lory asked, getting up from his place on the rug.

"Mine, too?" Hal asked hopefully.

"It seems you've got two more customers." Jake got to

his feet, envious of the boys' demand for attention. His heart pounding like a Comanche war drum, he gazed at his wife, and wished they were alone. "Thank you, Mattie," he said softly. He wanted to kiss her, but the way his body was reacting, he knew it would be difficult, if not impossible, to stop with a simple kiss. Instead, he bid her a hasty good night, then turned away and walked out the door.

"Good night, Jake," she called after him. For a moment she had thought he intended to kiss her, but she'd been mistaken. Yet, raising a fingertip to her mouth, she wondered what his kiss would feel like—a real kiss, not just touching his lips to hers like he had that night on the porch. Even that gentle brush of his lips had upset her equilibrium for days. A real kiss would probably set her back on her heels. But somehow she would have been willing to chance it.

The next day Mattie was still in a state of euphoria. Whether she did dishes or folded clothes, her mind seemed to drift from her task. The only thing she was fully conscious of was the memory of her hands on Jake's flesh.

"Mattie?"

"Yes, Jake," she answered dreamily. Then coming to herself, she asked primly, "What is it you need?" She briskly scrubbed the tabletop.

"I think we all need a change of pace. There's going to be a dance in town Saturday. How about you and me and the kids taking it in?"

"A dance?" She didn't know how to dance, but the chance to get away from the ranch even for a short while would be a welcome relief. "That sounds delightful. Tell me more."

"Actually it's a barbecue, too. Me and the other ranchers will provide the beef. You ladies are supposed to cook up the rest of the stuff. We'll close the street off and sweep it so nobody steps in any . . ."

"I get the picture," she said quickly. "What should I wear?"

"You might whip up something out of that blue stuff I got you."

"The calico. Yes, that would do nicely—if I have enough time," she amended, remembering her busy schedule.

"Well, tell you what I'll do. The boys seem to be occupied for a while. How 'bout I take the sprout and the girls into town with me? That might give you a chance to get started."

"Jake, I could . . ." *hug you*, she'd started to say, then caught herself. "Thank you."

His blue eyes twinkled. "You're welcome."

Mattie folded the fabric she'd cut and placed it to one side. The boys had been awfully quiet—which usually meant they were up to something. It might not hurt to check on them. Besides, she had a crick in her neck, and a little fresh air might do her some good. She scanned the yard, then, not finding them, headed for the barn, thinking they might be playing in the loft.

A few minutes later she left the two-story outbuilding and came back out into the sunshine. *Where could they be?*

The dirt pile. She rounded the house to check the large mound that Jake and the cowboys had removed from the old house, using a new puncheon floor to replace it.

The twins weren't there, either. She turned to go back inside when a gleam of glass caught her eye. *Cochise.* They couldn't be too far away.

Noticing how the snake had coiled in the very bottom, she lifted the jar, finding it so hot it burned her fingers. "Poor thing. You're about broiled." Thinking to cool the container, she carried it to the water trough in front of the house and doused the jar several times. Then, she opened the lid so the inside jar temperature would lower. "There, isn't that better?"

She carried the container to the back of the house. She would add some green grass for the snake to lie in, then place the jar in the shade, where the boys could find it, yet in a spot more comfortable for their pet. Her attention on the reptile, she didn't notice the rock until she was hurtling through space. She landed belly down on the ground.

The container, torn from her grasp, rolled away—the jar in one direction, the lid in another. The snake, taking advantage of his chance, quickly slithered away.

"Oh, no! Come back!" She scrambled to her knees.

"Whatcha yellin' about?" Lory asked, darting around the side of the house.

"Look! That's our jar," Hal yelled. "What did you do with Cochise?"

"You left him in the sun. I was trying to cool him off," Mattie explained.

"I bet she wasn't trying to cool him off," Lory said furiously. "She let him go!"

" 'Cause she didn't like him."

"I did like him." She saw the disbelief on the boys' faces. "All right, I didn't like him, but I didn't let him loose on purpose."

"I bet you did. I hate you!" Lory's face crumpled, then he turned and ran toward the barn.

"I hate you, too." Hal ran after him.

Mattie watched helplessly. First the mouse. Now the snake. How could she ever make it up to them? *By finding the damned thing.*

She covered most of the yard on her hands and knees searching for the elusive reptile. While she did find an assortment of bugs, spiders, a scorpion, and some very large worms, there was no sign of the snake. Finally, hours later, she gave it up as a lost cause. She struggled to her feet, brushed her dress off, and went back into the house.

When she entered the kitchen a piece of white paper on the table caught her eye. She picked it up and tried to decipher the childish scrawl.

Me and Lory don't lik it here no more.
Gonna liv wit Injuns.
Lory Hal

The note fell from Mattie's hand and fluttered to the floor. She didn't bother to retrieve it. The boys had run away, and it was her fault.

She hurried to the bunkhouse, but found it empty. The cowboys were all out on the range. The cook was asleep and snoring his head off. She noted the whiskey bottle cradled in his arms and knew she'd get no help from him.

Hoping the twins had changed their minds, she checked the rest of the house and the yard, but the youngsters were nowhere to be found.

The sun had dipped lower in the sky. Jake and the girls would be returning before long. But would they arrive before dark? A vision of the little boys, alone, frightened, possibly lost, came into her mind.

She shielded her eyes from the setting sun and stared at the sagebrush-dotted hills. The twins might be miles from here by now. Even if she ran, not knowing which way they had gone, she'd probably never find them.

A man on horseback could find them easily.

Or a woman.

The old terror of horses rose to confront her—along with the vision of her father. His body bloody and broken. The wild-eyed stallion standing over him. She shuddered.

She couldn't do it.

She had to. She was the only one home.

She couldn't wait for anybody else. It was her fault they were gone. It was up to her to find them. Her legs trembling, her mouth filled with fear, she headed toward the corral.

She stood for a moment, eyeing the animal. The bay horse swished his tail and continued to doze. He didn't look fierce. But he was big and, like all horses, unpredictable. Since there were no others to choose from . . .

Her mouth dry, she crawled through the bars, then slowly lifted a bright Indian blanket from the rail. Shaking so bad she could hardly stand, she approached the animal, murmuring a prayer for the Lord to give her strength. She slid the blanket over the animal's back.

He only flicked his ears.

Since she had forgotten about the bridle, she did it next, putting the bit in his mouth, the headstall over his ears, fastening the buckle. She tied the long leather reins to the railing of the corral. Staggering under the weight, she carried the saddle toward the animal and flopped it onto his back.

The horse jerked and sucked in air.

Startled, Mattie leapt back. Then she remembered Jake telling her how a horse would hold wind to keep the cinch from tightening. He'd showed her a trick the cowboys used. Hoping she was doing it right, she tightened the cinch, then waited. When the horse let out his breath, she tightened it some more. She checked, making certain the saddle wouldn't slip.

Now all she had to do was get atop the animal.

She also had to open the gate.

She did that first, but left the horse where he was, fearing he might get away if she tried to mount him outside the enclosure. Next, she untied the reins.

She hesitated. The horse certainly wasn't asleep now. He had taken on a wariness, his eyes following her every move.

The cowboys ride them all the time, she told herself. There was nothing to be afraid of. *Like hell!*

Dragging in a calming breath, she gripped the pommel with one hand, the back of the cantle with the other, and swung herself astride. She stared at the ground and swallowed, then slid her other foot into the stirrup. So far, so good.

"Giddap, boy," she said hesitantly, wondering if he would obey.

He did. Too well. No sooner had the words left her mouth than the horse bolted through the gateway.

The reins slid from her hands to flap in the wind. She grabbed the saddlehorn and held on for dear life. "Stop! Damn you!"

But this time he didn't obey. The horse stretched his neck and lengthened his stride, running dead out for the hills.

"Wow!" Lory said, watching from the loft of the barn.

"I thought she was afeerd of horses," Hal said in wonder. "Specially ones that ain't full broke."

"I don't know. She seemed to be doin' okay till he started runnin'."

"S'pose we oughtta go help her?" Hal stared at the trail of dust fast disappearing into the foothills.

"How? We cain't run as fast as that horse." Lory held up a hand to shield his eyes. "He's probably a mile away by now. 'Sides, I'm still mad at her."

"Uncle Jake's gonna be mad at us if she gets hurt."

"I don't want her to get hurt, neither," Lory said. "But what can we do?"

A wagon rumbled into the yard. After a brief stop at the house, it came on toward the barn.

"I guess we'd better tell Uncle Jake," Lory said solemnly.

"I reckon we'd better."

"She did what?" Jake stared down at the white-faced youngsters.

"She rode off on Cyclone. They went thataway." Lory pointed toward the hills.

"I think there's a lot more to this than you're tellin'. You get on into the house and stay with your sisters. I'll deal with you later." Jake clucked the team into a gallop, setting out in the direction Mattie had taken.

He couldn't figure it out. She was scared to death of

horses. Had been ever since one had trampled her father to death.

Something must have happened. What could make her desperate enough to saddle, let alone attempt to ride one of the critters? And then she'd ended up on a critter that even the cowboys tried to avoid. Jake's eyes narrowed as he pondered the possibilities. Those twin devils had something to do with it, he'd bet his boots on that.

He cast a glance toward the crimson sky. Soon it'd be dark. He had to find her before then. He topped a rise and paused to let the winded animals blow. He set the brake, then stood on top of the wagon seat to get a better view. He cupped his hands around his mouth. "Mattie?" He turned in the other direction and yelled again.

"Jake!" came a faint answer from a distance.

He unwrapped the leathers and released the brake, then he turned the team in her direction.

Mattie, her hair undone and streaming around her face, staggered toward him. "Jake! Thank God you came!"

He pulled the wagon alongside, then jumped down to confront her. "Damn it, woman. Don't you know better than to try to ride an unbroken horse?" he asked, the gruffness of his voice betraying his fear.

She lifted a dirty, tear-streaked face. "I didn't have a choice. I have to find the boys."

"The boys? What do they have to do with it?"

"They ran away."

"So they did, did they? Wait till I get back to the ranch, I'll tan me a skinny little hiney or two."

She gripped his shirtfront, her eyes wide with concern. "They're at the ranch? They're all right?"

"They're just fine."

She heaved a sigh, then winced.

"What's the matter?" he asked. "Are you hurt?"

"Just my dignity," she said, trying to manage a smile. "The horse threw me."

"I'm not surprised." He helped her into the wagon, then

took his seat beside her. More shaken by the mishap than he cared to admit, he picked up the reins. "Now you can tell me what happened."

Jake shoved a lock of hair out of his eyes, then pointed his finger toward the lantern-lit barn. "I want every one of those stalls cleaned out before you go to bed."

Their faces streaked with tears, the boys each picked up a pitchfork and set to work.

Massaging his stinging palm, Jake cast one more look over his shoulder, then he headed for the house. Might give them something to do besides get into trouble. After the walloping he gave them, he doubted if they'd be sitting for a while.

He entered the kitchen and poured himself a cup of coffee. He gazed across the supper table at Mattie. "The cowboys found Cyclone on their way back to the ranch."

"That's good. At least that's one animal I didn't manage to do in." She wrinkled her face and squirmed from one hip to the other.

"You appear pretty stove up. Didn't break nothin', did you?"

"No, the ground was soft," she said between gritted teeth.

"Didn't land on a rock?" he asked, watching her.

"If you must know, I lit in a bed of cactus."

"Oh." Envisioning that scene, he chuckled.

She shot him an indignant look, then her eyes filled with tears. "That's right. Laugh! It's not you with a bottom full of stickers."

"Hurts pretty bad, does it?" He came over to stand by her chair. She did look a mite peaked. "Maybe I'd better take a look." He glanced down at her hips.

"Not on your life!" She gathered her skirts primly about her.

"If you have thorns in there, they could get infected."

She glanced up at him, her brow furrowed in pain. She wiggled again.

"Might already be. Doesn't take cactus long." He set the cup down on the table. "Better let me see."

"No!" she said, her eyes widening with alarm. "You can take me into town in the morning. I'll consult the doctor."

"That old drunk!" Jake plopped down on the bench next to her. "Besides, he isn't there. Some miner broke his leg over to Leadville."

"There's got to be somebody." She studied on it a minute. "I know. How about the barber? He pulls teeth . . ."

Jake scowled. "Absolutely not! I don't want that lecher lookin' at *my* wife's bottom. Besides, how would you explain having him pull out the stickers when you have a perfectly good husband at home? Pretty loose behavior, if you ask me."

"Well, nobody asked you," she snapped. "I just never thought about that part."

"They ought to come out of there, Mattie. You could be in real trouble if they don't."

Frowning, she eyed him up and down. "If I do let you do it, you won't look?"

He rolled his eyes in exasperation. "Mattie, if I don't look, how am I going to pull out the cactus?"

She thought about that for a minute. "Well all right— you can do it." She held up a finger. "Long as you promise not to enjoy yourself!"

Jake, caught with a mouthful of coffee, strangled.

❧ FIFTEEN ❧

Jake coughed until he cleared his lungs enough to breathe. Wiping away tears, he watched her hobble across the floor and into her room. Enjoy himself? That was one promise he would not make, for although he hated to see Mattie in pain, he fully intended to enjoy the hell out of himself.

"You girls do the dishes and watch Joshua." Leaving the three to finish their meal, he rose from the table and followed Mattie into the bedroom. There, smiling, he closed and locked the door.

She whirled away from the lamp she had just lit. "What are you doing?"

"You don't want the kids poppin' in here, do you?"

"Of course not!"

"Well, I don't either." He gazed at her, noticing she looked about as comfortable as a june bug in a hot skillet. He strode across the floor and sat down on the edge of her bed. "Come on over here and drop your drawers, and we'll get you taken care of."

"Drop my drawers?" She sucked in a breath. "I can't."

"Hellfire, Mattie, you're a widow. It won't be the first time a man's seen your bottom."

"Yes, it is." She bit her lip, then quickly added, "Except of course for my husband."

That comment rankled like salt in a sore wound. "I'm

149

your husband now." For all the good it did him. "So get over here."

Her cheeks crimson, she walked across the room and turned her back to him. She hoisted her skirt and tugged her white cotton underwear just low enough to expose the extreme top portion of one pale hip.

Jake parted the armload of petticoat ruffles and peered down at the portion of flesh she had bared. "I don't see anything."

"That's because it's lower," she said, her voice muffled.

"This is not going to work." He dropped the layers back into place. "Lay down on the bed."

"On the bed?" she said, plainly appalled by the idea.

"Facedown," he insisted. "With all that foofarall back there, I can't get to the cactus." He stroked his chin thoughtfully. "In fact it might be better if you took your dress off."

Her eyes widened in shock. "No!"

"At least the petticoats?"

She shook her head.

Jake sighed in exasperation. He was beginning to get the idea that getting Mattie out of her clothes would be more difficult than separating a mama cow from a newborn calf. "It would make it easier," he coaxed. "Otherwise this could take all night."

"All right," she said with obvious reluctance. "I suppose I could take off the petticoats—but you have to turn your back."

Realizing she wasn't about to remove a stitch as long as he watched, he obligingly stood and faced the door. "I never saw anybody so bashful. Hell, if I didn't know better I'd think you were a virgin."

He heard a choked sound, then cloth rustled behind him. "You can turn around now," she said.

He turned and saw the pile of petticoats on the floor. Mattie, her face the color of a summer sunset, shyly peered up at him. "What is it you want me to do?" she asked in a whisper.

"Lay down. But before you get all cozy we're going to need a few things. Do you have a needle and some tweezers?"

"There." She pointed to the bedside table.

"And a little whiskey might help."

"Whiskey? Whatever for?"

"It will help ease the pain, and I'll need to use it as a disinfectant." It would also help her relax a bit. He sure didn't want her jumping all over the bed every time he touched her.

"I don't have any whiskey," she said primly.

"That figures," he muttered. "I'll be right back."

He unlocked the door and left the room. He returned seconds later with a couple of clean cloths and an amber flask. He pulled the cork and handed her the bottle. "Here, take a swig."

"Ladies do not swig," she said stiffly. "If you're sure it's necessary, I'll have a sip."

"Make it a big one. It's gonna hurt like hell, and you'll need it."

She eyed the flask, hesitated, as if thinking on what he'd said, then she put the bottle to her mouth and took a tiny sip.

"It's going to take more than that." Cupping her head with one hand, he tilted the end of the bottle up, forcing her to take a big gulp. Before that hit bottom, he tilted it up again. "There, that ought to do it."

He took the bottle from her hands. "Swallow," he ordered.

She swallowed. Then she swallowed again. Her eyes bugged like they would pop from their sockets. She forgot to breathe.

Noticing, he opened his palm and walloped her on the back. "Guess you ain't used to it."

She sucked in air and doubled in a spasm of coughing.

After a moment, she straightened. Tears streamed down her cheeks. She doubled a fist and punched his arm.

"What'd you do that for?" he asked, rubbing his shoulder.

"You hit me. On purpose."

"I had to do somethin'. You weren't breathin'."

"Well, I'm breathing now." She squared her shoulders. "Shall we get on with it?"

"Yes, ma'am. Whatever you say." Once again he locked the door, then he turned toward her. He took up his position on the edge of the bed and patted a spot beside him. "Right here will be just fine."

Her eyes flashed amber-green fire. Her chin tilted defiantly. She gave him a scathing look and raised her skirt. Then she loosened the ties on her drawers and flopped face-down on the bed.

Not enjoy it? He rubbed his hands together. He was looking forward to it. He leaned over and grasped the white fabric on either side of her waist.

She swatted his hands away.

"Now what?"

"One hip at a time," she said, twisting so she could watch him. "I won't have you ogling me."

He sighed. "All right." Under her rigid scrutiny, he slowly slid the fabric down barely far enough to expose one rosy hip. She blushed all over, he noticed with delight. He sat down on the bed and picked up the needle. He found the first spine, and carefully pried it out.

"Oww!" She rubbed the spot, then quickly drew her hand back. "That hurt!"

"It's hard to get to them like this. Here, let's try something different."

Before she had a chance to protest, he lifted her, placing her across his lap.

"Oh, what are you doing?" She twisted, trying to see.

He tossed the voluminous skirt up over her head. Before she could untangle herself, he had her drawers down to her knees and both boots planted firmly on the ties. "There, now I can see what I'm doing." *And enjoy the view at the same time*. She had about the pertyest little bottom he had seen in a long time. Sure seemed a shame to hide it under all those skirts.

"What are you doing?" She squirmed, trying to right herself.

"Hold still." He placed a palm in the small of her back to keep her from moving. There, in the middle of each perfect round, was a cluster of prickly stickers. The reddened area told him they were rapidly becoming infected. "Relax now. I'll try not to hurt you." He poked the needle under the first one and pried it out.

She uttered a muffled curse.

He grinned. He didn't know she had it in her. Carefully, he removed the easier ones first and placed them to one side. The others, broken off beneath the skin, were more difficult. "How are you doing?" he asked, after prying out a particularly deep one.

"It hurts."

"Here. This will numb the pain." He handed her the bottle. "Not too much at a time."

The flask in one hand, the other arm hooked over the foot post to support her weight, she took one swallow, then another—then another. She licked her lips. "Not bad once you get used to it. Feels warm all the way down. And it does seem to help."

When she tilted the bottle again, he took it away from her. "That's enough for now. Hold still." When she was flat again, he probed another thorn. Even though he tried to be gentle, he could tell by the way she jerked that it hurt like the devil.

Finally, when the last sticker was out, he took the whiskey and dampened one of the rags, then he wiped each blood-dotted hip. While he thought he had them all, he carefully examined each curvaceous mound to see if there were any he might have missed.

The flesh he kneaded under his hand was firm, the skin—except for the part where the cactus had been—was pale and smooth as new cream. He envisioned the rest of her body and imagined himself exploring, caressing each silky curve. His own body hardened with anticipated pleasure.

He trailed a hand down to the soft spot behind her knee, then ran his palm back up to her hip. He hadn't thought her legs would be so long, or so shapely, being as short as she was.

Her soft moan made him conscious of what he was doing. He jerked his hand away. He trickled more whiskey into the wounds, then, afraid he might yet yield to temptation, he quickly pulled her drawers up around her waist. "There, all finished," he said hoarsely.

When the clock in the kitchen bonged, Jake looked up in amazement. The removal of the cactus spines had taken less than twenty minutes. To him, it seemed like eternity. He carefully lifted her off his lap and placed her facedown on the bed. "Is that better?"

Her hair curling in disarray, she turned on her side and gave him a sleepy smile. "Much better," she sighed. "Thank you, Jake."

"You're welcome." He'd never noticed how long her lashes were or how her amber-flecked eyes seemed to change color: becoming tawny when she was angry; the color of new grass when she laughed. Right now, as she peeped up at him, they were a curious mixture of the two.

It was the first time she had allowed him in her room, and even though he knew he should leave and let her rest, he found he wanted to stay. His gaze touched on the personal things, a silver-backed brush, a small ceramic bird, her Bible, and a tintype of a young man.

He frowned. "Your husband?" He pointed to the dresser.

"Yes. Poor Jaime. He died the same day we were married."

"How?"

"Shot. A couple of miners were celebrating. We were coming out of the church. A ricocheting bullet caught Jaime in the chest. He died instantly."

Barely a bride, the same day a widow. He remembered how shy she'd been. Could it be—? He would have encouraged her to say more, but for an insistent pounding. He crossed the floor and undid the lock.

The door burst open. The hay-dotted twins stood in the doorway. "We found our snake. See." Lory extended the wriggling creature toward him.

"That's good."

Two blond heads peered around him. "What's wrong with Mattie?"

"She's tired. We need to let her rest."

Two pairs of blue eyes worriedly studied Mattie.

"She's all right," Jake assured them.

"We finished the barn. Can we have a cookie?"

"Yeah, come on. How about a glass of milk to go with it? Y'all get to the table. I'll be there in a minute."

After they had bounced out of sight, he gazed toward the bed where Mattie lay with eyes closed. She'd probably have a heck of a hangover tomorrow, but for tonight he'd let her sleep. He'd put the girls and baby in his room; he and the boys would share the barn loft. He unbuckled her shoes and pulled them off. Then he shook out a quilt and tucked it around her. "Good night, Mrs. Turnbull," he said softly. Unable to resist, he bent and touched his lips to her forehead.

"Good night, Jacob," she said with a sigh, then she turned on her side and snuggled down into her pillow.

He grinned and shut the door.

Mattie lifted her head, then wished she hadn't. She knew why her bottom hurt, but how had she injured her head? Had the horse kicked her, and she didn't remember? She didn't think so. They hadn't stayed together that long.

"Oh-h-h." She slowly raised her hand and gingerly ex-

amined her scalp to see if she could detect some sort of
wound. There wasn't any. Then what—? She peered
through a red-rimmed haze. There on her bedside table, she
saw a needle, tweezers—and an amber flask. "The whiskey . . ."

Now she knew why her skull felt like it had been parted
by a Comanche hatchet. She also knew why she had gone
to bed still wearing her clothes. She tried to get up but when
the room began to spin, she quickly resumed a prone position.

After a soft knock, the door opened and Jake stuck his
head inside the room. "Good mornin'. How do you feel?"

"Probably the same way I look," she said between gritted teeth.

"That bad, huh?" He grinned.

She wanted to shout at him to go away, but lacked the
energy. She also couldn't bear the noise.

"Want some coffee? It might help."

"Yes," she whispered, wishing he would do the same.
His voice, never soft, echoed inside her head. The pain . . .
She was beginning to wish the horse had kicked her, put
her out of her misery.

Jake stomped across the floor and clanged the coffee mug
down on the table. "How's the bottom?" he boomed.

"Shhh!"

He chuckled. "Let's take a look." Before she could stop
him, he rolled her over and hiked her dress, then much to
her horror, he was examining her naked behind. "Pretty
red, still. I don't think they're infected, but just to make
sure, I'll just dump a little more of this on them." He pulled
the cork on the bottle and poured some whiskey into his
hand. Before she could protest, he began smoothing the
liquid over her backside. She flushed with mortification,
then gasped. It stung like she'd just sat in a pile of nettles.
"Stop it!" she cried, slapping at his hands. "It hurts!"

"Course it hurts. But this will make it feel better.
There." He pulled up her bloomers and rearranged her

skirts, then he looked at her and grinned. "Mattie Turnbull, your face is as red as your bottom."

"Oh, you . . ." She raised herself on one elbow, then fell back on the pillow. "Thanks to you I hurt on both ends instead of just one."

"That's gratitude for you." He dumped a measure of the open bottle into her coffee and stirred it with his finger, then he licked his finger dry. "Here, this will fix you up." He slid his arm behind her and hoisted her into a sitting position.

She clamped both hands on her head to keep it from flying off. "Damn you, Jake."

He thrust the cup under her nose. "Drink."

Since she had no choice, she did. "That's awful." She tried to shove his hand away.

"All of it."

Condemning him to perdition, she finished the cup. Then and only then did he allow her to sink back onto the bed. "I hate you," she gasped when she was able to talk.

He grinned. "Go back to sleep." He went out and softly closed the door.

The whiskey slid through her veins, taking the edge off the pain, warming, numbing, till at last she sighed in relief and closed her eyes. Never in her life had she allowed a man to take such liberties, to touch her so intimately. Not even a physician. Just the memory of Jake's hands on her sent a quiver of fire racing through her veins. She drifted into sleep, knowing that whatever she felt for Jake Turnbull, it certainly wasn't hate.

❧ SIXTEEN ❧

In the week following the incident with the cactus, Mattie not only tended to her chores around the house, but attempted to make new clothes for them all. She'd finished britches and shirts for the boys, a shirt for Jake, and dresses for the girls. Now it was her turn. She had cut the fabric earlier and stitched up the seams. She only had to set in the sleeves and add the finishing touches.

She slipped it on to check the length and gasped in amazement. It didn't fit. Puzzled, she peered under her arms to examine the seams. They hadn't come undone. Then what . . . ? Since she had used the same basic pattern for several years, she knew it should fit. Unless . . . She removed the garment, then clad only in her chemise and bloomers, she examined herself in the mirror.

She'd lost weight. That's why the dress was so loose.

It was true she'd been working harder than she'd ever worked in her life. She'd seldom had time to sit except for meals. Intrigued, she gazed into the mirror again, then she smiled, quite pleased with what she saw. Why, she was slim, almost willowy—if someone of her small stature could attest to being such a thing.

And she hadn't even noticed.

Apparently, neither had Jake.

Not that she wanted him to, she told herself. If he had, he certainly hadn't commented on the fact. But then as long she kept the kids quiet, his meals were on the table, his clothes washed, and the house clean, she imagined she could dye her hair purple and wear feed sacks to the table, and he wouldn't blink an eye.

He paid her no more mind than if she were a piece of furniture. An old piece of furniture at that.

She picked up her needle and thread. A good two inches and then some. She quickly began to work.

The day of the dance Jake had left for town just after daylight to oversee the barbecue. Mattie had been busy all morning, making pies and tending to the rest of the fixings.

It was nearing noon and now that she had the children ready, it was time she, too, got dressed. Her behind, although still a little tender in spots, had healed nicely. She doubted if she'd even have a scar. The rest of her body . . . ? She finished fastening the last of the tiny buttons, then gazed into the mirror. She twisted and looked at herself from a different angle. She'd never look like Jolene, but . . . *Not bad. Not bad at all*.

Now if she could do something a little different with her hair. She eyed it critically. The color was all right, and while it was soft enough, it certainly didn't have any style. She yanked the pins and shook it out of the tight bun she usually wore, then she picked up the brush and ran it through, until her locks lay in shining sable curls around her shoulders. ''Hmmm.''

She picked up her scissors, taking a snip here, a snip there. Finally she laid the shears aside. *Like this—or like this?* She lifted the side sections and brought them to her crown and anchored them with a sky-blue ribbon. Tiny wisps curled around her face; a halo of ringlets brushed her forehead, softening the sharpness of her features. *Much better*.

She, who'd always considered vanity a sin, wished for a bit of Spanish paper to rub on her cheeks, or a dab of lip rouge for her mouth. Even if she did have such things she would probably look like she fell in a bucket of paint if she tried to apply them. Deciding to help nature a tad, she bit her lips and pinched her cheeks until they took on a rosy tint.

"Mercy me! Is that you, Mattie?" She smiled, then fluttered her lashes, trying to mimic the actions of other women she had seen. She snorted in disgust. She looked so silly that if she tried it, Jake would only ask if she had something in her eye. She was plain old Mattie, and the sooner she accepted the fact the better off she would be. Still, what she saw was a definite improvement. Would Jake notice?

"Mama, Joshua's eating a bug and he won't let me have it," Hope called from the doorway.

Mattie chuckled and snatched up her apron. *Nothing like children to bring a body crashing back to reality.*

"Now, remember," Mattie reminded when Slim pulled the wagon up at the end of town, "girls, you stay with me. Hal, Lory, you may find Uncle Jake, but stay out of mischief. You did leave the snake home?"

"Yes, ma'am."

"He's in our bedroom."

Mattie smiled down at them. "All right, then run along."

"You want me to carry that youngun', Miz Mattie?" the lanky cowboy asked while helping her down from the wagon.

"No, thank you, Slim. I can manage just fine." She hoisted Joshua to one hip and grabbed his bag of necessaries with the other.

"You shore do look purty today," the cowboy said, tucking his head. "I don't supposed you'd be willing to save me a dance?"

"I'd be happy to—if I knew how to dance," Mattie confided.

"Shucks, ma'am. Don't let that stop you. I'd be pleased to teach you," the cowhand offered with a shy grin.

"Thank you. That sounds delightful."

The homely cowboy blushed an even brighter red, then he stammered a good-bye and got back onto the wagon.

Mattie, one eye on the girls, the other on the lookout for Jake, strolled down Main Street toward the group of people gathered at the far end of town.

"There he is. There's Uncle Jake," Hope said, dancing up and down.

"Can we go say hello?" Faith pleaded.

"Yes. But don't get dirty."

"We won't," the girls called in unison, already dashing down the dusty street.

"Get away from there before you get burnt," Jake warned, pulling one of the boys back from the embers by his shirttail.

Two men—one short, one tall—lifted their respective ends of the heavy iron rod from over the pit and carried the roasted carcass to a large wooden slab at one end of an oversize plank table.

"Just wanted to touch it. Never seen a whole pig dead before," Hal said, striving to squirm away from Jake.

"Specially one with an apple in its mouth," Lory added, plainly fascinated.

"You can look from over here." Jake tightened his hold.

"Aww, Jake. Let the kids have some fun," the short stout man in overalls said. "Y'all come here. Ever tasted a pig's brains?"

Both boys solemnly shook their heads. They eyed the hog's head with horror, then glanced at each other. "I think I got to go pee," Lory said.

"Me, too. Right now!"

Both youngsters churned the dust in their effort to leave the area.

"I'd never have thought of that," Jake said, chuckling.

"You ain't got eight kids. You get real inventive when you do."

"Ain't that a fact?" Eyes crinkling, his taller companion

smiled. "You get positively fanciful when you've got nine girls. Here come some of my little darlin's now. Looks like they picked up a couple of yours along the way."

Jake squinted against the sun. Faith and Hope, their braids bouncing in time with their movements, skipped toward him. Four other girls about the same age led the way. Well, so far, he'd spotted all the younguns—except the baby, of course, and he'd be with Mattie. Where was she anyway? He peered toward several groups of women.

"Uncle Jake. Uncle Jake." The girls stopped in front of him. Both pairs of eyes stared toward the table.

"What is it?" Faith asked.

"Looks awful," Hope whispered.

"Looks good to me," Jake said. "Where's your mama?"

"Right there," Faith said, pointing.

Peering past Faith, he saw a pretty woman in blue walking toward him. He still didn't see Mattie.

With Joshua stashed in the shade with two more of his age, who were in the care of their older, teenaged sisters, Mattie felt almost girllike herself.

Several people who hadn't recognized her eyed her curiously; one even asked if she was new to the area. Others, having known her for years, nodded and said hello. Most whispered behind her back and giggled. All, she knew, speculated about her sudden marriage—and relationship— with Jake.

She strolled down the street, noting the changes—few for the better. The peeling paint on the storefronts, the flies, the noise. The town seemed smaller than she remembered—dirty, almost squalid. Someone had planted a few patches of wilting flowers between two buildings. Even that pitiful effort at beautification had grown more to ragged stems than blossoms.

The ranch, even with the mess of construction, seemed like paradise in comparison. The sage-scented air, the juniper-dotted hills, the spiky-topped cedars, and the snow-capped mountains in the distance; who could want anything more? At home, even the wildflowers grew in great profusion.

And the children . . . Her children, for she thought of them as such, had blooms in their cheeks. The town children looked pasty by comparison, as if the constant shifting of dirt had settled beneath their skins.

Where are the children? she wondered. She scanned several groups, then found the twins on their knees playing marbles with some other boys. She'd need lots of hot water tonight, she thought.

Finally, amid a bobbing flurry of calico braids and hair ribbons, she spotted Faith and Hope. Just beyond them, she recognized Jake. "Now is as good a time as any," she said softly.

Leisurely making her way toward him, she watched and waited for him to see her, to smile, call out her name—something. The nearer she got, the more he seemed to be preoccupied with something behind her.

"Hello, Jake," she said, determined not to be ignored.

He turned to gaze into familiar, dancing, amber-green eyes. "Mattie? Is that you?"

She grinned. He hadn't recognized her either. "Yes, Jake, it's me."

He looked her up and down. "What did you do to yourself?"

"Nothing special. Just a different hairdo and a new dress."

"Boy, if my wife could look like that I'd buy all the calico in Hiram's store," a stout farmer standing next to Jake declared.

Jake scowled. While he couldn't quite put his finger on it, he knew it was more than the hairdo and dress, although they did look mighty fetching.

"Howdy, missus. I'm Jodie Blaine," a tall man said, extending his hand.

"Hello, Mr. Blaine. I'm happy to meet you." She obligingly shook the man's hand.

The heavyset man immediately thrust his hand forward
for her to shake as well. "I'm Jackson Perkins."

"Of course. Millie Perkins's husband," she said smoothly, amazed that the man who now gazed at her so admir-
ingly was one of the bunch that before her marriage to Jake
had threatened her with tar and feathers.

When Mr. Perkins continued to hang on to her hand, Jake
glared at him so fiercely that his companion, noticing, attempted to lure Perkins away. "I could use a drink—of
lemonade," Jodie Blaine suggested quickly. "How about
you, Jack?"

"Never touch the stuff," Mr. Perkins said, his eyes never
leaving Mattie.

"I think that's enough hand shakin'," Jake said gruffly,
stepping between them. "I, for one, would like some lemonade. How about you, Mattie, dear?" He wrapped his arm
around her waist and led her away.

Dear? Mattie ducked her head to hide a smile.

The rest of the day, Jake hovered by her side, fetching
her lemonade, carrying her a plate of food. He arranged a
pallet in the shade for her, and even took care of the children when they needed it. By the time the barbecue was
over and the dance had started, Mattie thought she could
never have wished for a more attentive husband.

While exciting, the fact that he had been so attentive also
terrified her. It was as though they truly were newlyweds.

"Hello, Miz Mattie." Slim, hat in hand, smiled down at
her. "Reckon it's about time for that dance. I asked the
boys to play a slow one."

"Thank you." She held up her hand so he could help
her to her feet.

Jake, who had been playing mumblety-peg with the boys,
rushed back to her side. "Where are you going?"

"Slim has offered to teach me to dance," she explained.

"You're my wife. I'll teach you."

She could just imagine Jake bouncing her about the floor; her, treading on his shoes; him, stomping on her toes. "No, that won't be necessary. You go on back to the boys." She turned and smiled at the worried-looking cowboy. "Shall we go?"

Slim hesitated, looking from her to the glowering Jake.

"Oh, all right," Jake grumbled.

The tall, lanky cowboy breathed a sigh of relief, then led her onto the dance area, a raised platform that had been constructed at the end of the street.

Slim stood opposite her and smiled. "Now, put your hand in mine, the other one goes on my shoulder. Listen to the music. One, two, three. One, two, three."

Mattie did as he instructed. Although his hands were callused and his movements anything but graceful, under the cowboy's patient tutoring Mattie soon found herself able to dance. "Oh, isn't this nice?"

"Very nice. You're light as a feather," he said in praise.

"You're just being kind." She glanced over his shoulder to see Jake stalking toward them.

"Now that she's learned, it's my turn." Jake came to a stop beside them.

"Thank you, Slim." Mattie smiled up at the tall, gentle man who blushed with obvious gratification.

"My pleasure, ma'am." The cowhand respectfully tilted his hat, then walked away.

"Seems like you're having a good time." Jake took her into his arms.

"A wonderful time."

When he whirled her around the floor, she found him surprisingly light on his feet. She would have expected a man of his size to be more deliberate, almost clumsy. Jake was graceful as a cat. Unlike the cowhand, Jake held her possessively, and glared at anyone who even looked like they might ask her to dance. And unlike the cowhand who reeked of rosewater, Jake smelled of soap and macassar oil.

He also smelled a little smoky, from the barbecue he had tended all day.

They sat out reels, polkas, and the gallup. When the pace finally slowed into a waltz, he pulled her into his arms and cupped her head against his chest. He held her close, indecently so, but she made no protest. Content to be held in her husband's arms, she could have danced like that all night. But no sooner had the music begun than she felt a tug on the hem of her dress.

Hope stood on the ground, staring up at them. ''Joshua's crying, and I'm tired. When are we going home?''

She sighed and glanced up at Jake, who seemed as reluctant to end the dance as she was. ''I guess it's time.''

''Yeah, guess so.'' He bent his head and brushed a kiss against her cheek. ''Thank you, Mrs. Turnbull, for a wonderful day.'' He gazed at her a minute, then he smiled. ''Well, guess I'd better go hitch the wagon. Unlike us old married folk, the hands will be here until morning.''

Her hand on her cheek, she watched him walk away. Was this what it would be like if they were really and truly man and wife?

A dreamy smile on her face, she gazed after him . . . And wished she hadn't when a slender figure in white left the crowd. The woman slid her hand into the crook of Jake's arm and walked with him into the darkness.

Jolene.

Why? Why couldn't she leave us alone? Mattie felt as though a Comanche arrow had just pierced her heart. Mattie knew she had changed, but she also knew Jake hadn't. He still had connections with everything she detested. The saloon, the whorehouse, and Jolene.

Mattie knew that while Jake might be eager to take her to bed, he would never be the husband she wanted. She mustn't allow herself to forget that.

❧ SEVENTEEN ❧

Jake shot a resentful look toward the house. For a while at the barbecue he thought Mattie might be softening in her attitude toward him, but on the way home he discovered he'd been sadly mistaken.

At first he figured one of the kids had done something to upset her, but then he decided they'd been too sleepy to get into much mischief. Besides, she'd tenderly tucked them into the bed of hay in the back of the wagon and covered them with a quilt so they wouldn't get chilled. But when she'd joined him, she'd sat rigidly on her side of the seat, not caring if he was cold or not. Just her manner toward him was frigid enough that he danged near froze to death.

When they reached the ranch, still hoping he might have been mistaken, he helped her carry the kids inside, then he took the wagon to the barn. After tending to the horses, he returned to the house. Mattie stood by the stove.

"Hello, Mrs. Turnbull," he said softly. He went up behind her and put his arms around her waist. "Nice dance, wasn't it?"

"Humph!" She shot him a look of pure dislike, then shoved his hands away and hurried toward her room.

Bewildered, he followed. "Mattie, what is going on?"

"Good night, *Mr. Turnbull*," she said and slammed the door in his face, removing all doubt from his mind that it

169

was him that had ruffled her fur.

"Women." Jake scratched his head, trying to figure out where he'd gone wrong. Then he let out a sigh and headed for the barn. He had another itch he wanted to scratch, but if tonight was any indication, she wasn't about to let him anywhere near her.

"That bull is a real doozy. Big. Randy as hell. Locked up in that pen, he's near gone crazy. When do you want me to go get him?" Henry asked, peering across the cook-shack table.

Jake took a sip of coffee, then grimaced and set the cup aside. The bitter aftertaste made him long even more for a cup of Mattie's brew. He knew how that bull felt, for he was pretty much in the same predicament.

It had been three days since the barbecue, and things had gotten worse instead of better. Mattie sashayed around the yard, her bottom swaying, luring him like a fly to sugar bait. She smiled at the younguns and hugged them. Him, she ignored, which only made him ache for a sign of her affection.

The accusing looks she shot at him made him feel guilty, even if he didn't know what the hell he was guilty of. She wasn't speaking to him, that was for sure.

He'd asked the kids why she was so mad at him, but they had no idea what he was talking about.

Even though he tried to stay away, his feet always seemed to carry him to the kitchen, especially when he knew she'd be there. He'd manage some flimsy excuse or another as a reason for his presence, such as he wanted a cookie.

She didn't give him one.

He needed something cold to quench his thirst.

She told him to try the well.

Mealtimes she wouldn't even pass the potatoes, leaving it up to the kids to do it, even though he had said please and thank you.

She'd made chili again.

He'd been afraid to touch it.

That made her so mad, she wouldn't give him any dessert.

She wouldn't give him anything else either. Not a smile, a kind word, nothing.

The cowboys had noticed. And whispered behind his back. The mood he was in, they didn't dare say anything to his face. Henry, being braver, had ragged him unmercifully.

"Jake! Are you listening?" Henry asked, frowning.

"What?"

"When do you want me to go after the bull?"

Jake's brows furrowed, then he slapped his palms down on the table. "I've decided I'll go get him myself."

"Oh?" Henry grinned. "And when are you planning on going?"

When? "Today is as good a time as any." *No sense hanging around the ranch.* He sure didn't enjoy being miserable.

"Slim and Romero would probably welcome a few days away from all that remodeling," Henry suggested. "They've been complaining that you've made them stack so many rocks they feel like they're in prison."

"You're probably right." He had been working them pretty hard. Besides, with Mattie in the mood she was in there sure wasn't any hurry on that bedroom.

"May as well take Sandy along, too. With that bull being so rambunctious, you could use an extra hand. Besides, Sandy can cook."

"That'd be a welcome relief," Jake replied dryly. The last couple of days he'd been taking his meals in the cookshack with the rest of the hands. Mattie's disposition being so sour, he didn't trust her not to poison him. "Tell the hands to pack their gear. I've got a few things to do at the house, then we'll be on our way."

Jake got as far as the doorway, then he turned. "Henry,

I'd appreciate if you'd watch out for the family while I'm gone. Kinda give Mattie a hand if she needs it and keep an eye on the twins. Those boys can be a handful.''

"I'll take good care of them," Henry promised. "Besides, you'll only be gone a week.''

"Only takes a few minutes for those two to bite off more than they can chew," Jake said wryly. "Oh, and if you get a chance to go into town, check on Jolene for me, too.''

"Yes, mama." Henry shot him an exasperated look. "Anybody else you want me to baby-sit while you're gone?''

"Naw. Unless you think Bock Gee can't take care of himself?'' When the foreman cursed, Jake decided he'd better leave well enough alone. He hurriedly left the cookshack and headed for the house, certain that after a few days of dealing with not only the ranch, but the rest of the responsibilities, Henry would be a lot more sympathetic by the time Jake returned.

Around noon, Jake gave the cowhands final instructions, then sent them on their way. Slim and Romero went out first, driving the heavy cattle cart. Sandy followed with the pack animals.

Jake knelt before the children who had gathered on the front porch to bid him good-bye. He hugged Faith and Hope, then he shook hands with the boys. "You two are the men of the house while I'm gone. I'm counting on you to take care of Mattie and the girls," he said, figuring that would carry a lot more weight than just admonishing them to behave themselves. "Can you do that for me?''

Lory and Hal stared up at him, their small, freckled faces solemn. "You can count on us, Uncle Jake.''

He ruffled their hair. "Good, that eases my mind. Well, I'd best tell your ma and Joshua good-bye.''

Mattie had stayed inside, but Jake noticed her peeking through the kitchen window. When he entered the kitchen, she ignored him.

He bent by the high chair and nodded while the baby

engaged him in a language only Joshua understood.

The toddler shoved a soggy cookie into his mouth.

Jake waited until he swallowed it, then gave the child a hug before striding toward the sink. "I've asked Henry to keep an eye on things while I'm gone, so if you need any help—"

Mattie whirled. "I'm certain we will manage quite nicely without you. Did you also ask him to take care of the rest of your female *friends*?"

All of a sudden the light dawned. She had seen him with Jolene. Mattie was jealous. He grinned. "As a matter of fact, I did."

"I figured as much," she said, her eyes glowing as yellow as that of an outraged mountain cat. "Well, what are you waiting for? Your men have already left."

"You haven't told me good-bye yet."

"Mercy, if that's all it takes. Good-bye!" She twisted toward the dishes she'd been doing. Tendrils, escaping from the tight knot of her hair, hung in shining, damp curls, softening the rigid appearance she'd strived for. The nape of her neck appeared youthful, vulnerable, and he found himself battling the urge to kiss it.

He took a step nearer, inhaling the scent of soap from the dishes, lavender, and woman. "You've got to do better than that," he said softly. He took her arms and forced her to face him.

"What?"

"I won't leave until you've given me a proper good-bye."

"Proper?" Her voice scathing, she raised a brow. "I doubt if you even know what the word means."

He held her, watching conflicting emotions flit across her face. Anger. Confusion. And something else he couldn't put a name to. "I'm waiting."

"All right." She heaved a sigh. "Good-bye, Jake. I hope you have a pleasant trip," she said in the same tone she would have used to tell him she hoped he ate rat poison and dropped dead.

He shook his head. "Not good enough."

"What . . . ?"

Cupping her head with his palm, he bent and pressed his lips against hers.

She stiffened and pushed against him, getting soapsuds all over his shirt. "St—"

He took advantage of her parted lips and eased his tongue inside her mouth. She tasted as good as she smelled. He probed, exploring, drinking in her sweetness. His kiss deepened until he felt her relax, then one trembling arm crept to the back of his neck. Soon her other joined it. Pinning her against the countertop, he held her close, his hands caressing her neck, her back, her hips.

"Jake? I brought your horse up," Henry called from the doorway. "Oh, excuse me. I didn't know you were busy."

Mattie, her face red as a ripe tomato, struggled to be free.

Silently cursing the foreman to perdition, Jake let her go. "I was just telling my wife good-bye."

Mattie ducked her head and flushed even brighter.

Unable to resist, he tilted her chin and brushed her lips with one last kiss. "Good-bye, Mattie."

"G-go-od-b-bye, Jake," she stammered, her eyes mirroring her confusion.

Feeling like a fox after a successful raid on the henhouse, Jake followed his foreman onto the porch.

"You still want to leave?" Henry asked, grinning.

"I think I'd better before she recovers from the shock and starts flinging pans at me." He climbed into the saddle. He glanced toward the kitchen window and caught Mattie peeking through the curtain. He smiled and blew her a kiss.

She instantly disappeared from sight.

Jealous. He never would have guessed it. He urged his horse into a gallop, anxious to get the bull and get back home again. He thought about the kiss and grew warm, remembering the way she'd responded. He'd been amazed when she'd kissed him back.

He wondered what else might she have done if they hadn't been interrupted. Probably smacked him. With Mattie it never paid to take anything for granted. He sighed, hoping that when he returned in a week, she might just discover she'd missed him.

❧ EIGHTEEN ❧

She didn't miss him, Mattie insisted. She wouldn't care if he never came back. No, that wasn't quite true because of the children, but *she* was doing just fine without him. But somehow all during the following week, Mattie caught herself staring out the window or going onto the porch to peer into the distance, searching for a sign of dust. She longed for a distraction, something—anything to take her mind off Jake. She watched the twins hopefully, but instead of getting into any mischief, they smiled angelically and went about their play.

She knew Jake had talked with them before he left but had no idea what he could have said that would make such a profound difference. The boys hadn't fought with each other, or with their sisters—and they hadn't gotten into any trouble. Instead they had been so polite and respectful that on more than one occasion she had placed her hand on their foreheads to see if they might be coming down with something.

The girls had never given her many problems. Joshua, over his cranky spell now that he sported a brand-new tooth, grinned at her like a benevolent cherub.

Henry had been so solicitous of her needs that she almost dreaded to see the man coming. He'd brought in firewood, fixed the stove damper, recaulked the windows, and when he wasn't whistling some off-key tune, the foreman was singing Jake's praises. To hear Henry tell it, Jake should have been recommended for sainthood.

The children's good behavior and Henry's help with the heavier chores should have made her happy, but Mattie found it did just the opposite. She was bored to tears.

She folded the britches she had patched and added them to the stack in the basket. At least Jake's absence had accomplished something. She had gotten caught up on her mending. It was a good thing, too, for Henry had assured her that Jake would be back tonight or tomorrow morning at the latest. In spite of her declaration that it didn't matter to her one way or another, she found herself washing the front windows, sweeping the porch, weeding the garden or any number of other things where she could watch for his arrival.

Then, after the week had passed and Jake still hadn't arrived, she decided her wayward husband was apparently in no hurry to come home. Told herself he was probably having too good a time. By the end of the eighth day, Mattie was spoiling for a fight.

When two weeks had gone by and Jake hadn't come home, she began to grow anxious that something might have happened to him.

"Naw, Mattie. Jake can take care of himself," Henry assured her. "It's a hard trip from here to Salida. Maybe he's taking it easy because of the bull."

Even though the foreman tried to ease her fears, she could tell that Henry, too, was worried.

Mattie had given up any attempt at sleep, instead she spent her nights in the kitchen in the rocker by the fire. Her eyes grew shadowed, her figure even slimmer. Although she tried to hide her concern from the children, she noticed that they, too, had taken to spending long hours on the porch, watching the trail.

Henry continued to bring the wood in each morning, but he no longer plagued her with his infernally cheerful whistling. When the foreman announced that he and two other hands were setting out to look for Jake, she really became worried.

Two days later, her nerves shredded, she made another attempt at anchoring the coil of hair on top of her head, but her unsteady hands couldn't seem to manage the pins. Finally, she shook the mass of curls down, then drew them away from her face with a piece of blue ribbon.

"Damn you, Jake Turnbull. You had better be sick, dead, or at least mortally wounded. If you've put us through this worry for nothing . . ."

The bedroom door burst open and crashed back against the wall. "He's home!" Lory shouted, his face stretched in a wide toothy grin. After his announcement, the boy immediately raced back into the kitchen and slammed out the door.

"Home. Oh, thank God." Her knees dissolving beneath her, Mattie sagged against the side of the dresser, then much to her chagrin she burst into tears.

"Mama, come see the bull," Hope said, rushing in to grab her hand. "Why are you crying? Uncle Jake's just fine."

"Fine, is he?" Mattie took out her handkerchief, wiped her face, and blew her nose. "Let's go take a look."

The cart, with the enormous red bull still inside, sat at the entrance to the corral gate.

Surrounded by the twins and Faith, Jake stood next to it, talking to the foreman. Jake didn't appear sick, or hurt, or dead, any of the things she had been so afraid of. He did indeed look just fine.

Hoisting her skirt to keep it from dragging in the dirt, she walked toward them. "Well, I see you made it."

A thick layer of dust covered him from the top of his hat to the tip of his boots, but when he turned his blue eyes gleamed and his mouth split in a dazzling-white smile. "Hello, Mattie." He strode forward and pulled her into his arms. "Did you miss me?" Before she could answer, he proceeded to kiss her. Long and thoroughly.

He smelled like dirt, hard work, horse, and manure, but wrapped in his strong arms, Mattie didn't mind a bit. Jake was home, and he was all right. He tasted of coffee and jerky and the motion of his tongue bombarded her senses. She wrapped her arms around his neck and kissed him back. Even though she desperately wanted to prolong the moment, the children's giggles and the cowboy's catcalls made her aware that they had an audience. Mortified that they had witnessed such outlandish behavior, she tried to push him away.

When he finally did release her, a rush of heat infused her from her feet to her ears. Unable to meet his eyes, she ducked her head and stammered, ''I g-guess you're hungry. I'll go fix something to eat.'' Ignoring the cowboys' grins of delight, she darted around Jake and ran toward the house.

''More taters, Uncle Jake?'' Lory asked, lifting the bowl.

''You bet,'' he said, filling his plate for the umpteenth time. Compared to Mooney, Sandy might have been considered a pretty fair cook, but the cowhand couldn't hold a candle to Mattie, on cooking—or anything else. Hungry for far more than food, he looked at her and smiled.

She blushed and turned her attention toward her plate. ''It must have been a terrible trip, what with the wagon wheel breaking and the bull getting loose and trampling Romero and all.''

''Well, we're all home now, thanks to Henry. If he hadn't arrived with that wagon and extra cart wheel, we'd be out there yet.''

''Henry's a good man,'' she agreed. ''He was a lot of help while you were gone.''

''Not too much help, I hope. I wouldn't want you thinking he could take my place.''

''No danger of that,'' she said shyly. ''The ranch wasn't the same without you, was it, children?''

''Nope.''

''Sure weren't,'' the twins said.

"We missed you a lot, Uncle Jake," Faith said.

"Mama most of all. Why she didn't even sleep at night she was that worried," Hope confided.

"Eat your dinner," Mattie said quickly.

So she didn't sleep, huh. Not that he got much sleep either. *She missed me.* He missed her, too. That kiss he had given her before he left had been a bad mistake, for the whole time he was gone, he could think of nothing else. He studied her from the opposite end of the table, his gaze caressing her hair, her lips, her breasts . . .

He remembered the way she'd greeted him, the way she'd felt in his arms. The moment, far too brief, had only whetted his appetite. It was like giving a kid a lick of stick candy, then taking it away. Now he had developed a craving that wouldn't be satisfied until he had the whole damned jar.

He wanted to make her his wife—in every way—and to hell with any agreement. He wanted—needed—to take her in his arms and make love to her, but knew once he did he wouldn't be letting her out of his bed for at least a week.

He also knew it wouldn't be that easy. For one thing there was no place he could get her alone. The barn was always crawling with children. The house, even with the door locked, wasn't private enough either. She didn't ride—at least not voluntarily—and after that mishap on Cyclone, he doubted if he'd be able to get her close to a horse again. She was too straitlaced to ever consent to going to his room at the saloon. He let out a sigh of sheer frustration. Sometime, somehow, he had to find a way. Soon.

"Why is the bull makin' all that racket?" Hope asked, her blue eyes wide.

"He's, uh, lonesome," Jake answered, hoping that would satisfy the little girl's curiosity.

" 'Tain't neither. The cowboys' said he's ho—"

Jake clamped a hand over Lory's mouth. "We don't discuss such things in front of the ladies," he said sternly.

"Why?" Hal asked. "The cowboys said the bull was

hot. I'd be hot too if'n I been riding in that old cart all that long way.''

''Oh.'' Jake dropped his hand and glanced at Mattie, who in spite of her obvious embarrassment seemed on the verge of laughter. ''Let's don't talk. Let's just eat,'' Jake said, hoping to waylay any further such conversation.

The bull bellowed again, and a cow answered.

Jake, thinking discretion the better part of valor, forced himself to concentrate on his food. But the natural call of his body drew his eyes to Mattie.

She met his gaze, then after a moment looked away. He saw the pulse pound at the base of her throat, the nervous way she moistened her lips, and knew that she was not as immune to the mating call of the animals as she tried to pretend.

''Do you suppose you should check on him?'' she asked. ''Maybe take him a plate of food?''

''The bull?'' Jake asked, confused. He knew she'd been saying something, but he'd been too busy watching her mouth to be aware of the words.

''Romero,'' she said with a giggle. ''He *is* the one with the broken leg.''

''We'll probably be spoiling him, but I guess he deserves it after what he's been through.'' Jake waited until she'd filled the plate and covered it with a cloth. ''You could try spoiling me a little bit. No telling what I'd do in appreciation,'' he whispered, only too conscious of her warmth, her sweet wildflower scent.

''You're spoiled enough already,'' she said, commenting on the first—ignoring the second. ''Now take this food out before it gets cold.'' She shoved the plate into his hands, then went back to clean the table.

The bull bellowed again.

''Maybe you should check on *him*, too,'' she said, peering at him from the other side of the table. The light from the kerosene lamp held her in a golden glow, making him imagine what she'd look like in candlelight—or moonlight.

Wearing nothing more than a smile.

Before he embarrassed himself, he turned away and hurried out the door.

A noise, almost like whimpering, came from the corral.

"Tomorrow," Jake promised, knowing the animal would be rested up enough by then to be turned in with the cows.

Mattie's voice, lifted in a hymn, drifted through the kitchen window.

Jake sighed with frustration. He knew how to ease the bull's misery, but danged if he could figure out how to take care of his own.

❧ NINETEEN ❧

"I want you girls to do the dishes and keep an eye on the baby while I start cleaning out the fruit cellar," Mattie said, ignoring the scowls on their faces. She'd hoped she might persuade Jake to clean out the cellar, but since Romero had broken his leg, making them one man short around the ranch, Jake had been so busy that she hadn't the heart to ask.

She told herself it was silly for a grown woman to be afraid of the dark. But then thinking of the mice, the spiders, and quite possibly snakes that might be inhabiting such an area—just the idea of entering the dank hole in the ground filled her with trepidation. She firmly attempted to force such thoughts away.

As the woman of the house, it was her duty to help preserve food to carry them all through the long, snowy winters. If she didn't, they might starve—or at least have to do without the extras that made the cowboy fare of beef and beans more palatable. Besides, with the garden coming along so fast, she delayed the cleaning all she'd dared.

Donning her oldest clothes and covering her hair with one of Joshua's clean diapers, she grabbed her bucket and broom and headed out the door.

Faith, watching her go, slammed the dishrag down on the table. "I don't want to do the dishes again. And I don't

want to take care of Joshua, either. I want to go play with
Bridget.''

''I don't want to do them either.'' Hope dumped the
stack of plates into the sink, causing a wave of soapy water
to slosh over the edge of the basin and onto the floor.

''Now look what you did, Hope. She'll expect us to clean
that up, too.''

''You clean it up. I'm tired.''

Joshua whimpered from his high chair.

Faith whirled. ''Oh, hush up. You don't have no reason
to cry. You don't have to do dishes. You don't have to do
anything but play and eat.''

''Maybe he's wet,'' Hope suggested.

''He's always wet. I supposed I'll have to change him,
too.'' Faith lifted her brother out of the chair and carried
him toward the bedroom. ''Sometimes I'd like to leave here
and be a real orphan. With nobody, just me.''

''You wouldn't really leave, would you?'' Hope asked,
following her into the room.

''I sure feel like it sometimes,'' she said, diapering her
little brother. Sighing, Faith carried the baby back into the
kitchen, then she plopped him down on the floor and gave
him a pan and spoon to keep him occupied.

''Are you going to leave?'' Hope persisted, her face
twisted with anxiety.

''No, I reckon not,'' she answered, shoving her hands
into the dishwater. ''It would be different if Jake and Mattie
acted like a real mama and papa, but they just moon at each
other all day, then at night Mattie keeps me awake by
moaning and talking in her sleep. Then the next day they're
both cranky at us.''

''How come you're not calling her mama?''

'' 'Cause I'm mad at her, that's why.''

''What's all the fussin' about?'' Jake said from the doorway.

''We have to do dishes—*and* take care of Joshua,'' Faith
complained.

"Is that so? I don't think that would hurt you." He glanced around the kitchen. "Where's your mama?"

A high-pitched scream answered his question. He whirled and ran out the door.

She screamed again.

"Mattie? Where are you?"

"Jake!"

Grabbing up a stick, he raced toward the cellar, then plunged down the stairs and into the gloom. "Mattie?"

She hurled herself into his arms. "Oh, Jake. It was awful."

"What? Where?" Thinking she might have run into a snake, he cautiously peered into the shadowy shelves, the spaces along the wall. Except for a row of canning jars, a few burlap sacks, and some woven fruit baskets, he didn't see a thing.

"It was awful. Big as a saucer and fuzzy. It jumped on me."

"You're shaking." He drew her even closer in an attempt to comfort her. "It's all right." He strained to see into the darkness wondering what she'd found to make her so afraid. "What was it?"

"A spider. I swatted it off, then it ran out the door."

"Well, if it's gone, then what's the problem?" He pulled the rag off her head and stroked her hair, threading the softness through his fingers.

"There might be others." She shivered and pressed closer.

He'd welcome an army of them, if it kept her in his arms.

"Shall we?" Faith said from beside the entrance.

"Yes!"

Suddenly the light above them dimmed. With an ominous groan the heavy cellar door slammed shut. Darkness descended like a black shroud.

"Hey, what are you kids doing?" Jake rushed up the stairs and heard a metallic clang as the heavy bolt slid home. He pounded on the rough wooden planks. "Open this door!"

"Think we ought to let them out?" Faith asked.

"Not now. He'd wallop us for sure," Hope argued. "I think we'd better go see about Joshua."

"Faith! Hope! You get back here," Jake bellowed.

"Jake. Please don't leave me," Mattie whispered.

"I'm right here, honey." He reached out and pulled her close. He ran a hand down her back and felt her shiver. "Shush, it's all right. I wouldn't let anything hurt you."

"Why would they do such a thing?" she asked.

"I don't think they like doing housework."

"I have put more on them than usual, but it is only because I've been so busy in the garden. Do you think they will come back?"

"Since they know they're in deep trouble, I doubt it. And even if they were of a mind to, the girls aren't strong enough to open the doors. The hands won't be back until dark, so it won't do any good to yell. I guess we are stuck until then."

Realizing it was too dark for her to see him, he grinned. Instead of giving the kids the walloping they deserved, he felt like giving them a medal, for in their mischief they had accomplished the one thing he couldn't. They had given him time alone with his wife.

He trailed a hand down her back, tracing her spine with his fingers. No corset. And no thick layers of petticoats. She must have left them off because of the job she'd planned to do and the heat. His body hardened in anticipation. Afraid she might notice and bolt, he shifted away. "Since we can't very well stand here until they come back, what say we make ourselves comfortable?"

"How?"

Jake lit one of two matches he'd found in his pocket. Then examining the shelves, he came upon a slender stub of candle and lit it. "There. Now for someplace to sit."

"The steps?" she suggested.

"Naw, too hard." He peered at the pile of sacks. Scratchy, but they could make do. He took them over to one corner of the cellar and shook them out, finding them clean if a mite dusty. Then he carried them back and arranged them in the middle of the floor. "There, how's that?"

"You're sure there are no spiders?"

"Nary a one. I looked."

"I still prefer the steps." She gingerly took a seat and arranged her skirts around her.

"Suit yourself." He stretched out on the makeshift bed.

The candle flickered, then went out, making it appear even darker than it had seemed before they had the light.

"Jake?" She reached out in the darkness and grabbed his arm.

He took her hand and pulled her toward the pallet.

She took a seat on the farthest edge. "Aren't you going to relight the candle?"

"Don't have any more matches."

"It's so dark," she whispered as if something unseen were listening.

"Why don't you scoot over here by me."

"It's a bit itchy," she said, moving next to him. "But not that bad."

Jake stripped off his shirt. "Raise up a minute." He spread it out beneath her. "Now, how's that?"

She patted the area, then scooted onto the shirt. "Much better."

"Maybe you should lie down and rest. We might be in here a long time." He shifted onto his back and closed his eyes.

She stayed where she was.

Skittish as an unbroken filly. He had to do something. He thought a minute, then he reached out, patting the dirt until he found a small rock. He tossed it across the room. It clanked against a fruit jar, then plopped to the floor.

"What's that?" she asked, reaching out to touch him.

"Oh, maybe a mouse—or a big rat."

"A r-rat?" She scooted closer.

Something rustled in another corner, this time it wasn't his doing. "Might have a family of them in here," he said matter-of-factly. "They'll more than likely be over to investigate us, but don't worry, they probably won't bite."

"Jake."

"Come here." He drew her down beside him and wrapped his arms around her. "There. Isn't that better?"

"Yes," she murmured.

It might be better for her, but his body was complaining something fierce. A rock lay somewhere in the region of his spine and her nearness was making him crazy. He drank in her scent, her softness, the way she felt in his arms. When holding her wasn't enough, he brushed a kiss against her temple. His hunger rising, he kissed her forehead, her nose, and finally her mouth.

His tongue traced the outline of her lips, then parted them to stroke the edges of her teeth. He thrust his tongue into secret crevices, plunging, then retreating.

She pushed against him.

He kept kissing her. His lips traced her jawline, savoring the softness of her skin, the smoothness of her cheeks, then he moved down to her lips, smothering her feeble protests. After several long moments she relaxed, and he felt her arms creep up and around his neck. He raised himself and rolled her beneath him.

"Jake," she murmured, her lips becoming warm, pliant, eager. He plundered the honeycombed depths. Like a bee with a flower full of nectar, he was determined to sample every last drop.

Captivated by her sweetness, he cupped her face in his hands, kissing her eyelids, the base of her throat, touching his tongue against the butterfly beat of her pulse. He nuzzled his way back to her chin, coming again to her mouth.

She trembled beneath him.

He raised his head. "Don't be afraid, Mattie. I would

never do anything to hurt you.'' He knew he had to be gentle, even though it took every ounce of willpower he possessed to hold his passion in check.

Mattie was his love, his woman, his wife, and he wanted to make their joining pleasurable for her. Even though she was a widow, he knew she had never been with a man before. She was too innocent for it to be otherwise.

''I'm not afraid of you,'' she whispered. ''I'm just . . .''

''I know, sweetheart.'' Almost reverently he slowly undid each button down the front of her dress, pressing his lips against each exposed bit of flesh. ''You taste so good.'' When he reached the end of the row, she allowed him to slide the garment over her head. He placed the dress under her, then his fingers traced the lacy edge of her camisole. Finding a satin bow, he untied it, then slipped his hand in next to her skin.

She gasped and made to push him away.

''Sweet Mattie, let me love you.'' He buried his head between the soft hills, and brushed gentle kisses against the top of her bosom, then slowly, deliberately his tongue lathed the soft bud until it grew taunt, the fabric over it wet. He pulled the chemise down, freeing the marbled mound, then drew her flesh into his mouth and began to suckle. His other hand caressed its mate until it, too, rose into a pointy crest.

She moaned and tangled her fingers in his hair, pressing him even closer.

He moved his mouth to cover the other peak. Her heartbeat drummed against his palm.

''Wait,'' Mattie said breathlessly. She pushed him away and yanked the garment over her head, as if she couldn't stand to have anything between them.

He cupped the breasts she had bared to his touch, savoring their shape, their satin fullness. She was exquisite and the idea that she belonged to him added to the swell of his loins.

Her fingers roamed down the bare skin of his back, then

his front, tangling in his chest hair, her palms touching, searching as if she sought to know every inch of him.

"Mattie, you are so beautiful." He explored the flat plain of her belly, then loosened the strings holding her petticoat and caressed his way to the junction of her thighs. He cupped the soft mountain of her femininity, stroking, fondling until the fabric was damp and she arched against his hand.

He undid the ties of her underwear, then removed the rest of her underclothing and tossed it away. He slid his palms down her legs, first removing her shoes, then her stockings, and set them aside.

On fire with desire, he massaged, nuzzled, and explored with tiny nibbling bites. Soft, sweet, delicious. He couldn't get enough of her.

"Jake," she said, her breathing ragged.

"Yes, darlin'?" he asked, his own voice unsteady.

Her hands tugged at his waistband, but she couldn't undo it.

"Let me." Reluctantly, he left her and skinned off the rest of his clothes.

He knelt, his legs on either side of her, when he leaned down to kiss her, he felt her outstretched arms. She pulled him close, as if welcoming him home. He flattened his length against her, supporting his weight on his elbows, wanting her close, yet afraid he might smash her. He captured her mouth and pressed his tongue against her teeth. She opened for him, allowing him entrance. Hesitantly, shyly, her tongue touched his.

He drew it into his mouth, encouraging her exploration, leading the way, teaching her to follow. His hands cupped her breasts, bringing the nipples to turgid points. He sampled each one until she pulled his head up, reclaiming his mouth. Their tongues met in a wild frenzied mating, while Jake's hands roamed her body with the same frantic need.

He bent his head, his tongue tracing the outline of her navel. His hand massaged the soft mound below it, then delved into the nectar, igniting a fire that threatened to consume him. He gently stroked, then plunged and retreated, until she arched and cried out coming to a shuddering collapse in his arms.

He kissed her, slowly, persuasively, rekindling her passion. Her trembling hand went to his throbbing staff, touching, sending an entreaty he could no longer deny. He rose above her, his kiss conveying his intention and his love. His fingers slid into the sleek part of her that embraced him, then knowing she was ready, he poised himself on her threshold and eased inside. He reached the barrier that told him she was innocent and felt her grow still. Then she clasped her arms around his waist and arched her body to meet his. He pierced the veil, making them one. She gasped.

Gently, tenderly, Jake kissed her, giving her time to grow accustomed to the fullness. Then with slow, measured strokes, he sacrificed his own need as he introduced her to the pleasure he had so longed to give her.

Soon Mattie began to meet each thrust, giving and taking, demanding ever more until at last he felt her quiver, then she cried out, calling his name.

Now that she had found fulfillment, he, too, sought the release he'd long been denied. He plunged again and again, the pressure building until he thought his heart would burst. He exploded with an intensity he'd never before known, pulsating time and time again as he filled her with his seed. Finally, his passion spent, he withdrew and collapsed by her side.

He pulled her close, his breathing coming in spurts, his heart pounding against hers, skin to skin, her cheek tucked in the hollow of his neck.

Gradually he became aware that the air around them was warm with the scent of their mating. He wanted to talk to her to see if she'd experienced the same wonder, the joy . . . but the soft evenness of her breathing told him she had fallen asleep.

He lay there in silence, marveling at what they had shared. In his lifetime he had lain with many women, most of them trained to give men pleasure. But never before had he been with a virgin. He would have expected their joining to be restrained, unsatisfying, but to his delight, Mattie accepted his love, loving him back with a wild primitive abandon. Their union had been beautiful, like a miraculous rebirthing. He had never before experienced anything even close to it.

Jake opened his eyes, wondering what had disturbed his sleep, then he heard the voices of the cowhands and knew they had returned to the ranch.

Mattie, still asleep, snuggled against him. He held her close for a moment, then, not wanting the hands to discover them like this, Jake gently kissed her. "Darlin', wake up."

"Hmmm?" She stretched like a lazy cat, then he felt her stiffen. "Where am I?"

"The fruit cellar, remember?" He nuzzled her neck, then brushed his lips against her breast.

"Ooh!" She gasped, then shoved his head away.

Jake frowned. Well, maybe she was just feeling shy. Much as he wanted to continue his seduction, he didn't dare. Neither he nor Mattie would want to be caught bare-assed in front of a bunch of ogling cowpokes. "Sweetheart, I think we had better get dressed. Somebody's bound to be opening that door any minute."

"Oh, my goodness," she said, realizing she wasn't wearing a stitch. "Where are my clothes?" She bolted upright.

"Stay put, and I'll see if I can find them." He got to his feet and bent, patting the darkness until he found one thing and then another, but danged if he could tell what they were without any light. "Here you go. Better hurry."

She attempted to sort through the things he gave her. "I still don't have my drawers. And I can't see how to put my chemise and dress on, let alone my stockings."

"Maybe you'd better just concentrate getting on the

dress and your shoes. Slip the rest of your stuff under the sacks and I'll get them for you later.''

"I'd feel half naked. I can't do that.''

"Jake!" Henry called from outside. "The kids said you were locked in.''

"Just a minute. Mattie?''

"Oh, good grief!'' She frantically yanked on the chemise, then found it was backward. She had no way to tie it. Not daring to take the time to correct the problem, she slid it down over her hips and then pulled on the dress.

Jake yanked on his own pants, then whirled toward Mattie. "Are you decent, honey?''

"I can't get my dress buttoned,'' she said in despair. "And my hair's a mess.''

Jake helped her fasten the tiny buttons, having more experience doing such things in the dark than she apparently did. As his fingers touched her soft flesh, for she had nothing on under the garment, a flood of desire made him tremble. A loud pounding on the door chased it away.

"There, sweetheart,'' he said, managing the last tiny fastening. "Are you ready?''

"Tell him to open the door, then go away. I don't want anybody to see me like this.''

"Henry, you can open it now.''

The wood creaked and groaned, then one side of the double door banged back against the ground. A second later the other door opened, revealing a moonlit night sky, bright with stars.

The foreman stuck his head through the opening. "Are you two all right?''

"Better than that,'' Jake said too soft for Mattie to hear. "Thanks for giving us a hand. You can go about your business now,'' he said more loudly.

Henry grinned. "Guess I can take a hint,'' he whispered. "See you later, boss.''

"Is he gone?'' Mattie asked from where she was hiding in the darkness.

"Yeah, he's gone. Nobody here now but just you and me," he said huskily, reaching out to pull her into his arms.

"Uncle Jake? You down there?" Lory asked, sticking his head through the opening.

"Why ain'tcha comin' out?" Hal peered over the other side.

"Damn," Jake muttered in frustration when Mattie twisted free and headed for the steps.

"Are you children all right?" she asked.

"Better than they're gonna be," Jake growled. "Where's those girls?"

"They've done gone to bed," Hal said. "We waited up for Henry to come home. The girls was awful scairt you'd give 'em a lickin'."

"Well, I ought to," Jake said. But remembering the "ordeal" he and Mattie had shared, he felt more like giving them a hug.

"You ain't gonna hit my sisters," Lory said, glaring up at him.

"No. I'm not. But they will have to do dishes for a month," Jake declared, remembering how much they hated the job.

"You won't forget?" Mattie nodded toward the cellar, reminding him of the rest of her things.

"I'll take care of everything," he assured her. "How about a good-night kiss?"

"Jake. Not in front of the children," she hissed, pushing him away. "Come along, boys. Time you went to bed, too."

"I could wait up for you," he suggested hopefully.

"Don't bother. Good night, Jake." A boy by each hand, she hurried toward the house.

Jake groaned. He felt like a bear who had just tasted honey. Now he wouldn't be satisfied until he had the whole pot.

❧ TWENTY ❧

Mattie groaned and turned over in her bed, so that she faced the wall. How could she ever have been so foolish? Or behaved so wantonly? Worse yet, how could she ever face *him*?

The girls would be stirring any minute, and the boys were probably already up. She knew they all would be expecting her to fix their breakfast—including Jake.

What she really wanted to do was soak in a hot bath, then go back to bed and never get up. She plucked a piece of straw from her dirt-matted hair and noticed even her hands were filthy—and this was after her attempt to wash up the night before.

Her body ached in places she never even dreamed of, and her cheeks felt as though she had a bad sunburn—from Jake's whiskery caresses, no doubt. Her lips were still swollen from his kisses. Thinking of those kisses and everything that followed, a rush of heat infused her body.

Somehow she thought when she lost her virginity it would be in a bed—atop a down mattress and immaculate linen. She had imagined herself fresh from her bath, her hair still damp, but brushed until it lay about her shoulders like a cloud of shining silk. She would be wearing a soft, embroidered nightie in virginal white. Adding to the sense of romance, the bedroom would be lit by the soft glow of a candle. And the air would be scented by a vase of fragrant roses that sat on the dresser.

Her husband would be handsome, clean-shaven, and smell of soap and macassar oil. He, too, would be clad in a soft linen nightshirt. He would tell her how beautiful she was, quote poetry, and feed her wild strawberries, or some other kind of sweet. Then he would gently make love to her—and be in love with her.

That's the way she had always imagined it. The way it should have been.

In reality, she'd been covered with cobwebs and dirt from her cleaning. The cellar had smelled moldy, musty, and of something faintly reminiscent of rotten apples.

Instead of a bed, she'd wallowed, naked, on the sack-covered dirt floor with an equally naked man, who not only hadn't bothered to shave that morning, he'd also smelled of horses, barnyards, and leather.

He had told her she was beautiful, but she imagined most men would have said the same thing in such a circumstance. He had never told her he loved her. It had been lust, pure and simple. Like two animals, coming together, mating for the first time. And the horrible part was, she had enjoyed it.

Tears of mortification filled her eyes and trickled down her cheeks. Even if the man was her husband, such a thing wasn't supposed to happen. She had made a vow that she would never share Jake's bed as long as he owned that dreadful saloon—not to mention being involved with that house of ill repute. And she never would have, if she hadn't been so frightened of the dark, the rodents, and the spiders.

It wouldn't have happened if Jake had been a gentleman. It was all his fault. He had deliberately violated their agreement, broke his word, taking advantage of the situation—as well as her fear—to seduce her.

She should have known she couldn't trust him. Now that she had given in to him, she had no doubt that before long he would be trotting back to sample the wares at the Miner's Delight. After all, what did he have to lose? Men like Jake would never be satisfied with one apple—not when they had a whole tree ready for the picking.

But her conscience nagged that she couldn't put all the blame on Jake. She could have staunchly and firmly said no. He wouldn't have forced her if she hadn't been willing. And she had been willing, eager in fact. Her cheeks burned with the memory of her practically ripping his clothes off. And the way she'd touched his body . . . Good grief, she had behaved no better than those soiled doves at the Miner's Delight.

In Jake's arms she had learned of passion of the most physical nature. And even now in the cold light of day, her body still burned from the touch of his hands, his seductive mouth, and the fierceness of their joining. She shook her head trying to deny the yearning that made her pulse race and her body ache.

She had discovered something in the cellar that frightened her more than the dark and the spiders—her own sexuality. Now that she had experienced such a revelation, she feared she might not be able to resist if the opportunity presented itself again.

Her lips thinned with determination. She could not, would not, allow that to happen.

Thank God, it had been dark last night when they had finally been released. She couldn't stand the idea of anybody knowing her shame. By the time she came in, the baby and the girls had been asleep, and angry as she was, she thought it might be better if she didn't waken them. She also gave thanks that the twins, while they'd commented and teased her about how dirty she was, were too young to understand.

Just she and Jake knew the truth.

And Henry . . .

While the foreman hadn't actually caught them in the act, he had seen enough to guess. If he told anyone else . . .

Imagining the cowboys' looks and snickers, she buried her face in her hands.

"What's the matter, Mama? Are you sick?" Hope asked from her position beside Mattie in the bed. The little girl peered up at her with anxious eyes.

"I'm not feeling very well," Mattie admitted.

"I'm sorry," the little girl wailed. "It's all our fault. We locked you in that awful place. We were mad because you made us do all that work."

Mattie drew the child to her bosom and stroked Hope's lemon-colored hair. "Shh. It's all right. Sometimes I get angry, too."

"You do?"

Mattie gently wiped the child's tear-stained cheeks. "Yes, I do." Thinking of Jake and his seduction, right now she was furious.

Jake paced the area between the table and the stove, his attention continually shifting between the boys, who squirmed in their seats at the table, and the still closed bedroom door. *Why isn't she up? Is she all right? Had he hurt her?*

"I'm awful hungry, Uncle Jake," Lory said.

"Ain't Mama gonna fix us any breakfast?" Hal asked, his freckled face wrinkled in a frown.

"I sure hope so." Jake hesitated, then he strode to the door and knocked softly. "Mattie. You awake?"

"Go away!" a muffled voice cried.

She sure didn't sound like herself. He slowly turned the doorknob, then stuck his head inside. "Good mornin', darlin'."

Mattie, her face crimson, stared at him and let out a shocked gasp. "Jake Turnbull, you get out of here. Don't you have any decency?"

"Decency?" He frowned. "Hell, Mattie, what's indecent about a man saying good morning to his wife? We are married, you know." Noting her kiss-swollen lips, her rosy cheeks, the pointy crests beneath the nightgown, he gave her a seductive grin.

"Really married, now."

"You don't need to remind me!" She yanked the pillow from behind her and sailed it toward his head.

Afraid she might follow it with something else a little more substantial, he jerked his head back and closed the door. Skittish as a half-broke filly. Well, with a virgin that was probably natural. He'd give her some time. Talk to her soft and low and give her a stroke or two. She'd settle down.

In the meantime . . . Just the sight of her aroused him so much he had to grit his teeth.

"Is she gonna fix breakfast or not?"

"Well, I kind of doubt it, but I reckon we can manage on our own." Ignoring the grimaces on the boys' faces, Jake took out the skillet and set it on the stove. "How about some pancakes? Then, what say we go fishing?" Until he had Mattie broke to the bit, he had the feeling he'd be spending a lot of time in the creek.

"He's just like that old bull," Mattie fumed, taking another swipe at the sticky table. Last night Jake had an itch; she just happened to be the one unlucky enough to scratch it. She had the feeling any female would have served the same purpose. By the leer on his face this morning, she could tell he had every intention of repeating the experience if given the opportunity. But she would never allow herself to be caught in such a position again. No sireee. She had her principles to consider. But still, she couldn't deny the way her heartbeat quickened when she contemplated the unlikely possibility.

Mattie spent most of the day hovering in the kitchen, ready to bolt toward her room if Jake stepped through the door, but he and the boys stayed gone all day. She told herself she was glad, and that it wouldn't have done any good for Jake to try to approach her, for she absolutely would have rejected any overture he might have made. Still, she couldn't help feeling a bit irritated that he hadn't even made an attempt.

That evening when the twins returned to the house, Mattie noted that Jake didn't accompany them, instead he went straight to the barn.

The little boys, their faces grubby as a pair of street urchins, grinned up at her.

"We went fishin'," Lory said proudly.

"Did you catch any?" she asked, gratefully observing that they hadn't brought any of the slimy creatures home.

"Caught a bunch."

"Ate 'em right on the spot," Hal declared.

"Cooked, I hope." Mattie grimaced at the smell of dirt and fish emanating from the pair.

"Injun style," Lory boasted. "Stuck a stick through them and roasted them over the fire."

"How nice." She struggled to hold back a shudder. "The water's hot, so let's get you two in the bath."

"What for? We ain't dirty."

"We went swimming. So did Uncle Jake. We pert near stayed in the water all day."

"Swimming or not, you're dirty now, so let's get at it."

"We ain't half as dirty as you was last night. You didn't take no bath."

"Well, I took one today." After Jake and the boys had ridden out, she'd bolted the door and scrubbed herself so hard it was a wonder she had any skin left.

"Cain't we just wash the dirty spots and go to bed?" Lory pleaded. "I'm awful tired."

Mattie gazed down at the twins who did indeed seem to be struggling to stay awake. "All right. I'll fix each of you a pan of water. You wash good, now. And when you're finished you can each have a piece of apple pie."

"I'm too tired to eat pie," Lory said, holding a dirt-encrusted hand over his mouth to stifle a yawn.

"And I'm still full of fish," Hal said, rubbing his eyes.

"All right, I guess the pie will keep until tomorrow."

The twins scrubbed their hands and faces, then both hurried off to bed.

Too restless to sleep, Mattie doused the light and sat in the darkness, staring through the window at the moonlit sky.

She must have dozed off for when she opened her eyes, Jake held her in his arms. "What are you doing here?" she hissed, raising her fists to pound on his chest. "Let me go this instant!"

He captured her fists in one hand and drew her close with the other. "Now, Mattie, you don't really mean that." He took tiny nibbles from her jaw and neck, then took her earlobe between his lips. "Um, you taste good. Better even than fresh trout."

Mattie stiffened. Now he had the nerve to compare her with a dead fish. "Let me go."

"Why don't we both go," he suggested. "I've got a nice little pallet fixed down in the barn. That hay is softer than any bed." He cupped her breast and gave it a squeeze. "And it sure beats a dirt floor." He ran his other hand down to her hip.

Pulled tight against him, she felt the heat of his arousal and the quickening of her own desire. Frightened by her own yearning, she fiercely shoved him away. "I'm not about to share your bed—straw, dirt, or otherwise. Last night was a mistake. A mistake I won't be repeating. I vowed I would never sleep with you as long as you owned that saloon, and while I may have yielded once, you can bet I won't do it again."

"Well since I'm not about to sell the Golden Nugget, we have a problem." He reached out and trailed a finger down her jaw. "You slept with me once, and you enjoyed it."

She twisted her head, but he gripped her chin, forcing her to meet his eyes. "Don't try to deny it."

"I do deny it." She slapped his hand away. "You disgust me! I'll never share your bed. Never!"

Jake's eyes narrowed, freezing her in their cold fury. "Well, Mattie, if you won't sleep with me, I know plenty of women who will." He turned on his heel and stalked out, slamming the door behind him. A few moments later she heard the drum of hoofbeats headed toward town.

She leaned against the door facing and stared out into the night. Bitter tears dampened her cheeks. The saloon was an abomination, a curse upon the town. The promise of strong drink lured men away from their families; its gaming tables took food from their children's mouths. Sometimes the very roofs from over their heads. Look what it had done to her own father. She remembered her childhood; the nights she'd spent, cold and alone. Her father hadn't been a bad man. It was the drink that did it.

She couldn't give in. If she did they would all be lost. Why couldn't Jake see that?

Maybe he just didn't care.

"Well, I see you made it home," Mattie said, staring up at her husband. Meeting his bloodshot eyes, she snorted in disgust and forced her attention back to the cake she was attempting to ice, but the trembling of her hands betrayed her.

He weaved toward the stove and poured himself a cup of coffee. He yanked a chair from the table and turned it around, then, straddling it, he sat down, hooking his arms over the back. He took one sip of coffee, then another, watching, waiting.

She lay the knife down and whirled to face him. "Did you visit the whorehouse?"

"No."

No? "Why not? I thought that was your intention." She crossed her arms and glared at him.

"I changed my mind."

"Oh?" He was telling the truth, she'd bank on it. He couldn't lie worth a darn.

He shoved a lock of blond hair out of his eyes. "I'm a grown man, and whatever I do—or don't do—is none of your business. But since you're so interested, I'll tell you this, if I decide to visit the Miner's Delight, I will. Especially since I have a wife who won't see to my comforts."

"*Comforts?* Is that what you're calling it now?" she asked scornfully.

Jake set the cup down and rose to his feet, towering over her. He smelled of whiskey, horse, and cigar smoke. His clothes were rumpled, and he hadn't shaved. In spite of that, she wanted him more than she had ever wanted anything in her life.

"And what would you call what happened between us?" he asked huskily, his blue eyes blazing.

She lifted her chin. "A mistake. A big mistake." Not daring to stay any longer, she hitched up her skirts and fled the room.

When the next three days passed and Jake still kept his distance, Mattie became more perturbed than if he had been hanging around the house making a nuisance of himself.

Why was he ignoring her? Had he found someone else to see to his *comforts*? No, that couldn't be true, unless he had left in the dead of night and returned before dawn, and since she was getting very little sleep these days, she would have heard him.

Could it be that he, too, was having second thoughts? Maybe even a little ashamed of his act of seduction?

Somehow she doubted that. More than likely he'd reveled in the experience.

Maybe he had been disappointed in her. Or maybe he'd lost interest. After all, Jake was a man of the world, he had probably made love to more women than she had fingers to count. Since she had no previous encounters with men and had nothing to compare it with, she didn't know the answer.

Even though she tried to deny it, she did know that distance had not quelled the fire that burned inside her. It smoldered, needing only his touch to send it bursting into flame.

Determined not to yield to temptation, Mattie buried herself in her work, cleaning the house from top to bottom, emptying the cupboards and refilling them again. She washed and ironed clothes and patched quilts. She engaged in boisterous games with the children.

Anything to keep her mind off Jake.

From his perch atop the roof, Jake held the cedar shingle in place with his foot. One hand holding the hammer, the other the square iron nail, he anchored the slender slat into place. Taking up another board, he sneaked a peek at Mattie who stood in the backyard, hanging up her laundry. He grinned at her modesty when she hung her underwear on the inside line, making sure they were out of view of himself and the cowhands.

He wondered what she'd do if she found out that the undergarments she'd lost in the cellar were tucked under his pillow in the barn. She'd never asked him for them. He had the feeling she never would. In either case, he had no intention of giving them back.

She hung another sheet, her gaze shifting from the top of the line to the roof of the house. For the barest second, their eyes locked, then she ducked her head, grabbed her basket, and scurried back into the house.

She was curious; he could tell that by the way her eyes always seemed to find him. Of course, he never let on that he'd seen her watching. Although one part of him wanted to confront her, to demand his rights as a husband, another, more saner part told him to hold his ground. Told him to keep his distance and make her come to him.

He held another of the shingles in place and raised the hammer.

The kitchen door slammed shut, and Mattie carried

Joshua out to the big oak tree and put him into the swing.

His concentration disrupted, Jake brought the hammer down—square on the middle of his thumb. He cursed and popped the stinging member into his mouth. Captivated by the child's giggles and the woman's laughter, he sat back on his heels and watched. She swung the child high, then, on the return, captured him in her arms and smothered him with kisses—much to Joshua's delight. Just witnessing the scene made Jake warm all over. Mattie was a natural-born mother, whether she cared to admit it or not.

The roof forgotten, he set the hammer aside. He imagined her, not slender as she was now, but with her middle swollen with child—his child. And after the passion they'd shared that day in the cellar, he knew she might already be pregnant. He found himself hoping she was. He also wondered how she'd take that discovery.

"Jake! You takin' a nap?" Henry called from the ladder. "I've been yelling for ten minutes." He hoisted another bundle of split cedar shingles onto the roof.

"No, I'm not taking a nap. Can't a man take time out to catch his breath?" Jake picked up the hammer and reached for another shingle. He tried to focus on the job at hand. But with the memory of that day imprinted in his mind, it sure wasn't easy.

❧ TWENTY-ONE ❧

"Would you please pass the potatoes?" Mattie asked, maintaining the same rigid politeness she had all week.

Jake handed the bowl to Faith, who in turn passed it to Mattie. She helped herself to a spoonful, then handed it back.

His plan wasn't working. Instead of coming to him like he had hoped, Mattie seemed more distant than ever. The woman was about as unyielding as tempered steel. Sometimes he wondered if he had dreamed that day in the cellar. Dreamed the woman that shared his desire, his passion. He stared across the table at her stiff face and wondered what he would have to do to find that woman again.

He figured he could solve all their problems if he could just get her alone, but as if sensing his intentions, she never allowed herself to be without at least one of the children.

He'd considered bribing the kids to lock them in the cellar again, but after her previous experience, he doubted if he could get Mattie within twenty feet of the place.

He'd even thought about backing down and telling her he loved her. But not wanting to be laughed at and not having a clue as to her feelings for him, he'd remained silent. She haunted what little sleep he managed to get. And all day he found himself watching for her, straining to hear the sound of her voice, or inhaling when he came into a room, trying to catch a whiff of that elusive something that was Mattie. He was becoming nervous and grumpy—a mental and physical wreck.

He'd hoped that when he had completed the repairs on the house, she might look at him a bit more kindly. But the remodeling had taken far more time and money than he expected. With his finances already stretched to the extreme, he'd had to cut expenses and forget some of the niceties he'd hoped to include, such as the big brass bed and fancy, carved wooden commode like he'd seen in the catalog at the general store. He'd also had to forget about the crystal lamps, and made do instead with a simple pine-framed bedstead, chamber pot, and coal-oil lamps. And even those would have to wait awhile.

He'd already pushed the good-natured cowboys to the point where they were ready to quit. Even if he worked them day and night, he doubted if the room would be completed in time for Mattie's birthday.

"Are you finished?" she asked, standing beside him.

"Yeah." He glanced up, surprised to find he was the only one left at the table. "Where are the kids?"

"Joshua's asleep. The rest are outside, playing tag. The evening was too nice to make them stay in." She arched her back, then rubbed her neck. She removed his dishes, washed and stacked them with the others on the drain board.

He took advantage of the time to study her, taking note of the circles under her eyes, the way her body drooped with weariness. Apparently she hadn't been sleeping too well, either. "I'll bet you'll be glad when your room is done." He rose and stretched like a lazy cat, his own body crying out in exhaustion.

"With the warmer weather, the children have been more restless than usual," she admitted. "They will probably be glad of the extra space as well." She rubbed her neck again, her face twisting with pain.

"Here, sit down. Let me see if I can help it." He pulled a chair away from the table and motioned for her to sit.

She eyed him warily, but did as he asked. He placed his palms on her shoulders, then slowly drew circles on her back and neck with his thumbs. "Relax. You are as stiff as that broom handle over yonder."

Gradually the tenseness left her body, and once she even tilted her head, placing her cheek against the back of his hand. Catching herself, she jerked upright, then got to her feet. "That's much better, thank you."

"Glad I could help." He could help with a lot of other things if she'd let him. But since that didn't seem too likely, he decided not to fret about it. He hesitated, torn between the desire to take her in his arms and the common sense that told him to say good night and get out. He sighed. "I reckon I'd better get to bed. If you want I'll send the kids in."

"Thank you," she said softly.

"I'm always here for you, Mattie. All you have to do is ask."

Her eyes mirroring her confusion, she gazed at him, then she ducked her head and muffled a yawn. "Good night, Jake."

"Good night, Mattie." He put on his hat and strode out the door. Her resistance was cracking. All he had to do was be patient. He only hoped he could survive the wait.

"Will there be anything else, Mattie?" Sara Gibbons asked before wrapping the package.

Mattie knew Sara was hoping to prolong her stay in the mercantile, especially since Mattie had managed to evade so many of her questions. She had no intention of satisfying Sara's curiosity. Her marriage—and her relationship with Jake—was something she had no intention of sharing with the town gossip.

"I'll take a half dozen of those peppermint stick candies. Oh, and two of the licorice," she said, pointing to another of the jars. "Jake's partial to them." She glanced around the mercantile, her gaze lighting on a pair of china dolls with painted-on black hair and ruby-red lips, exactly the kind of doll she'd longed for but never received when she was Hope's age.

"Aren't they pretty?" Sara asked, holding out one of the two for her to examine.

Mattie wistfully fingered the dolls' satin skirts and stiff bonnets, wishing she had enough money for their purchase.

"With a small deposit, I could put them back, save them for you until Christmas," Sara suggested.

"I'm not sure what Jake would think about that." While he'd never been a pinchpenny, she knew things were tight as far as money was concerned. Apparently the saloon wasn't as prosperous as she had first believed. She glanced at the dolls again, then reluctantly shook her head. "I'm afraid we'll have to wait on those."

"Speaking of Jake. Haven't seen him around much," Sara said, leaning close. "You two getting along pretty well now? You know . . ." She glanced around the room, then said in a lower voice, "I kind of thought you might be knitting little things by now."

"Sara!" Not wanting to offend her friend, but not wanting to divulge any confidences, either, Mattie gathered up her packages.

"Oh, I almost forgot. Knowing how interested you are in religion and such, I thought you might want to see this." Sara handed her a folded piece of paper.

"What is it?"

Sara grinned. "A tent meeting is arriving in Leadville a week from Tuesday with a real hellfire and brimstone preacher. Since you were the head of the temperance league, I thought you might want to send a note up with one of the miners. Maybe you could persuade the reverend to pay us a visit while he's in the area. I had thought about doing it myself, but you're so much better at that sort of thing. Goodness knows, we've got a lot of souls needs saving around here."

Mattie smiled, delighted with the news. "An answer to

a prayer. I'll do just that. Good-bye, Sara—and thank you.''

A tent meeting. She hadn't attended one of those in years. It wouldn't be much out of the preacher's way. If she worded her request right she was certain he might consent to do it. She and the children would definitely attend the services. Maybe she might even convince Jake to make an appearance.

A real sure-enough preacher, she thought with excitement. *It must be a sign.*

The letter penned and sent on its way, Mattie waited impatiently for a reply. She'd also got around to answering the letter she'd received from the missionary service back east. That one had told her that although they could see a definite need, they had no one interested in volunteering for the hardship of such a mission.

Mattie had thanked them for their time and asked that they keep Sweetheart in mind—in case they ever did have a soul brave enough to attempt such an undertaking. She thought it a good thing the Almighty hadn't been so faint-hearted or they'd all be doomed to perdition.

A couple of weeks later on a return trip from town, Jake strode into the kitchen and handed her a letter. "This came for you. Any idea who it's from?" he asked, plainly curious.

Her hands shaking with excitement, she opened it and read the contents. "He's coming!"

"Who?" Jake asked with a frown.

"The preacher. Brother Abraham. He says so right here in the letter." She danced toward Jake and grabbed the front of his shirt. She gazed up into his blue eyes. "Do you know what this means?"

"I can't say as I do, Mattie."

"He's bringing his tent revival here after he finishes in Leadville. It means we're finally going to get some honest-to-goodness preaching in Sweetheart." She whirled away and began counting down the days on her fingers. "Two weeks."

"I can hardly wait," he said in a dry voice. Leaving Mattie to her chores, he left the house and stalked across the yard to the barn. A psalm-singing preacher. Just what he didn't need. He remembered the last time Mattie had been inspired to righteousness, she'd damned near wiped out his saloon. With this Brother Abraham getting her all worked up, heaven only knew what she might decide to do.

✦ TWENTY-TWO ✦

"That's the biggest tent I ever did see," Myrtle declared, her upper half dangling out of the upstairs window of the Miner's Delight. "Looks like half the town is helping put the thing up, and the other half is down there watching."

"Let's hope they don't all get religion or we'll be out of business," Jolene said wryly.

"Maybe we could entice that preacher man up here. Give him a good taste of sin so he'd know what the hell he's talking about." Daisy batted her eyes and traced her ample curves with her palms.

"You girls stay away from there," Jolene warned. "I don't want any trouble." They got plenty of that without asking for it. She shoved a pearl-tipped hatpin into a tulle-draped straw hat, anchoring it into place atop her head, then she picked up her list and her reticule. "I've got to go out for a while. Is there anything you ladies need from the mercantile?"

"Some of that good-smelling soap—Lily of the Valley. The fellers sure do like that," Daisy said.

"Anything for you, Myrtle?"

"I don't believe so." The tall brunette joined her blond cohort at the window. "Wonder if that's him? My, ain't he gussied up?"

"Let me see." Daisy stood on tiptoe to get a better view. "Oooh, he's a biggun, all right. He's got on one of those

215

Prince Albert coats and a tall silk hat—and would you look at that beard? Looks like he's got a bush tied to his face.''

''Come and look, Jolene.''

''You two are gawking enough for all of us. Besides, I don't have time.'' She checked her appearance in the mirror and straightened the lace-trimmed collar on her shirtwaist. Satisfied, she headed down the stairs.

When she reached the front entrance of the Miner's Delight she paused by an abandoned ore wagon where she'd planted her petunias. The flowers were a bit bedraggled to be sure, but considering the conditions they had to grow in, it was a wonder they bloomed at all.

She'd threatened the miners with dire consequences if they spit tobacco anywhere near her precious blooms. And she had found it necessary to move the cart away from the hitching rail out of reach of the horses.

After the blossoms kept disappearing, she knew the miners were taking them home to brighten their own domains. She hadn't the heart to castigate them for it. Their lives were dreary enough. She solved the problem by saving the seeds and planting a few extra each year.

She removed one of her immaculate white kid gloves and pushed a manicured finger into the dirt. The plants needed water. She made a mental note to see to them as soon as she got back. She plucked a faded pink blossom and placed it to one side. She did love flowers, even if they were straggly and planted in a rusty wagon.

Someday she dreamed of having a white house, two-storied and edged with gingerbread trim. It would have lots of windows, and from those shining panes she would look out and see other neat houses, beyond which would lay a grassy valley with lots of trees. Her home would have a covered porch running across the front and down one side. And there, under a vine-draped veranda, she would have a swing where she could sit and enjoy balmy summer breezes. A white picket fence festooned with red rambling roses would enclose the perimeter of her property, and the rest of her yard—except for a patch of emerald-green lawn—would be a fragrant bower of flowers of every kind and color.

She knew down to the last detail how the house would be furnished—even to the color and texture of the curtains and rugs, the pattern of her dishes, the design of the lace on her crocheted doilies. Everything, even to the smallest knickknack.

She had thought about the place so long that it seemed real, like she had actually visited—no—lived there.

The hardened, more practical side of her knew it was a fantasy, an escape from the ugly, seamier side of her life. A dream. That's all it was. All it would ever be. She had no more chance of having a house like that than she did of being a virgin again. And there had been far too much water under that bridge.

When she reached the mercantile, she found the establishment locked and a crudely printed sign tacked to the edge of the door: "GONE TO THE TENT RAISING."

Since she wasn't anxious to rejoin the two gossipy females who had invaded her upstairs bedroom, she decided to see for herself what all the uproar was about. Lifting the skirt of her green and white striped bombazine dress so that the hem didn't drag in the red dust, she strolled down the boardwalk, passing the restaurant, the sheriff's office, and on to the end of the street.

Up the hill and off to the right on a barren patch of earth lay the gospel tent—half of it up, the other half getting there. Men yelled at each other, their muscles straining as they pulled the outside walls of the canvas structure into place. Other men tethered the ends of ropes to pegs they had driven into the ground.

Looks like a sure-enough circus, she thought, observing the enthusiastic crowd of people. Even though the tent revival meant a loss of business for her establishment, Jolene couldn't begrudge her fellow townspeople a little excitement in their lives. Living in Sweetheart was about as exhilarating as watching grass grow. But then considering the barren hills and dirt yards, even watching grass grow would be a change of pace.

Spying Sara Gibbons among a small group off to one side, Jolene made her way toward her to ask when the mercantile would reopen.

"Brothers and sisters," a rough voice boomed behind her. "Thank you kindly for your help. And now that our prairie church is in place, let's bow our heads and give thanks for this joyous occasion."

The deep, raspy timbre of the reverend's voice froze Jolene in place. Mind-numbing fear slid up her spine. She told herself it was coincidence. After all, a lot of men's voices sounded the same. Dread raised goose bumps on her flesh as she turned, her gaze seeking out the man who had spoken.

Dressed in unrelieved black, the tall man hunched his shoulders and the tail of his suitcoat flapped in the wind. He reminded her of a vulture hovering over its prey. With the hat covering his head, and the gray, rust-streaked beard hiding the lower half of his face, she couldn't distinguish his features. Older and thinner. It had been years. But still . . .

Then the reverend raised his head, his hawklike gaze scanned the crowd. The fierce fanatical gleam in those eyes removed all doubt.

Jolene felt the blood drain from her face. *Dear God, no! Not him! Not here!*

Her mouth dry, she backed around the corner, then hiked up her skirts and raced toward the sanctuary of the Miner's Delight.

"All right, Mattie. Now you can open your eyes."

Her heart pounding in excitement, Mattie peered up at Jake whose paint-splattered face wore an ear-to-ear grin.

"Well, how do you like your new room?"

Her new room. She could hardly believe it, especially

since she hadn't been allowed near it since the beginning of the remodeling. Jake had wanted to keep it a surprise.

"It's wonderful!" she said, stepping through the doorway. "So big and bright. Why, I hardly even need a lamp." With its freshly whitewashed walls, and a large window facing the mountains, the room did seem to have a glow of its own. The floor, formerly dirt, now gleamed with honey-colored puncheon planks whose boards, along with the cedar logs spanning the ceiling, lent a fresh tangy fragrance.

"Oh, a window seat," she cried with delight, lifting the lid to discover a storage area for blankets and quilts. Once she had made a cushioned pad for the top, it would be a perfect place to sit and watch the sunset.

Even though the room was wall-to-wall bare, Mattie could hardly wait to move in. She ran her hand down a shelf Jake had attached to the wall, then spying a small circlet of light on the floor, she gazed upward and saw it was made by the sun shining through a hole in the ceiling. "What . . ."

"I left it on purpose. I ordered you one of those small parlor stoves, but it hasn't come in yet. The hole is for the stove pipe."

"Oh, my goodness, a parlor stove in the bedroom. Won't that be cozy come winter?" Without waiting for an answer she twirled about, intent on examining every inch of the room. "I'll make rag rugs for the floor, calico curtains, new quilts . . ."

"Now hold on. I didn't do this so you would work yourself to death. I wanted you to have a place to rest." He stepped close and gently ran a paint-speckled fingertip under her eye. "Might help get rid of these dark circles."

She grabbed his hand and held it between her own, feeling its warmth, its callused strength. She noted the thumbnail blackened where he had hit it with the hammer. The gash on his wrist from a jagged splinter. "Oh, Jake," she murmured. He had worked so hard for so many hours, and he had done it all for her. Tears blurring her vision, she moved closer and wrapped her arms around him and placed her head against his chest. "How can I ever thank you?"

He touched her hair, then lifted a stray lock back over her temple. "I'd say you're doing a pretty good job."

She gazed into his eyes. Memories of the day they'd shared made her ache with awareness. When his eyes darkened to sapphires, she knew he was thinking of it, too. Just when she thought he might kiss her, she heard the thump of bootsteps in the hallway, then Henry stuck his head into the room.

"Jake, I need to see you outside. Pronto."

He touched her cheek and sighed. "Sounds serious. I suppose I'd better go see what's wrong." He left her and went outside to talk with his foreman. After a few minutes he returned, a deep frown etching his forehead. "I have to go into town. Better not wait supper on me. I could be late." He hesitated as if wanting to say more, then apparently changed his mind. "I'm sorry, Mattie." Then he was gone.

She ran to the door to tell him it was all right, that she would keep supper hot anyway, then she heard Henry say something about Jolene.

Without even pausing to wash his face or comb his hair, Jake swung into the saddle of the horse Henry had brought up from the corral. He kicked the animal into a gallop and headed toward town.

Anger and jealousy twisted her insides into knots as she watched him ride away. A moment ago they'd seemed so close. Jake was her husband, but their relationship was so young, so fragile. She was hoping that he would come to care enough about her and the children that he would be willing to abandon that other life.

Why couldn't Jolene leave him alone? All *she* had to do was beckon her perfectly manicured finger and Jake would drop everything to rush to her side. It wasn't fair.

Jolene. Hair like a summer sunset, eyes like new spring

grass. Young. Willowy. Seductive. Everything Mattie herself could never be.

She spun away from the empty prairie and hurried into the house, into the room where only moments before Jake had held her in his arms. She closed her eyes, trying to recapture that special feeling, that sense of closeness they had shared before Henry had interrupted.

But the only image her mind could conjure was the one she had witnessed that day so long ago, that of Jake—and beautiful, wicked Jolene.

"What's the matter with her?" Jake asked, taking the stairs two at a time.

Bock Gee, running to keep up with him, shook his silvery head. "Never seen her like this before."

Jake reached the door at the end of the hall and tried the handle. "Jolene." He rattled the knob again. "Jolee, honey, open the door."

"Damned impatient, aren't you, Jake?" The lock clicked and the door swung open.

"My God!"

"God has nothing to do with it," she said, her crimson mouth lifting in a sarcastic smile. She tilted the bottle she carried by the neck and poured a measure of the amber liquid into her mouth.

Jake stared at her, then looked at Bock Gee.

The elderly man gave him an almost imperceptible shake of the head.

"Better get some coffee," Jake said softly. Then, leaving the old man, he went inside the room and closed the door behind him. His gaze took in the scantily clad woman, the scarlet dress cut so low it was almost as disgraceful as if she wore nothing at all. He watched her hoist the bottle again.

"You want to tell me what the hell you think you're doing?" He strode forward and yanked the bottle out of her hands.

"Plying my trade," she said, sidling up to him. "I'm good at it, but then you wouldn't know that, would you?" Her eyes heavily outlined in kohl, she gave him a seductive look. Her fingers slid inside his shirt and began undoing the buttons.

Plying her trade? Although she owned the brothel, he knew she had never entertained any of its clients, or anybody else in that way. Completely at a loss to explain her behavior, he jerked her hands away. "Stop it!"

Her green eyes narrowed. Her lips tilted in contempt. "What's the matter, Jake? Got religion?" She laughed, the sound coarse, ugly. "I forgot. Only *Mrs*. Turnbull has that affliction."

"Leave Mattie out of this."

"She doesn't share your bed, does she, Jake? And you haven't been with any of the girls in a long, long time. Must be hard on a lusty man like you."

"That is none of your business."

"I wouldn't send you away." She unfastened the dress and let it slide to the floor. She stood before him, glorious in her nudity. She held out her arms. When he didn't move, she dropped them to her sides. "So you don't want me? Well, there's plenty downstairs that do."

He stared at her, trying to find any resemblance to the sweet childlike woman he had known. Failing, he turned away in disgust.

He strode to the door, yanked it open, then slammed it hard behind him.

Her laughter, high-pitched and mocking, followed him down the hall.

Henry met him on the staircase. "Well?"

"She's drunk. And wearing enough makeup to paint a barn. She tried to seduce me. *Me!* I'm like her brother!" Jake met his foreman's troubled gaze. "Something has happened. She seems determined to go straight to hell, and I can't do a thing to stop her."

"Think if I talk to her . . . ?" Henry asked. "We've been friends for a long time."

"Talking ain't what's on her mind. Henry, I'm scared for her. If she lets any of those men downstairs . . ."

"That's one thing I won't let happen." A determined look on his thin face, Henry strode up the stairs.

❦ TWENTY-THREE ❦

After Jake ran off to be with Jolene, Mattie turned to the only source of solace she had ever known, her religion. The first revival meeting was scheduled for tonight and she intended that she and the children would be there—right smack in the front row, her presence stating her position loud and clear for everyone to see.

Just because she had married a saloon owner didn't mean she had relaxed her morals—or her opinion of the saloon and the brothel—especially the brothel. She had seen in her own family just how disrupting those influences could be.

Since Jake and the cowhands had been working every day on the house, the boys quite frequently used such bad language that she had to threaten to wash their mouths out with soap.

While Joshua was too young yet to know the difference between right and wrong, she had no doubt he would soon be following in his brothers'—and Jake's—footsteps.

Even the girls had to be chastised for their manners and lack of decorum. Why if it wasn't for her, Mattie fumed, the whole kit and caboodle would be running wild.

"Hurry up, children. We have to be there early. I want you to help me hand out pamphlets before the meeting."

"We don't want to go," Lory complained.

"Besides, these old clothes are hot." Hal yanked at the freshly starched collar of his shirt.

"Leave it alone. You'll get it dirty," Mattie ordered, straightening his neckline again.

"Uncle Jake ain't goin'. How come we have to?"

"I won't have you growing up to be a heathen. The matter is settled. Now get in the wagon."

"I like heathens," Lory argued. "Bock Gee is a heathen. Don't you like him?"

Not about to argue the matter, she took the two by the hand and led them from the house.

"Come to the gospel tent. Find salvation before it's too late," Mattie yelled, shoving the leaflets toward everyone who happened her way. She nodded encouragement to the boys, noting that they were managing to dispose of quite a few. Apparently the miners were more eager to accept the pamphlets from the twins than they were from her. Some of them even sought the boys out, she noticed with delight.

"Can we have some more?" Lory asked, running toward her.

"Why bless my soul, what a good job you are doing." She eyed the little boy curiously. "How did you get the men to take them?"

"Shucks, that was easy. We just told them there weren't no paper in the privy. After that, they wanted a handful."

"Oh!" She snatched the leaflets back. "That's disgraceful. How could you do such a thing?"

The proud grin disappeared from the little boy's face. "You told us to hand them out, and that's what we did."

"You can't blame the kids," Jake said, coming up behind her. "I told you it was a waste of time and money."

"It's my time," she said tersely.

"And my money." Jake pointed out the fact that she had charged the printing bill to his account. "Half the men can't read, and those that can wouldn't read that stuff anyway." He stalked off after the boys.

Filled with resentment, Mattie gathered up the rest of the flyers, then noticing the twilight sky she set off in the direction of the gospel tent. Why couldn't Jake see? Why couldn't she make him understand? And now with his pig-headed attitude she'd doubted if she could even get the boys to attend the meeting.

She joined the girls who were attempting to hand out flyers at the other, more respectable end of town. While they had managed to dispose of a few, nobody seemed especially interested in religion there, either. She suspected the preacher's haranguing of the miners in the days since he'd arrived had a lot to do with that, for ordinarily they would have shown up just to see what all the fuss was about.

After giving Joshua a spit and polish wash job with her hankie to remove smudges of cookie from his face, she lifted the toddler out of the bed of the wagon where he had been playing, and carried him into the makeshift church. Wide-eyed, the girls followed, talking in whispers.

Mattie found the tent dark, hot, and oppressive; the wooden benches hard, uncomfortable, and full of slivers. She made a note not to squirm no matter how torturous the seat became. Remembering the incident with the cactus, she refused to give Jake another excuse to explore her nether region.

"Sister Turnbull, I'm glad to see that you arrived a bit early."

Startled, Mattie glanced up to see the evangelist hovering over her. "Good evening, Brother Abraham. I'm sorry there doesn't seem to be much of a turnout."

"No matter. Quite often there is only me and the Lord." He scanned the sparse crowd, then his sharp-eyed gaze fastened on her. "Besides, it is you I am concerned about. A grievous matter has come to my attention. A matter most critical to your salvation."

"*My* salvation?" she asked with a frown.

"Yes." The big man ran his hand over his beard, his forehead furrowed in a frown. "Are you related to Jake Turnbull?"

"Jake? He is my husband."

"So you don't deny it?"

"Why should I? We are married," she answered, at a loss to why he was asking her such questions.

"You are living with this man as his wife, even though you know he is a sinner, a fornicator, and is encouraging others to follow the same path?"

"Jake isn't like that. He is a good man."

"A man who sells the devil's drink and associates with whores of Babylon!" he spat out, his eyes gleaming like shards of green glass.

Before Mattie had a chance to reply, the minister's attention was caught by others entering the tent.

"We will discuss this later." He gave her a cold smile, then he left her and strode forward to greet the new arrivals.

"Mama, let's go home," Faith said, tugging at her sleeve. "I don't like that man. He scares me."

Hope, on Mattie's other side, had scooted so close the child was almost behind her.

"Sometimes tent preachers do appear a bit frightening. I guess they figure they have to shout and wave their hands to make themselves understood," she said, giving the children a reassuring smile.

The man scared her, too, but she wasn't about to admit it. Besides, from his point of view, everything he said was true. Jake did sell whiskey and he did associate with loose women. But his actions didn't make *her* a sinner. She refused to be branded by the same iron. Mattie took her Bible and opened it to a familiar passage. "We came here to worship," she told the children. "And that's what we are going to do."

The twins scooted through the tent flap just as the sermon began and slid into the seat next to Faith.

All during the sermon not one of the congregation let out a peep—not a cough, not a sigh, not a sound. The twins sat unmoving, mesmerized, their eyes large, their faces pale. Despite the minister's zealous delivery of his sermon,

Joshua, snuggled against Mattie, remained sound asleep.

When it was over and the last prayer had been said, the audience silently filed out the opening.

Mattie, fearing she might be waylaid by the man, hurried toward the wagon where, wonder of wonders, Jake sat waiting.

"Well, how was the meeting?" he asked.

"Scary," Lory whispered, scrambling over the tailgate.

"Let's get out of here," Hal added, quickly taking his place beside him.

Faith and Hope, too, couldn't wait to get on board.

For once Mattie noticed there was no shouting, pushing, or arguing about who was to sit where. The children seemed anxious to be gone from the place.

Jake arched a brow, but Mattie just shrugged and shook her head. Knowing her husband's temper, she didn't dare repeat what the minister had said, especially when she wasn't quite sure she knew what to think of it either.

The trip home was made in silence, another rarity for the family.

"Would you like a cup of coffee?" Mattie asked Jake when the children were all tucked in their beds.

"Naw. I'm pretty beat." He gave her a curious look. "I don't know what went on in that tent tonight, but I've never seen such a change in the younguns." He grinned. "Maybe that tent meeting wasn't such a bad idea after all." He winked at her, put on his hat, and went out the door. A moment later the wagon rattled off toward the barn.

Still too shaken to sleep, she poured herself a cup of this morning's coffee and sat down in her rocker, taking a sip of the bitter brew.

Bridget, who had been dozing in her basket next to the stove, left her pillow and curled up in Mattie's lap.

She absently stroked the purring animal, her mind on the preacher's words and his actions. All during the sermon his eyes had fairly bored into her, making her decidedly uncomfortable. The children had clearly been intimidated by all the ranting and raving.

Since she had been the one to invite the man to Sweetheart and had been so enthusiastic about going to the gospel meeting, she couldn't very well say that she didn't want to attend. Not without having to explain why. And why she felt that way didn't even make sense. Because a minister, a man of God, had called Jake a sinner, a fornicator?

It wasn't the Brother's words as much as his manner when he said them that made her so uneasy. He actually hadn't done anything, and words were only words, she told herself. Still, she shivered, chilled in spite of the fire. Raising her cup to her lips, she took a swallow of the steaming brew.

She had battled Indians, fought drunken miners, killed deadly snakes, and conquered her terror of horses. She'd never thought herself to be a coward.

Yet, she, Mattie McFearson Turnbull, who had never cowered before any man in her life, was afraid.

The next night at twilight, Mattie made certain that she and the children weren't the first to enter the tent, and neither did they sit in the front row. When Brother Abraham approached their bench to shake her hand and wish her a good evening, she found herself tense as a frog held over a skillet full of hot grease.

The hand gripping hers felt cold, clammy, and unpleasant, but the minister seemed to be going out of his way to be congenial. When he left her to welcome another small group, she let out a sigh of relief. It was only when she saw that he had no intention of coming back her way did she begin to relax.

During the sermon she was grateful to see that she wasn't the one singled out for the minister's attentions. She gleefully noted that it was the banker, Ben Satterfield, that had caught the good Brother's eye.

Ben squirmed in his seat, and more than once tugged at

his collar. Then when Mattie thought the banker might bolt
from the canvas building, the preacher's message took on
a softer tone.

At the end, they actually sang a hymn, something they
hadn't done on the previous night. And when the evening
was over, she wondered if she might not have misjudged
the reverend.

When the last Amen had been said, Mattie rose from her
seat and followed the children through the doorway. Just
outside the tent, she heard someone call her name.

"Mattie," Sara Gibbons gasped out, rushing forward to
grab her by the hand. "I was afraid I wouldn't catch you
in time."

"What is it, Sara?"

"Tomorrow Brother Abraham and some of the town
women plan to picket the Golden Nugget and the Miner's
Delight. We wanted you to lead the procession."

She glanced toward the wagon where Jake's familiar figure was silhouetted against the light of the rising moon.

She had led the march before, and it had gotten her ar-
rested. It was only because the sheriff didn't know what to
do with her that he had immediately turned her loose. Back
then she'd been angry and bitter, and if someone had supplied the bucket, she would have been the first to apply the
tar and feathers to Jake Turnbull's hide.

But now things had changed. He was her husband. And
while she still didn't condone his business, nor especially
the establishment next to it, she did feel she owed him a
certain loyalty.

She looked from Jake to Sara, then she shook her head.
"No. I'm sorry, but I can't do that." Ignoring the mercantile owner's gasp of surprise, Mattie hurried toward her
family.

"What was that all about?" Jake asked, nodding toward
Sara who appeared as riled as a wet banty hen.

"She wanted me to lead a march against your saloon,"
she said matter-of-factly.

Jake wheeled the wagon, making a U-turn in the road, and headed toward the ranch. "What did you say?"

"I told her I wouldn't do it."

He looked at her in amazement. "Well, I'll be damned."

She smiled. He probably would be.

But then, remembering Brother Abraham's wrath, so would she.

❧ TWENTY-FOUR ❧

The next day both Hope and the twins came down with a case of the sniffles, so any idea of attending the tent meeting or taking part in the march, even if Mattie were of a mind to, was out of the question. As nightfall grew nearer, she alternated between drying the dishes, pacing the floor, and chewing her fingernails.

Fearing the town ladies' demonstration could get out of hand, Jake had decided to stay at the Golden Nugget until the temperance protest was over.

Mattie, torn between loyalty to Jake and her religious beliefs, had mixed emotions.

She gladly would have marched against the Miner's Delight, for she had come to detest Jolene and everything the woman stood for. But Mattie felt it would have been hypocritical to lead a protest against Jake's saloon, especially when it not only paid for the roof over her own head but also provided food for the mouths of their children.

The ranch itself was not yet prosperous enough to do either. Jake had assured her that someday it would be, but until that time the Golden Nugget was all they had. And with the bank holding the mortgage on the ranch, she knew Ben Satterfield would not hesitate to put even little Joshua out on the street if he had the chance.

Thinking about the banker, she wondered if he would be attending the service tonight, especially after the way the minister had singled him out in the previous gospel service. Old Ben sure squirmed, she thought, wondering who would be pulling the splinters out of the banker's skinny behind. Imagining that scene, she giggled.

"What's so funny?" Jake asked.

Startled, she whirled, almost dropping one of the new dishes. "Jake! My goodness, I didn't hear you ride in."

"Better put that down," he said, removing the plate and laying it on the cabinet.

She clutched his sleeve, grasping the muscled arm beneath the fabric as if to reassure herself that he was in one piece. "Is everything all right in town? The march . . ."

"There wasn't any. At least not much of one." He tilted his hat back, allowing a shock of blond hair to fall down onto his forehead. His blue eyes sparkled. "Seems without you there to give them some backbone, the ladies thought better of the idea."

"But the minister . . ." She couldn't imagine him giving up that easily.

"Oh, he yelled a lot and spouted some kind of gibberish, but when everybody ignored him, he fizzled out. He was still carrying on when I left, but I don't imagine it will be long before he gives up, too."

She frowned. Even from the little she'd seen of the "good" brother, she feared he wouldn't take such an insult lying down.

Jake sailed his hat toward the rack, then plopped himself onto the seat of a ladder-backed chair and tugged it up to the table. "Honey, I'm hungry enough to eat my boots. Got anything around here a starving man could chew on?"

Honey. The name matched the warm syrupy feeling she got every time he was near her. "I imagine I can find something. How about a thick slice of ham and a few eggs? I have some biscuits left over from supper, too."

"I think I've died and gone to heaven." He grinned. "And about those eggs, could you make it a couple more than a few?"

She nodded and beamed a smile in return. Well, she knew the way to her husband's stomach—now if she could only capture his heart.

Peeking from the edge of the curtain of her upstairs bedroom window, Jolene watched the minister shake his fists and shout to the heavens calling down the wrath of God upon the Miner's Delight and Golden Nugget. He was so vehement in his spiel that she half expected a bolt of lightning to shoot from the sky. Finally when his ravings failed to draw an audience, he threw his banner into the thick dust and marched back toward the gospel tent.

Jolene let out a sigh of relief. "Well, girls, I guess it's over."

Daisy released a nervous giggle. "After that preacher caught old Satterfield giving me a poke down by the river, I half expected him to come up here and grab me by the hair of the head." She and Myrtle told Jolene good night and headed for their own rooms down the hall.

Jolene moved away from the window, stunned to find herself trembling.

In her profession, she had witnessed similar scenes that had turned violent, ending in destruction of property, injury, and sometimes even death. She was glad, this time, not to be the object of the crowd's ire.

Apparently Jake had been right. Without Mattie, their temperance leader, there to rally support for the cause, the march had been short-lived and ineffective. While it surprised her that Mattie had refused, Jolene was grateful, for whatever reason she had decided not to take part. Otherwise the evening might have had a far different ending.

Why had she refused? Because of Jake? Jolene thought of Mattie and Jake and their marriage of convenience. Somehow she had the feeling that while neither of them seemed ready to admit it, it had turned into far more than that. Jake had changed, grown more settled, and while she was glad for him, she also resented being replaced in his affections.

That wasn't really true either. Mattie hadn't stolen Jake from her. If his attitude had cooled, Jolene knew she had no one but herself to blame.

Jake had always been there when she needed him, and she'd grown used to, even taken advantage of that fact. Instead of facing her fear, her weakness, she'd piled her burdens on his shoulders, using his concern as a crutch.

Now he had other responsibilities, Mattie and the children. They had to come first. And in spite of Mattie's attitude toward Jolene's profession, she admired the woman. At least Mattie had the backbone, the nerve, to stand up for herself and what she believed in.

Mattie wouldn't be hiding in her rooms.

But thinking of the failed march that evening and the preacher's fury, Jolene did hope Mattie had the good sense to stay at the ranch, at least until the man left town.

Even though the preacher wasn't scheduled to move on until the end of next week, Jolene hoped his lack of support from the townspeople would make him fold his tent and leave early. If he left that very night, it couldn't be soon enough for her.

Since he had arrived, her emotions had been in turmoil, running the gauntlet of fear, anger, hatred, and rebellion, with fear being the most prevalent. Like a frightened child, she'd hidden behind the walls of the Miner's Delight, afraid of what might happen if she ventured onto the street. Her self-imposed isolation had made her restless and edgy.

At night, she hadn't dared close her eyes because along with sleep came the nightmarish visions, imagined or real— she no longer could tell the difference—that hauled her back through time and into the depths of hell.

A knock sounded on her door. She jumped, then reached toward her dresser where she kept her gun.

"Jolene?"

Recognizing the voice as Henry's, she crossed the room and released the latch.

When he entered the room, he took her into his arms. "Are you all right, sweetheart?"

Nodding, she gazed into his silvery eyes. "I'm fine."

"The old coot finally gave up." He chuckled. "The whole thing turned out to be a lot to do about nothing. Just one crazy old man, shouting and waving signs. I almost felt sorry for him."

"Don't. If he had been given any encouragement at all, he would have pulled this place down around our ears." She laid her head against Henry's chest, taking comfort from his goodness, his strength, like she had every night since the tall, lean man had made Bock Gee lock him into her room. The same night her drunken, desperate actions had driven Jake away in disgust.

Henry had stood firm against her rage. He'd ignored her threats, her attacks on his person. And finally, when her outburst was over, he'd held her in his arms, asking no questions, only offering comfort when she'd cried. Then in the wee hours before dawn they'd made love.

She still felt awed by the wonder of it. She'd been with many men and knew all about lust and the heat of passion. But only with Henry had she experienced the tenderness, the gentle giving and taking between two human beings.

What they shared wasn't love, but then she'd never had anything even close to judge it by. She and Henry had a mutual understanding, a respect for each other. He knew what she was, and he accepted it without trying to change her, and in her eyes that was even better.

Henry kissed her temple, then lifted a lock of her hair and used it to tickle her face and nose.

She grinned.

"That's my girl. Couldn't leave without seeing you smile," he teased.

"You're leaving?" The idea that he might not be there that night filled her with dread.

"No. I'll be back later on. The boys in the saloon were riled some about that preacher's threats. Since Jake has gone home, I think I'd better keep an eye on them in case some drunk decides to deal out a little damnation on his own."

"Some of the girls were a little uneasy, too, so I told them we'd lock up early."

"That's good news. Leaves more time for us." He kissed her on the tip of her nose. "I'll try not to take too long."

Feeling almost carefree, she watched him go through the connecting door that led to the saloon. She turned in the opposite direction, going down her own set of stairs and into the corridor where her girls' bedrooms were located. She knocked on each door, then after ascertaining there were no late-staying patrons, she went into the front entry parlor and locked the large double doors. She doused the oil lights, then peered through the windowpane to the darkened street outside.

The wind wailed around the eves of the building, coating the horses that stood patiently by the hitching rail and everything beyond in a shroud of dust.

Remembering that she still hadn't watered her wilting petunias, she removed her watering can from a cupboard in the corner. She figured that now was an okay time, seeing that the preacher had just stormed off. She unlocked and opened one of the front doors, pulling it shut behind her as she stepped onto the walk outside.

The town seemed eerily quiet for so early in the evening. No piano tinkled from the saloon next door, no ribald shouts or laughter, just the soft murmur of voices, between the howling gusts of wind.

Anxious to get her watering done and get back inside, she started toward the horse trough that sat in the alleyway at the end of her building. But as she approached the area, the darkness made her wish she had saved the chore until morning, or at least had delayed extinguishing her parlor lights.

She had almost reached her goal when something white fluttered up from the street, took wing, then plastered itself against her thigh.

She cried out, dropping her can. She whirled and raced back to her doorway. Her hands trembling, she fumbled with the knob. Once she had gained entry, she slammed the door shut and slid the bolt. With scarcely a moment's hesitation, she also drew the heavy oak bar and dropped it into place, even though it hadn't been used since that trouble they'd had with the Indians.

A glimmer of white against the scarlet carpet made her gasp, until she realized it was only a paper. The same paper that had made her run like the devil himself had been hot on her coattail. One of the preacher's discarded signs. It had blown inside when she'd opened the door.

Feeling foolish, she leaned against the door facing and brought a hand to her bosom to still the frantic pace of her heart. Then recalling that the back door to her building was still unlocked, she took the paper by the corner and carried it into the kitchen and laid it on the table. After she had secured the door she picked up the sign, intending to stuff it into the fire. Curiosity drew her gaze to the crude scarlet letters.

Whore. Daughter of Satan.
The hour of judgment is at hand.

He knew! She retreated from the paper as if it were the devil himself. It fluttered, mocking her.

"No!" She reached out and crushed the paper into a ball, then opening the door to the large iron stove, she thrust it into the fire. The paper hissed and curled, tinting the fire with a blue-green flame.

Jolene watched until nothing remained of the sign but a fluttering gray ash.

❧ TWENTY-FIVE ❧

After the night she'd burned the sign, Jolene waged a battle with her demons. She cursed, cried, and walked the floor, then finally, in desperation, she prayed. She didn't pray to *his* God, a God of hatred and vengeance. She prayed to a more merciful being, a God of compassion and forgiveness, and in doing that, she managed to achieve a sort of inner peace. And with that peace came a grim determination, to confront her past and the horrors it contained, then go on with her life.

Jolene checked her appearance in the mirror, the emerald-green dress, the dainty lace collar. Modest as the primmest schoolmarm. Why had she taken such pains? Deep down, did she still seek his approval? Not that it mattered. He wouldn't have given it to her anyway, not even if she had been pure as driven snow.

Noting the shadows, she dusted another layer of powder under her eyes. After everything else, she'd not give him the satisfaction of knowing that he'd caused her to miss any sleep.

All week, she'd remained in her rooms, not going out for fear that she might be seen. Might be recognized.

Why? What was she afraid of? What could he do to her that he hadn't already done?

Kill her perhaps. She scoffed at the notion. Even death would be preferable to the torment, the fear she had lived

241

with all these years. Then there were the nightmares, shadows from her childhood. For her own sanity, she had to
know the truth.

And he was the only one who could tell her.

She anchored the broad-brimmed hat to her head, then
hooked the strings of her reticule over her wrist. Noticing
her hands were trembling, she took in a deep breath and
told herself she was no longer a frightened little girl. Besides, it was broad daylight. What could happen?

Once on the board walkway she squared her shoulders,
nodded good morning to several of the townspeople, and
headed uphill, every step taking her nearer to the gospel
tent. She would not cower any longer.

Jolene lifted the heavy canvas and stepped into the
gloom. After waiting a moment for her eyes to adjust to
the lack of light, she made her way down the aisle. The
tent smelled of dust, and mold, and lamp oil, and tangy
pitch-pine from the newly constructed benches. Bombarded
by the mixture of scents, she was unable to stifle a sneeze.

"Who's there?" A tall man in black on his knees in the
front of the room glanced up from the lanterns he'd been
refilling. Spying her, he got to his feet and brushed the dirt
from his trousers.

Jolene swallowed back the metallic taste of fear and
walked forward.

He tilted his head to one side, as if studying her. "I don't
believe I've seen you before. You haven't attended any of
the meetings."

She walked to within a few feet of him, then she raised
her head and gazed into his eyes.

"Welcome to the Lord's house," he said, holding out a
bony hand.

How ironic, she thought. All this time she'd been afraid
for no reason. He didn't even know who she was. Jolene
glanced at his hand, but made no attempt to touch him.
Instead she moved around him and stepped up onto the
platform. There she walked a few paces forward until she

stood behind the pulpit. She rested her arms on the scarred surface and stared out over the multitude of empty benches.

"Young woman, may I ask what you think you are doing?"

"I'm seeing what it feels like to play God."

"How dare you." He rushed forward.

She whirled to face him. "Does it make you feel important? More powerful? Do you still frighten little children?" she asked, hating the tremor in her voice.

"Little children?" He peered at her and his brow furrowed. "Do I know you, my child?"

"My child?" she asked, her lip curling in contempt. "Don't you recognize me—Father?"

His eyes bulged until she thought they might pop from his head, then his lips drew back in a snarl. "You!"

"My, my. And for a minute I thought we might have a civilized conversation."

"What do you want? How did you find me?"

"Oh, I didn't find you. You found me. I hoped I'd never set eyes on you again." She gazed about her, then she looked back at him. "Come down some in the world, haven't you?"

"Thanks to you," he hissed, spittle showing white around the edges of his mouth.

"Me? What did I have to do with it?"

"They thought I was too harsh on you. They took my church away from me," he said, his voice increasing to a roar. "Said I was demented."

"So there is some justice in the world."

"Justice? I was trying to save you, Mary Kate."

"Save me?" she spat. "You stripped me naked in front of the whole congregation. You beat me with a belt. And for what? Because I shared an innocent kiss with a boy." Her first kiss, just the barest touching of lips. Something so innocent, so beautiful, and her father had made it vile. He had shamed her in front of the whole town. And not having the courage to face them again, she had run away.

"Given the chance, you would have done more. You would have been just like *her*. I couldn't allow it to happen again, that's why I had to do what I did."

"Mother?" She watched the expressions flit across his face. Hatred, cunning, self-righteousness.

The nightmares, the awful dreams—became reality. A shiver snaked up her spine. She swallowed back the fear. She wouldn't let him win. She couldn't. To regain her own sanity, she had to have the answers. "She didn't leave you, did she?"

"You don't remember." He smiled as if pleased by the idea. "She tried. But I found her. She begged for forgiveness. And I did forgive her, in the end—after she paid for her transgressions."

Jolene clutched the pulpit, using it to support her weight, for without it she surely would have fallen. A kaleidoscope of images whirled, flooding her mind, then, one by one, they fell into place. No longer muddled, but vividly clear. Now she remembered what she'd tried so hard to forget— a truth more horrible than any nightmare.

She stared at her father, her eyes conveying her hatred, her contempt, and her horror. Then, with a cry of anguish, she darted around him and raced down the aisle.

"Come back, Mary Kate!"

She lifted the tent flap. He would catch her before she got to town. She had to hide, then go home when it was safe. She glanced behind her, then darted across an open area and into the brush. She took the river path, running as though the devil pursued her, until her breath was gone and her legs wouldn't carry her anymore. She staggered off the trail and stopped in a grassy glen beside the river. There she fell to her knees and buried her face in her hands.

She wore her ugliest dress that day, the one her father always made her wear when they were going to visit the sick. An indeterminate grayish color, plainly made, without even a touch of lace to relieve the somberness of the frock. She hated it.

"Why must I wear ugly old clothes? The other girls don't have to," she argued.

"The other girls aren't the minister's daughter. You must set an example. I will allow no vanity in this house," her father told her sternly. "Now get in the wagon, Mary Kate."

She hurried to the wagon. Even though she was only five, she knew better than to argue. She didn't want to suffer from a "delicate constitution" like her mother. At least that's what her father told the parishioners the times when her mother was too beat up to accompany them on his rounds.

Mary Kate had heard the telltale noises the night before, the muffled cries of her mother, her father's angry tirades, and other sounds, sounds that even hiding her head under her pillow had not been able to erase—that of fists upon flesh. That's why her mother wasn't going. Why Mary Kate and her father had to go alone.

The visiting had taken longer than usual, and it was late afternoon when they returned home. The house had been cold, for the fire had gone out. Her stomach rumbled with hunger, but there was no food prepared and waiting on the stove.

Her father stormed into her mother's bedroom. He returned a moment later, a piece of paper in his clenched fist. "The whore is gone!" he shouted, his face red and twisted with rage.

Fearing his wrath might be turned on her, she cowered in a corner, trembling. She had always been afraid when he raised his voice. It was as though God himself thundered down from the heavens.

But after that one furious statement, her father had grown quiet, almost calm. The very strangeness of his silence filled her with mind-numbing terror.

He took the shotgun down from the mantel and

shoved a box of shells into his pocket.

She wanted to tell him it was nearing sunset, almost dusk. It would soon be too dark to hunt. He wouldn't be able to see the birds. But something in his eyes kept her from speaking.

She didn't even protest when he took her back outside and placed her in the bed of the wagon. It was growing cold, and she had no coat, but he hadn't noticed.

He'd driven out of town, racing the team, using his whip until the horses' sides were covered with blood. Pitying the poor animals, she'd begged him to stop. He had slapped her. It was the first time he'd ever struck her.

Then they came across another wagon by the side of the road. Mary Kate recognized it as belonging to the nice man who had delivered the hymnals. The wheel had broken and Mr. Jones was trying to fix it.

She'd wanted to get out and say hello, but Father ordered her to stay in the wagon.

Then she saw her mother. Mama was crying. Father screamed curses at Mama and Mr. Jones. Mr. Jones yelled back. There was a fight, but her father was bigger, and soon Mr. Jones lay on the ground. Father came back to the wagon and took out his gun.

Hating the noise the gun made, Mary Kate had hidden under the seat and covered her ears. But still she heard the shots, one blast—then another.

Father carried Mama and put her in the back of the wagon. Mama wasn't crying anymore. Father said she was sleeping, but Mary Kate knew that wasn't true because her mother's eyes were open, and her dress was all red and sticky with blood.

Her father turned the wagon toward home. But after they traveled a short distance, he pulled the team to a stop. He told Mary Kate to get out, then he and Mama drove away.

She'd stood alone in that dust-covered road, silently sobbing; she'd been too afraid to cry out loud. Then full darkness came, along with the animal noises and the terror. She needed to relieve herself, but fearing something might get her if she stepped into the bushes, she hadn't dared to move. She wet herself.

Whether the wagon returned or not, she didn't know. The next memory she had was of the doctor coming to the house and telling her she'd been a very sick little girl. She'd asked for her mother. Father said Mama had gone to Philadelphia to take care of her grandfather, but Mary Kate didn't remember having a grandfather. Father insisted they write Mama letters. So many letters. Never any answers.

Then one day Father told her that her mother had gone to visit the angels. Lots of people came to visit and Mary Kate remembered having to sit very still. They all hugged her and told her how sorry they were that her mother had died. Then they left and she and Papa were alone.

After that day, she had never written another letter.

As time went by and she grew older, she actually believed that her mother had died of pneumonia. It was only in the dead of night, after the nightmares began, that she began to have her doubts. She had asked her father once about the dreams, by then only bits and fragments with nothing making any sense. He'd explained it away, calling it childhood delusions as a result of the high fever she'd had during her illness. Being a dutiful daughter she had accepted his explanation.

Dutiful daughter? Jolene scoffed at the idea. She'd been a coward then and a coward now. The idea of confronting him still terrified her.

Something rustled in the bushes.

Startled, she gasped and jumped to her feet. She twisted toward the path.

"There you are, Mary Kate." His breath harsh and rasping, her father parted the bushes with his cane and hobbled forward.

"My name's not Mary Kate," she said bitterly. "I left that behind when you drove me away from home."

"What do you call yourself these days?"

"Jolene. I've found it's better for my business."

"Business?" he asked contemptuously. "What sort of business?"

"A very prosperous business. The big white house in the center of town—I think you know it as the Miner's Delight."

His face reddened, his eyes narrowed. "That's— that's . . ."

"A whorehouse? Can't you say it? Whore." She ran her palms suggestively over her figure. "Perfect example of a minister's daughter, don't you think?" Her lip curled. "But then you aren't much of a minister, are you, *Father*? *Mother* could tell us all about that."

"So you remember?" he said softly.

"I not only remember, but I intend to make you pay," she spat out between gritted teeth. "I'll be in the front row when they hang you. Hell, I might even sell tickets."

She dodged around him, heading for the path.

"You'll be the one who pays. You and that Turnbull woman."

Mattie? Her step faltered. She never saw him raise the cane, she only felt the blow. She fell to her knees, her head engulfed in blinding pain. He struck her again, once— twice—then again and again, until finally she was swallowed in a merciful, swirling, red-rimmed darkness.

❧ TWENTY-SIX ❧

Jake curled his hand around the handle of the hammer, gave the board a final tap into place, then lay the tool aside. He glanced over at his foreman who was helping with last-minute details. "Damn, I knew there was something. With everything that has been happening in town and all the preparations for the party, I plumb forgot to pick up Mattie's present."

"Kind of late, isn't it? The party's tonight," Henry said, inspecting the room for one last time. "You sure she doesn't suspect anything?"

Jake shut the door and followed Henry onto the porch. "Naw. Bock Gee's been keeping her too busy. He's been a most demanding patient."

"Looks like she'd catch on to him," the foreman said, grinning.

"That old fake can look plumb pitiful when he takes a notion. He looks so bad even I worry about him, and I know the whole thing is put on."

"Well, that's to be expected. You're so gullible even the twins could pull the wool over your eyes. But I expected Mattie to have better sense," Henry said, dodging the block of wood Jake chucked at him. "What are you giving her for her birthday?"

"A brooch. An ivory cameo set in filigreed gold. Real pretty. Ordered it all the way from Chicago. I got her some of that French perfume to go with it."

"The brooch sounds nice, but I don't think Mattie is the French perfume type."

Jake raised a brow. "And just how would you be knowing what type she is?"

"Well, I don't," Henry drawled. "It just seems like Mattie's real respectable and that perfume is—well, sorta—sexy."

"Mattie can be sexy, when she wants to be."

"I reckon she could, now that I speculate on it," Henry said thoughtfully.

"You just keep your speculatin' to yourself, especially when it concerns my wife."

"I'll be. You're jealous!"

"I'm not either. Besides, I don't have any reason to be jealous—do I?" He studied his friend who grinned back at him.

"Jealous as a green-eyed frog." A wide grin on his face, the foreman slapped his leg. "Who'd a thunk it?"

"I ought to take a poke at you."

"You haven't got time," Henry pointed out, backing away. "Not if you intend to get that present."

Jake scowled at his old friend. "Lucky for you."

"Get out of here." Henry stepped off the porch and stretched his arms over his head. "I guess I'd better see if the boys are through with their decoratin'."

"I hope they got that building cleaned up good. If they didn't, Mattie will take one look and grab a broom, party or no party."

"They cleaned it all right," Henry assured him. "Had it so spotless, Mooney was scared to cook, least he get a speck of grease on the floor. I think he's trying to stay in the cowboys' good graces. After tasting Mattie's cooking, the boys are getting plumb particular. They won't even let Mooney use the soup kettle to wash his dirty socks."

"That explains why his soup always tasted so bad."

Henry laughed, then his manner became more serious.

"Jake, I won't be going back to town tonight, could you . . ."

"I'll tell her." He pointed toward the cookshack. "From the ruckus going on in there, I'd say you'd better hustle before they decorate the building right down to the ground."

Watching Henry hurry toward the noise-filled building, Jake chuckled, then headed for the corral to saddle his horse.

Perplexed, Mattie watched Jake ride away from the ranch. "Did your uncle say anything about going to town?"

Faith looked up from the book she was reading to her sister and Joshua and shook her head. "Not to me."

"Me neither," Hope added.

Maybe his sudden decision had something to do with the rest of the strange goings-on. All week Mattie had felt like she might be growing horns or warts or something, for everyone coming in contact with her giggled or gave her a silly grin.

She ladled the chicken soup she had made for Bock Gee into a bowl. Then she added a spoon and a napkin to the wooden tray and carried it toward the boys' room. Since the old man had taken ill, the twins had been sleeping in the barn with Jake, which delighted them to no end, but made Mattie fear she'd have a hard time getting the pair back into a real bed once the old man recovered.

She paused in the hallway and reached for the knob, then she noticed the door was already ajar.

"You don't have to play sick anymore," Lory said, leaning close to the bed.

"Besides, it's almost time for the party," Hal whispered.

"Did you bring my clothes? I cannot go anywhere dressed like this," the old man complained, his thin fingers plucking at the scarlet long johns.

"Yeah, we got 'em." Lory placed a bulging cloth sack

on the bed. "Better hurry up and get 'em on. Everybody else is all ready over at the cookhouse."

So the old scoundrel had been playacting. That explained why he suddenly grew much worse when she entered the room. But why had he found it necessary to pretend? Had he been doing it for attention? And what was that about a party?

"We'll save you a seat," Lory said. "Come on, Hal."

Not wanting to be caught eavesdropping, she scooted back into the darkness.

The twins bolted from Bock Gee's room and slammed out the kitchen door.

Mattie knocked, then opened the bedroom door. "I brought you some chicken soup, Bock Gee," she said, trying to keep a straight face. She set the tray on a bedside table, then stood back and observed him.

"Aww, Mattie, don't need soup," the old faker said brightly. "Feel much better. In fact, feel so good I think I get up."

"Oh, no, you don't." She pushed him back in the bed and drew the covers up to his chin. "You were practically at death's door, remember? You had me burn that smelly incense to keep the evil spirits from invading your body. Made me mix up that awful goo for your chest, which, by the way, I know you didn't use because I saw Jake carrying that same pot toward the barn later in the day."

The old man tucked his head. "Stuff smell so bad even horse refuse to use it."

"You might claim you feel better, but I insist you stay in bed for at least another week." The expressions crossing the elderly man's face were so comical, Mattie had to look away to keep from laughing.

"But I fine—now. What I have to say to convince you?"

Mattie gazed into his eyes. "Well . . . you could start by telling me about the party."

"Party?"

"Party. I overheard you and the boys talking a minute

ago, so you may as well confess.''

"So you listen at keyhole like nosey person.''

"I must admit I was curious.''

"It supposed to be surprise,'' he said indignantly. ''How can it be surprise if you know?''

"I thought you wanted to get up.''

Bock Gee scowled.

"It can still be a surprise,'' she said. ''You're not the only one who can pretend, you know.''

The old man gave her a shamefaced look. ''You still say, Oh. Ahh. What wonderful surprise?''

"I promise. I'll be completely amazed. Now tell me.''

Leaving the elderly Chinaman to get dressed, Mattie picked up the soup tray and headed toward the kitchen. She glanced down at her own faded dress. How could she change without making it obvious that she knew about the party?

By getting dirty of course. Hearing the girls' voices in the kitchen, she smiled, and dumped the bowl she carried down her front.

"That's even prettier than the picture,'' Jake said, turning the cameo this way and then that to admire it.

"I know she'll love it. I'll wrap it up in some of that fancy paper I ordered for the occasion,'' Sara said, tucking the ornament back into the box.

"Don't forget the perfume.''

"I won't forget anything,'' the mercantile owner assured him.

While she was busy with the presents, Jake strolled onto the porch to have a cigar.

Against the brilliant sunset, the barren red hills surrounding the town appeared to be drenched in blood. In the distance dark cedar-spiked spears pointed the way toward lavender, snowcapped peaks.

Then his gaze drifted toward the gospel tent. The last

service was scheduled for tomorrow night. As far as Jake was concerned, the minister's departure couldn't come soon enough. Apparently from what he'd heard, the rest of the town felt the same. Sara had confided that the numbers of attendants had dwindled with each service.

A few miners, most of them hecklers, continued to attend, along with the regular hard-bitten Christians. One of the devout was Ben Satterfield, a fact that both puzzled and amazed Jake for he considered the banker to be a sure-enough sinner.

Mattie, too, had surprised Jake. For after the first couple of sermons, she had not mentioned wanting to attend the meetings again. In fact, she had made up excuses not to, which seemed strange, especially when she'd been the one who had urged the reverend to come to Sweetheart in the first place.

"Jake?"

He glanced toward the mercantile doorway. Sara beckoned him inside.

"Got it finished?"

"Yes." She reached beneath the counter and with a flourish handed him the present. "The violet paper is hand-painted and Mattie can use the bow later for her hair."

"Mighty fancy," he said, eyeing the parcel.

"I wanted you to see it before I put it in the bag. The bag will be an additional five cents."

"What do I need a bag for?"

"So the present doesn't get dirty," Sara said in the same tone of voice he'd heard Mattie use when explaining something to the twins.

"All right." He reached into his pocket and handed her a nickel.

"That's not quite enough," Sara said, continuing to hold out her palm. "The decorated paper is twenty-five cents; I think I told you it was hand-painted. The velvet bow another fifteen. The two bows I put on the perfume box were another ten cents each."

"Why did it need two bows?"

"For the two girls, of course. You wouldn't want them to feel left out. I threw in a few licorice sticks for the boys."

"Of course." He eyed his pocket change, hoping he'd have enough. "How much altogether?"

"Sixty-five cents, but since you already paid the nickel, you only owe sixty."

Jake hurriedly counted out the coins. Good thing the presents were already paid for or he wouldn't have had enough money. Sixty-five cents to wrap the dang thing. The brooch only cost two dollars, and he thought that was mighty expensive. The perfume another dollar and a half, but since it came all the way across the ocean, he reckoned he could make an allowance for that.

He shoved the receipt into his pocket, then picked up his package, anxious to be on his way before Sara dreamed up anything else she could charge him for.

"Good night, Jake. You come back real soon, you hear. And don't forget to tell Mattie I said, 'Happy birthday.'"

"I'll tell her."

As he tied the bundle behind his saddle, he eyed the Golden Nugget, wishing he had time for a drink. Then he thought better of the idea. Mattie sure wouldn't like it if he showed up with whiskey on his breath. "Gonna be late enough as it is." He grabbed the pommel ready to swing himself into the saddle, then he remembered the flowers— and his promise to Henry.

Jolene had saved some of her precious petunia seeds for new starts. He had talked her out of one of her tiny plants for Mattie's birthday. He'd have to hustle, but if he just ran up and got the plant and ran back down. No, he'd have to stay a little longer than that, he didn't want to hurt Jolene's feelings.

He hurried to the back door of the Miner's Delight, figuring he might as well grab a glass of lemonade while he was there, at least it would quench his thirst.

When he reached for the screen door, he heard a mewling sound. Grinning, he glanced toward the bushes. Jolene had apparently found herself a kitten. Wondering where she had come by the animal, he opened the brothel door and stepped inside.

❧ TWENTY-SEVEN ❧

"Jake Turnbull, what for y'all come creeping around my back door and scarin' me half to death?" the elderly black woman asked, blandishing a spoon in his face.

"Could be I came after some fine brown sugar," Jake said with a grin.

"I knows better than that, you rascal." Even though the big woman knew he was teasing, she flashed him a pleased smile. "Now what y'all really want?"

"I sure could use some of your lemonade, Delilah. I'm plumb parched." When she nodded and turned away to fill his glass, he heard the cat again. "And while you're at it, maybe you could rustle up some milk for Jolene's cat?"

"What cat? Miss Jolene don' have no cat." The cook handed Jake his lemonade. "Last cat we had around here belonged to your Mattie."

The cat mewed again.

"Well I'll be," Delilah declared, arching a brow. "Maybe Jolene do have a cat—if'n I can catch it." She poured a saucer full of milk and carried it out the door. "Here, kitty."

"Jake? Is that you out there?" Myrtle came through the doorway, her face twisted with anxiety. "Have you seen Jolene?"

"No. I've been out at the ranch all day."

"Jake, I'm so scared. She went for a walk this morning

and nobody's seen her since.''

"Are you sure?'' He frowned. Jolene rarely stayed away
from the Miner's Delight for more than a few minutes, and
he'd never known her to be gone for much more than an
hour.

"I asked everybody.'' The white-faced woman wrung
her hands. "The bootmaker and his wife, the folks at the
mercantile, the banker, the miners. Everybody in town. I
even asked that preacher feller—from a distance of course.
I figured he wouldn't want the likes of me coming anywhere near him. I tell you, nobody's seen her. She's flat
disappeared.''

Hearing the panic in Myrtle's voice, an uneasiness
crawled up his spine. "Did you tell the sheriff?''

"He's out of town. Some trouble down Dog Gulch way.
Jake, what are we gonna do?''

Delilah heaved her bulk back into the room and set the
saucer on the kitchen counter. "I can't find no cat. If it
was a cat I guess it took off.'' Her eyes wide, the black
woman hugged herself and shivered. "Spirits walkin' out
there tonight.''

"Did you ask Delilah about Jolene?''

"No,'' Myrtle admitted. "I didn't want to upset her.''

"What's that about mah honey lamb?'' Delilah asked,
waddling forward.

"Jolene's—missing,'' Myrtle said reluctantly.

Delilah grabbed Mrytle by her shoulder and spun her
around. "What you talkin' about, girl?''

"Jolene's disappeared—vanished. Nobody knows where
she is.''

"Oh, my poor little lamb,'' Delilah wailed. "I knew
somethin' was goin' to happen. I knew it. Oh, Mistah Jake,
you gots to find her. I just knows somethin' terrible done
happened to my sweet Jolene.''

"Now, Delilah, we don't know that. She might be visiting, or maybe somebody needed her help. We'll find her.''
But even while he was attempting to reassure the old

woman, Jake had an awful feeling.

"The girls are too scared to work tonight," Myrtle said.

"Probably just as well," he declared. "Tell Jobe to close the doors and lock them."

He awkwardly patted the two women on their shoulders. "I'll get a search party organized in case she might have had an accident or something."

Jake went up to Jolene's room to see if he could find a clue as to where she might have gone. No sign of a struggle. Nothing out of order. She simply went for a walk and hadn't come back.

She must have had an accident, he told himself. She'd been here for years and didn't have any enemies that he knew of. If anybody wanted to hurt her they would have done it before now.

He left the bedroom and went through the connecting door and into the saloon. From the top of the stairs, he surveyed the room. The usual racket. The same old crowd. He put his fingers to his mouth and let out a shrill whistle.

All activity ceased. The startled patrons gazed up at him.

"Men, something's happened. I need . . ."

"Fire!" a man screamed, rushing through the swinging front doors of the saloon.

"Where?" Jake bellowed.

"Right here!" The man pointed. "The whole damn back of the building is afire."

Cursing, Jake stripped off his hat and coat and tossed them on a table. "Sound the alarm," he ordered. He stooped, grabbing a bucket from behind the bar, then he charged through the swinging doors.

Jake dropped the wet sack back into the horse trough, then wiped a grimy hand across his face. Thanks to Old Joe giving the alarm, they had stopped the fire before it had done much damage. He'd have to replace a few charred boards and the back steps, but that didn't amount to much. It could have been worse, much worse. Whoever had set the fire could have waited until they were all asleep. That the fire had been set, he had no doubt. The smell of coal oil still filled the air. After the town had burnt to the ground twice already, everyone who lived there was too conscious of the danger for it to have been an accident.

But why would anybody do such a thing? And how could it have happened so damn quick? He'd been at the back of the Miner's Delight only moments before. It was forty feet or less from Delilah's kitchen to the back door of the Golden Nugget. Which meant that the same time he was sipping lemonade, somebody had been setting fire to the saloon.

"Check around out there, boys, and see if you can find anything," he shouted to the group of men examining the scorched building by lantern light.

"Sure smells like lamp oil," a man said, sniffing the air. "And here's the can. I'll see if they left anything else behind."

"I see a bunch of old rags over here," another said from the bushes.

"Must be a cat out here somewhere. Hear it?" The man waded through a clump of weeds. "That ain't no cat. My God! Jake! Get over here quick!"

Jake covered the ground before the man's words had ended. The man knelt by something on the ground. Another man held a lantern so the first could see.

"It's a woman."

Jake pushed them aside and knelt beside her. He stared at the woman, then his stomach churning, he turned away. Jolene? He couldn't tell. Her face was so battered she hardly looked human. The dress she wore was ripped and covered with musky-smelling, green slime. The red mud covering her hair and her clothes told him she had been in the river.

He held his fingers to the side of her neck and detected a faint, fluttering pulse beat. "Get a blanket and we'll carry her inside."

"Who is it?" one man asked another.

"I can't tell. Whoever she is, she's bad off."

Jobe, his arms full of blankets, his brown eyes wide and tormented, stared down at the woman's body. He let out a cry of despair and fell to his knees. "It's my Missy."

"How do you know?" Jake asked, praying the black man was wrong.

Jobe extended a trembling finger and pointed. "The ring."

Jake's gaze fastened on the woman's slender white hand and the ruby that winked in the light of the lanterns. He recognized it instantly. He had given Jolene the ring for Christmas. "Spread these blankets, hurry. Now, help me lift her. Careful! She's probably all broken up inside. All right, now, slowly. God help the man that runs into anything."

The men carried her, holding the blanket even, watching every footstep so that her battered body would not feel even the slightest jar. Jake led the procession up the staircase, finally laying her on the immaculate linen of her own bed.

"Somebody get the doctor!" Jake ordered.

"He ain't here."

"I don't care if he's in Denver, you find him and bring him back." He whirled toward the rest of the men. "Get out. Find the coward that did this. But don't kill him," he said, his voice deadly. He wanted the pleasure of doing that himself.

"We'll find him, Jake." With a murmur of angry voices the men headed down the stairs.

Jake drew a hand over his eyes, then sensing another presence, he spotted Myrtle hovering by the doorway. "We'll need lots of hot water and bandages."

When the room had emptied, Jake knelt by the bed and took her hand. "Jolee, baby?" He fumbled with her buttons, trying to make it easier for her to breathe.

Jobe helped his grieving wife into the room. Delilah hurried toward the bed. "Mistah Jake, let me do that."

"I'm trying to help her."

"I know. But there is a time when a woman's touch is more gentle than a man's."

Jake nodded, then got up and went to the window. A fury more terrible than anything he had ever known shook him from head to feet. Who had done this? And why?

He thought about the miners Jolene had grubstaked when they'd been down on their luck. The endless pots of soup cooked in her kitchen and carried to the sick. The blankets, purchased from the mercantile and left in her vestibule so that anyone needing one on a cold winter's night could help themselves without being embarrassed. The countless other things she'd done without thought of thanks or payment.

Not all, but still far too many of the sanctimonious townspeople, including his own wife, scorned Jolene because of her profession. If the truth be known, Jolene had more Christian charity in her little finger than the lot of them put together.

Which one of them could have done this? Which one could have beaten her and left her to die? God have mercy on his soul, because, Jake vowed, whoever did it would certainly find no mercy in him.

"Let's sing 'Happy Birthday' and then we can cut the cake," Lory suggested, his blue eyes shining with excitement.

Mattie, sitting in the chair of honor, struggled to keep her gaze from straying toward the doorway as it had done so many times in the past few hours. By now it was obvious to everyone that Jake wasn't coming.

Henry had told her not to fret, that Jake had only ridden into town after her present and that he should be back anytime. That had been hours ago. The party was almost over and Jake still hadn't returned. Why?

If she shouldn't worry, then why did the foreman continue to pace the floor, peer out the window, and check the time on his pocket watch?

"Blow out the candles," Mooney urged, his round, be-whiskered face as excited as any of the children's.

"Help me, you two." She clasped each of the twins around the waist and drew them close. "Let's count. One. Two. Three. Blow." With the help of Lory and Hal the flames were quickly extinguished, then Mooney cut the large lopsided creation and served it up on tin plates. He handed the first slice to her.

"Don't worry," Henry whispered, handing her a fork. "We watched him cook it and made sure everything was clean."

Relieved, she nodded and took the first bite. And swallowed, and swallowed. "Very tasty, Mooney," she lied, for in reality the cake had the texture and taste of sawdust.

"How about some punch?" Henry winked and handed her a glass. "I made this myself."

"You didn't . . ."

"Naw, we kept a batch separate for you and the kids."

She took a drink. "Very good. I'll have to get your recipe."

"Well, it's not really my recipe. Actually, it's Jolene's."

Jolene. Mattie gritted her teeth, wishing she could get through one day without hearing that woman's name.

"Smile, Mama. Aren't you happy? Don't you like your party?" Hope asked, a frown on her sweet face.

Mattie forced a smile. "I am very happy, and I love my party." She squeezed the child tight. Then noticing other anxious eyes on her, she smiled . . . and smiled . . . and smiled.

After the cake had been eaten, everyone insisted that she open her presents. She did, finding dried wildflowers from the girls, and shiny rocks from the boys. Henry had given her a book of poetry; Bock Gee, an intricate handmade puzzle. From the cowboys, she'd received a set of fancy earrings made from silver *conchas*. They had also given her a hand-braided quirt, a leather coin purse, and a deco-rated bookmark. The cook, Mooney, presented her with another cake, a smaller version of the first, so that she didn't have to share, he'd whispered.

Hoping the first piece didn't soak through her pocket and give her away, she nodded graciously and thanked him.

The cowboys insisted on several more games of "pin the tail on the mule," but Mattie knew the play was more to keep her from dwelling on Jake's absence than any desire on their own part to play the game.

Finally, having no excuse to prolong the festivities any longer, she got to her feet. "It has been a wonderful party and I want to thank each and every one of you. I will cherish the gifts you gave me, as well as the wonderful cake Mooney made."

She gazed at each face, realizing how dear they all had become. The children, the little Chinese man—her family now. The cowboys, despite their ages and their rough ways, seemed little more than grown-up children, full of pranks, quarrels, and so eager to please. She loved every one of them. "I know you men have worked hard all day and must be anxious to get to bed. I see the children are yawning, so I think it's time we said good night."

"It was a grand party, Miss Mattie," Slim said solemnly.

"That it was," she agreed. One she would never forget.

Their arms loaded with presents, the boys and Hope led the procession back to the house. Faith and Bock Gee followed with the cake.

Henry, walking beside Mattie, hoisted Joshua to his shoulders and gave him a ride to the kitchen porch. "Do you want me to ride into town?" the tall man asked softly.

"No. I'm sure that isn't necessary," she said, feigning a lightheartedness she certainly did not feel. "Something probably came up. A couple of drunks might have gotten into a fight. Who knows? Or the preacher might have staged another protest against the saloon."

"I, for one, will be glad when that man's gone." Henry lifted the toddler from his shoulders and placed him in Mattie's arms. "Bye, squirt. Good night, ma'am."

"Good night, Henry." Mattie carried Joshua inside, then washed the cake and punch from the baby's face and hands, and after making certain the other children were washing up as well, she went to her room and tucked the little boy into his crib.

"Can we sleep with Bock Gee tonight?" Lory asked, peering up at her.

"It's kind of scary in the barn without Uncle Jake," Hal said solemnly.

"Well, I don't know . . ." She glanced at the little man.

"I would be most honored to share sleeping space," Bock Gee said. "Show you how we do it in China. There, many people sleep in one room." A small blond boy on either side of him, the old man shuffled off to bed.

Mattie peeked in at the girls, and found them already in bed and asleep. Joshua, too, slept peacefully.

Knowing that she would not be able to close her eyes until Jake came home, she took her shawl from the peg, then eased through the kitchen door and went out onto the porch.

She inhaled the night air, finding it sage-scented and nose-nipping cold. Overhead, scores of diamondlike stars glittered against an ebony velvet canopy. A magical night, a night for lovers and romance. For everyone but her.

She settled onto the porch swing and hugged her shawl tighter in an attempt to ward off the cold. In the distance a coyote let loose with a mournful howl. Each quivering note dying on the wind found an echo in her own heart. Where was he? Why hadn't he come home? Her thoughts bitter, she gazed at the road leading toward town.

❧ TWENTY-EIGHT ❧

Jake, Jobe, and Delilah spent the night standing vigil beside Jolene's bed. Myrtle, Daisy, and the other girls hovered anxiously at the foot of the staircase.

Dust-covered and trail-weary, the doctor arrived shortly before dawn. After a few terse words, he told everyone to wait in the hall while he examined Jolene.

A while later, his thick gray brows drawn into a fierce scowl, Dr. Welden motioned Jake off to one side. "Personally, I can't understand why the girl is still alive. She has a concussion, a broken arm, and several broken ribs. It's a miracle one of them didn't puncture a lung. Most men would have died after the sort of beating she has taken. But if she makes it through the next few hours, then I'd say she might have a chance."

The doctor's brown eyes filled with anger. "I've never seen so many contusions. It looks like whoever did it wasn't content to just beat her, he kicked her. Stomped on her, by the look of it." He gazed up at Jake. "Do you know who did it?"

"If I did, do you think I'd be standing here?" Jake growled.

"No. I guess you wouldn't." The physician opened his bag and took out a bottle. "It's laudanum. Keep her sedated, otherwise she won't be able to stand the pain. I'll check on her every couple of hours. If there is any change—any change at all—send somebody to get me."

The slender man snapped his bag shut, took one more look at his patient, then left to get some much needed rest.

"Need more ice?" Jake asked Delilah who was bathing Jolene's bruised face with a soft cold cloth.

"In a little bit."

Not having anything else to do and too agitated to sit and watch, Jake went downstairs to the saloon. There, several men sat at a table, not drinking, not gambling, just waiting.

"How is she?" one of them asked.

"The same." He saw the question in their eyes and continued. "If she makes it through the next few hours, she'll live." She had to live.

He poured himself a cup of coffee and gazed out the window. His horse still stood by the hitching rail where he had tied it the night before. He noticed the package tied behind the cantle. *Mattie's present. The surprise party.* He'd forgotten.

He downed the coffee and set the cup back on the bar, then he took the horse to the livery and told the stable boy to rub the animal down and give him some grain. Jake removed the sack containing Mattie's presents and headed back toward the saloon.

Bridget jumped into Mattie's lap, the motion waking her from a sound sleep. She ran her palm down the purring cat, then yawned and glanced around, surprised to find herself in the kitchen. She didn't even remember coming into the house. She got to her feet and placed the cat back in the seat of the rocking chair, then raised her hand to massage the stiffness out of her neck. She stoked up the fire in the cookstove and put water on to boil. A ray of faintest pink shone through the kitchen window. Dawn. She'd waited all night. She glanced toward the corral, but Jake's sorrel wasn't in it. He hadn't come home.

Not wanting anyone to see her in the same clothes she'd

been wearing the night before, she took a dress from the laundry she had ironed but not yet hung in the closet, and put it on. Then she went to the sink and washed her face, and patted some semblance of order into her hair.

By the time the household was stirring, she had coffee in the pot and potatoes and bacon frying on the stove.

"Mama. Mama," whimpered a small voice from the bedroom.

She opened the door and took little Joshua into her arms. "What is it, sweetheart? Are you hungry?" Not wanting him to awaken the sleeping girls, she eased open the bureau drawer and removed a diaper and some clean clothes, then quietly left the room.

She bathed him in the sink, watching his chubby hands slap the water in his exuberant effort to burst the iridescent soap bubbles. After he tired of the game, she dried him off, then dressed him and set him in his high chair and handed him a piece of toast.

"Good morning, Mattie," Bock Gee said, entering the room.

"Good morning," she said brightly. "How about some coffee?"

"Coffee sound very good."

"Are the boys still asleep?"

"Nope. We're right here," Lory said, wiping the sleep from his eyes as he staggered through the doorway.

"Where's Uncle Jake?" Hal asked, peering around his brother.

"I—I guess he was detained in town," Mattie said, hoping they wouldn't ask any more questions. "You two, wash, then sit down and have your breakfast."

"Jake not home?" Bock Gee stood by the window and drank his coffee, then he set the cup on the table. "I think I take a little walk. Work up appetite for breakfast," he said, giving her a smile.

A while later he reappeared, Henry by his side. "You need anything from town, Mattie?" the foreman asked. "I thought I would take Bock Gee in and pick up the mail.''

''You're leaving?'' she asked, gazing at the elderly man. ''But you haven't had breakfast.''

''I really not very hungry. Not take much food for so small a body.'' He bowed. ''Thank you for your hospitality, Mattie.'' He went to gather his things.

''What is it you're not telling me?'' Mattie asked Henry. ''Do you think something has happened to Jake?''

''Of course not,'' he said, avoiding her eyes.

''Then why didn't he come home?''

''I don't know,'' Henry said, trying to appear nonchalant. ''Could be he got to celebratin' a little ahead of time and clean forgot where he was supposed to be.''

She didn't believe that for a minute and neither did Henry.

''Okay. I am ready,'' Bock Gee said, carrying his bundle into the room.

Mattie and the children gave the old man a hug.

Henry touched the brim of his hat. ''I'll be back after a bit.''

She nodded. Henry and Bock Gee climbed on the horses and rode out of the yard. She'd never seen the elderly man on a horse before. He'd always ridden in a wagon.

Why hadn't Henry taken the buckboard? Because horses were faster. Apprehension knotted her middle.

Jake alternated between pacing the floor and questioning anybody who entered the saloon, but nobody seemed to know any more about last night's happenings than he did. Weary beyond words, he ran a hand over his face, then thinking the fresh air might revive him, he started for the saloon door.

Henry and Bock Gee hurried down the boardwalk toward him. ''We just rode in from the ranch and heard what happened. How's Jolene?'' Henry asked, gripping his arm.

''Alive. Barely.'' Jake shook his head, finding words difficult. He motioned them back inside, then went behind the bar and filled another bucket full of ice for Delilah. On the way up the stairs, Jake told his two friends about Jolene's beating and the fire.

Shortly after noon, Romero rode into the yard. Mattie headed for the barn to question him. Another of the hands was already there.

"You missed Mattie's birthday party last night," Slim said.

"I know, and I sure feel bad about that, but we kind of had a party of our own in town."

"Do you know Jake didn't come home all night?"

"Yes. Jake spent the night with Jolene. We had some doings in town—"

Mattie brought a hand to her mouth to stifle her cry, then she turned and ran toward the house. She had stayed up all night waiting, beside herself with worry that something might have happened. She'd pictured Jake hurt, maybe even dead. All the while he had been with Jolene.

Well, she didn't need a stone wall falling on her to tell her exactly how she stood in her husband's affections. Jolene had beckoned, and he'd stayed. And he hadn't even been discreet. Everyone knew.

She loved him. Didn't he know that? Even though she'd never said the words, couldn't he have guessed? They could have had a life together. A good life for them as well as the children. She'd had such hopes, such dreams. She should have known it was too good to ever come true.

She could no longer be his wife. Not after what he had done. Her pride and her principles would not allow her to stay, now that Jake had broken the faith.

But what about the children? She closed her eyes against the pain. God help her, she loved them so. Right now they were too young to understand. But later . . . It was better this way. The children would soon forget her.

Leaving the children to play outside, she hurried to the house and packed her few meager belongings, then stowed the satchel by the foot of her bed.

As she smoothed the wrinkles from the coverlet, she thought about the new bedroom that Jake had worked so hard on. She had hoped that someday they would be sharing it. She remembered his gentle caresses, his kisses, and his passion the day they had made love. She had believed he cared for her, but it had apparently been an act. For if he truly had cared, he wouldn't have spent the night with Jolene.

What if things weren't as they seemed? an inner voice nagged at her. *What if she was mistaken*?

How could she be mistaken? She'd heard Romero speak the truth with her very own ears.

She fed the children early, then did the dishes and cleaned the kitchen. Jake still had not come home. She figured he probably felt too guilty to face her, until she remembered that Henry hadn't returned, either. She knew the foreman hadn't planned on being gone long. An uneasiness crept up her spine. What if something terrible had happened?

She could send someone else in to find out, but if something had happened, she doubted they would tell her the truth. Besides, even if she could bring herself to ask one of them to check on her wayward husband, the hands were out on the range. They wouldn't be in until late.

After repeatedly pacing the kitchen and glancing out the window for the umpteenth time, she knew she couldn't stand another minute of not knowing, wondering, waiting. If necessary, she'd go into town and find out for herself. Mooney could help her hitch the wagon. He could also keep an eye out for the kids.

She went onto the porch and gazed up at the saffron-colored sky. She shivered, finding the light eerie. The air seemed unusually hot, sticky. A trail of perspiration trickled between her breasts. Midafternoon. Still time enough to go to Sweetheart and get back before dark—if she hurried.

*   *   *

Doc Welden wiped his spectacles with his handkerchief, then blew on them and wiped them again.

"Well?" Jake demanded.

"Looks like she'll make it." He put his glasses on, then peered at the rest of the group that had gathered in the room. "But the rest of you look like hell. I suggest you all get some rest."

"But what if she needs something?" Jake protested.

"Right now the thing Jolene needs most is to be left alone. The laudanum I gave her will help her sleep—provided you don't keep fussin' over her."

"You're sure she'll be all right?"

"I said so, didn't I?" The doctor gave him a stern look, then pointed toward the door.

"Okay, we're leaving." Jake ushered Delilah, Jobe, Henry, and Bock Gee from the room, then after one more glance toward the bed, he, too, left, following the doctor and closing the door.

"Have you learned who's responsible yet?" the doctor asked.

"Not a clue," Jake answered.

"Bock Gee and I are going to ride out and talk to some of the miners, see if anyone noticed anything unusual around that time," Henry said.

"I'll be glad when they catch him," the doc said. "Whole town is fit to jump out of their skins."

But Jake knew he had to go home first. After talking with his foreman and the elderly Chinaman, he had to see Mattie and try to explain. Mattie had been real hurt when he hadn't arrived for her party. Then when he didn't come home—well, he could imagine what she thought about that.

Even though he was bone-tired both in body and spirit, he saddled the horse and headed for the ranch.

❧ TWENTY-NINE ❧

Her arms feeling like they had been pulled from their sockets, Mattie left the main road, taking the horses down to the edge of the river to drink. That way, she figured, after she got to town she could avoid the livery and any inquisitive stares and questions from the nosey townsfolk.

Since she had never driven a team before, the trip had been difficult and had taken much longer than she had expected. Her palms had blisters from tugging on the rough leather reins. She climbed down and plunged them into the river, allowing the cool water to soothe the pain. Not wanting to arrive looking like a harridan, she brushed the dirt from her sweat-stained dress, then dampened her handkerchief and wiped her dust-covered face and arms.

The air had grown thick, suffocating. Massed clouds now rolled over the snow-crested peaks and spilled into the valley; their black underbellies flickered with spasms of lightning. Thunder boomed; an endless drumroll echoed down the range.

A storm. Just what she didn't need. She thought about the children and for a moment considered giving up the trip and returning to the ranch. She glanced at the bridge leading into town. No. She was already here. It would be foolish to turn back now.

Overhead, the leaves of the cottonwoods lining the riverbank rustled, then the branches whipped, leaving bits of white, like falling snow, in the rising wind. The horses danced nervously. Mattie reached out and tightened her hand on the nearest one's bridle and hoped they wouldn't bolt. After allowing them a few more minutes to finish drinking, she led them in a turn to straighten the wagon, then climbed back onto the seat.

She heard a clip-clop of hooves from a horse crossing the bridge. Whether the rider was headed into or out of town, she couldn't tell. A thick cloud of dust made it impossible to see either the rider or the direction he had taken.

Hoping she wouldn't encounter any further traffic on the narrow wooden structure, she maneuvered the horses back onto the road and across the bridge. In Sweetheart, she avoided Main Street and took the alleyway that led behind the livery. There, she tied the horses to a post at the back entrance of the stable, then, taking a path beside the building, headed for the street.

A gust of wind whipped down from the rocky hills, blowing dirt, rattling shutters. The back door of the stable slammed shut. She hoped it hadn't frightened the horses. From the weathered walkway beside the shadowy barn she glanced across the street to the Golden Nugget.

Ladies did not enter a saloon, the voice of propriety nagged.

Ladies didn't marry saloon owners either, she silently argued. Besides, she'd been in the place before.

And look what happened. The idea that she might again find Jake and Jolene together sent anguish ripping through her heart. It was time for the truth, no matter how painful it might be. She took a deep breath, then before her courage deserted her, she crossed the street and pushed through the swinging doors.

The place was empty, which surprised her. Then she heard a clattering of bottles coming from the back room. She tiptoed forward and saw Charlie busily counting a crate of empties.

"Better make that two cases next time," the bartender

said to someone who stood just out of view. "The men drank dang near all we had last night."

"All right. I'll double your order on that one."

Not Jake. A whiskey drummer, Mattie decided. She took a step closer to the staircase.

"I heard you had a fire here last night. I didn't see much damage."

A fire? The man's words froze Mattie in place.

"Yeah. Somebody tried to burn the place down. But Jake and the men managed to put it out. Scorched the back side of the building, but no real damage."

"Anybody hurt?" the drummer asked.

"By the fire? Naw. A few minor burns, and somebody got hit with a shovel. What with everything else that was going on, I guess we were lucky." The bartender straightened. "Well, I guess that's all we'll be needing."

Not wanting the men to catch her, Mattie hurried up the stairway and entered Jake's office. He wasn't there, but an empty whiskey bottle and glass sat on the desk. She glanced out the window and gazed at the narrow avenue of shops. Outside of a few stray dogs, even the main street seemed deserted. Where was everybody? The bartender had mentioned a fire. Was that why the saloon was empty?

Puzzled, she left the office and strode down the hall. She raised a shaking hand and tapped on the door of Jake's bedroom. No answer. She turned the knob. The foot of the bedspread was rumpled as though someone had sat on the end of it, but the bed didn't appear slept in. A soot-streaked shirt lay on the floor. From the look of things, Jake had been here briefly, then left.

If he wasn't here—then where? Her gaze went to the door at the end of the hall. At the Miner's Delight, of course.

She tried the handle. The entry swung inward, revealing a hallway. To the right, she found another door. She turned the knob.

The shades were still drawn, but even in the muted light

she noticed the bedroom had been tastefully decorated, the furnishings elegant. Such a room could belong to only one person—Jolene.

Mattie stood on the threshold, then when her eyes grew accustomed to the dim light, she stared at the large brass bed. Was that where Jake had spent the night? Was he still there? Filled with jealousy, she studied the mound of covers. Too small for Jake. Jolene apparently—still asleep.

Determined to get answers, she closed the door and walked toward the bed. A peculiar, almost medicinal smell hung in the air. Strange, she would have expected the madam's quarters to have the scent of perfume.

She reached out and touched the woman's nightgown-clad shoulder. "Jolene? Wake up. It's Mattie Turnbull. I want to talk to you."

"Wa-ter," came a hoarse feminine whisper.

Water? Mattie glanced at the china pitcher on the small bed table, noticing the cloth on the edge of the bowl, the vial of laudanum beside a glass. Was the woman ill?

Mattie bent close to the bed. Then she saw the white bandages around the woman's head. *Burned in the fire*?

"Wa-ter." The woman moaned as if in great pain.

Mattie's anger dissolved in a flood of compassion. She poured a glass of water, then she carefully lifted the woman's head and held it to her swollen lips. After the poor creature managed a sip, Mattie gently laid her back against the pillow.

"La-mp," she croaked.

Mattie lit the bedside lamp and turned it down low. "There, is that—" She recoiled in horror. "Oh, my God," she whispered. Jolene's face! Or was it Jolene? "What happened?"

Bandages swathed the woman's forehead. A line of neat stitches ran down one cheek. Her face bore plum-colored bruises and although the swelling made her face unrecognizable, the slits of green eyes told her the person was indeed Jolene. Below the neckline of the nightgown, thick bandages wrapped her chest. One arm, apparently broken, bore a cast.

"Oh, my dear," Mattie whispered, realizing that whatever had happened to Jolene had not been the result of the fire or any accident. It was evident that someone had cruelly, deliberately tried to beat the woman to death.

"Mat-tie?"

Mattie pulled the chair closer to the bed. "I'm right here. Can I get you anything? More water?"

Jolene made an effort to nod.

Mattie gave her another drink. "I can't understand who would do such a thing."

"J-ake?"

Mattie sucked in a breath. "Jake did this?"

"No."

Thank God. But he must have known about it. That's why he hadn't come home. Why he had spent the night with Jolene. She certainly couldn't leave him for that. "Jake isn't here. I really don't know where he is." Mattie carefully straightened the covers. "You should rest now."

Jolene clutched at Mattie's hand. "Lis-ten," she gasped. "W-arn . . . T . . ."

"I don't . . ." Mattie shook her head. Every word the woman uttered came out a croak, a hiss, almost unintelligible, but still she struggled trying to make herself understood. "Are you trying to tell me who did it?"

"T-ent."

"Tent?" Some of the miners lived in tents. The only other tent around was . . . "The gospel tent?"

"Ye-es."

Mattie leaned closer. "Are you saying the reverend knows something about this?"

"Ye-es. Wa-rn . . ."

Warn? Did Jolene want her to warn the minister? She knew the man was wild-eyed and fanatical, but she couldn't imagine anyone wanting to do him harm. But if Brother Abraham knew who had beaten Jolene—from the looks of it, tried to kill her—he might very well be in danger.

Mattie squeezed Jolene's hand, then tucked it under the covers. "Don't worry. I'll warn him." She rose and put the chair back where she had found it.

"N . . . Mat-tie, lis . . ."

Mattie returned to the side of the bed. But there was no answer. Jolene, exhausted by her efforts to speak, had fallen asleep. Not wanting to disturb her further, Mattie turned out the light. Then she tiptoed from the room and closed the door.

She had never liked Jolene, even though the woman had never done anything to her. Examining her feelings, Mattie decided that even though she was loath to admit it, she'd been jealous. Jealous of Jolene's face, her figure, her beauty, and most of all her hold on Jake. Now she felt ashamed.

Jake. Jolene had called out for him. Maybe Jake knew something that would shed some light on the beating. Then there was the saloon fire. Arson, from what the bartender had said. Both occurrences frightening; both mysteries.

She had the feeling the whole thing was connected, if she could just figure out the answer. She sensed that whatever Jolene had been trying to say had been important. An eerie feeling slid up her spine. A feeling that Jake might be in danger, too.

She went through the connecting door and entered the saloon. Once again she checked Jake's bedroom and office. He wasn't there. She ran down the stairs. "Have you seen Jake?"

"No." The bartender turned, his eyes widened in surprise. "Mrs. Turnbull, what are you doing here?"

"I'm trying to find my husband."

"I thought he had gone home."

"No." He hadn't gone home; she would have passed him. "If you do see him . . . never mind." This wasn't getting her anywhere.

Since Jolene couldn't talk and Jake was nowhere to be

found, the only person left who knew anything about the matter was the minister. Determined to get to the bottom of this, she left the saloon and strode down the boardwalk.

"What do you mean she took the wagon? She doesn't even know how to drive a team," Jake bellowed, not that that would have stopped her. "Where did she go?"

"To town I reckon," Mooney belligerently yelled back. "She asked me to watch out for the kids, then she took the wagon and left."

"Damn." Jake ran a hand through his hair. He would have passed her on the road—unless . . . He had noticed a wagon down by the river. It never occurred to him that it might be Mattie.

She wouldn't go off and leave the kids, not if she didn't intend to come right back. What was so all-fired important that she needed to go to town in the first place? Couldn't she see it was fixing to storm? Maybe she hadn't made it to town. She didn't know how to handle a team. If it started lightning . . .

He scowled at the billowing dark clouds overhead. She'd never get back before the storm broke. Mooney told him she hadn't appeared mad, just quietlike. With Mattie, being quiet could mean any number of things, all of them worrisome. Maybe she left a note. He sprinted toward the house.

Entering the kitchen, he checked the table and the cabinet, then the floor, thinking it might have blown there when he opened the door. No note. He went into her bedroom, scanned the neatly made bed and the dresser. No message there either.

He rounded the bed, heading for the door, then he noticed the carpetbag sitting in the corner. He knelt and opened it. Dresses, underwear, comb, brush. She wouldn't pack those things unless—unless she was leaving him. Battling a wave of pain, he stuffed the things back inside and buckled the latch. If she was leaving him, then why hadn't she taken her bag?

After him missing her party and not coming home last night, he figured she'd be hurt and spitting mad—but he didn't think she'd move out, especially without giving him a chance to explain.

"She can't leave," he reasoned. "She has no place to go." His words echoed in the stillness of the house. Already the place felt cold, without heart, as if it were Mattie's presence that had given it life. He tried to imagine him and the children without her. He couldn't. A knot twisted his middle. Damn it, she couldn't go. The children loved her, they needed her. *He* needed her. He loved her.

Going onto the porch, he peered into the distance, his eyes searching the narrow road that led into town. Deep cloud shadows raced over the sage-dotted hills, making it appear dark as twilight. No matter how hard he stared, Mattie's wagon was nowhere in sight.

He didn't like this. He didn't like it one bit. He thought about the fire at the saloon. Then about the severe beating someone had given Jolene. No telling what other kind of trouble might be brewing in town, and Mattie, unknowingly, had ridden right into the thick of it. What if some lunatic was on the loose? The idea that Mattie could be in danger made his blood run cold.

He raced toward the cookshack. Whether he could convince her to stay or not was something they'd have to settle later. Right now he wanted Mattie back here at the ranch where he could protect her.

"Mooney, take care of the kids," he yelled through the cookshack door. "I'm going after my wife."

Jake took his sorrel to the corral and turned it loose, then he saddled a fresh horse, one who possessed both strength and speed. He swung into the saddle and pointed the gray gelding toward town.

Around him lightning jabbed downward with forklike spears; thunder followed, shaking the ground. Ignoring the danger, Jake leaned low in the saddle, urging even more speed from the gelding.

The horse stretched out, his silver nose pointed into the wind, his swift gallop eating up the miles. But the closer Jake got to Sweetheart the more his apprehension grew.

Mattie was in danger. He could feel it.

❧ THIRTY ❧

Jolene opened her eyes and stared around her bedroom. "Mattie," she whispered, her throat aching. The room was empty, making her wonder if Mattie's appearance had only been part of a dream. *Thirsty.* Her body pulsing with agony, Jolene struggled to sit up, to reach for the half-full glass. There on the table, next to the china water pitcher, lay a white linen handkerchief. She picked it up and saw the "M" embroidered in the corner. Beside it lay the cloth Mattie had moistened and used to wipe Jolene's face. It hadn't been an illusion. Mattie had been here. But she wasn't now.

Jolene managed to get the glass to her lips, downing enough water to quench her thirst. Why had Mattie come? Had she been looking for Jake? She remembered Mattie's shocked face, her compassion and her anger toward the person who had done the beating. She had been surprised at Mattie's reaction, since most of the townspeople would have considered it no better than a whorehouse madam deserved. But then Mattie had never been one to conform to convention. Maybe that's why she was so perfect for Jake, although neither of them seemed ready to admit it.

She tried to remember the purpose of Mattie's visit. A blinding flash of pain sent Jolene's fingertips flying to her forehead. She pressed her temples, hoping to ease the hurt. They had been talking—at least Mattie had.

Jolene remembered how hard she'd fought to say the words. *"Wa-rn. Te-nt."*

"The reverend knows something about this?" Mattie had asked.

"Yes." But before she could finish the warning, weakness carried her into darkness. And now Mattie was gone.

Oh, God. She doesn't know. I wasn't able to tell her. What if she went to the tent? Jolene slid from the bed, every movement a spasm of agony. *Got to stop her, tell her.* Gripping the bedpost, she struggled to her feet, then lurched to the wall. She inched her way to the window and slumped to her knees. Pressing her face to the windowpane, she strained to see the tent at the end of the street.

By the flare of lightning, she saw Mattie's wagon pull out from behind the livery and come to a stop where the alley formed a junction with the main street.

"Turn left," Jolene prayed. "Go home to your children." But even as she spoke Jolene knew it was too late.

The woman on the wagon seat had already guided the team toward the tent and headed up the hill.

The wind whipped Mattie's hair, flinging stinging strands against her cheeks. Clouds of grit rose from the rut-laden street, filling her eyes, blurring her vision. She ducked her head and leaned into the gale.

Ahead the gospel tent moaned, its canvas billowing, then slacking, breathing as if the wind had given it life. Another gust hit. It shuddered and strained against the creaking ropes.

A zigzag flash ripped across the sky. A deafening roll of thunder vibrated the earth. The horses pranced nervously, neighing their terror.

Mattie guided the team to the only shelter available, the far side of a misshapened juniper. Hoping the tree wouldn't be a target for lightning, she tied the horses to a sturdy limb.

The animals tossed their heads and rolled their eyes. She

rubbed their satiny necks. "There, there. It shouldn't take long," she crooned. "A few minutes at the most."

Thunder boomed again. The horses strained against the tether. Praying the team would still be there when she returned, she straightened her shoulders and strode toward the canvas church.

When she lifted the tent flap, she stepped into inky blackness for the lanterns inside the enclosure had not yet been lit. "Reverend Abraham?" she called, her voice somewhat breathless.

No answer.

He isn't here. More than likely the services had been canceled because of the storm. Lightning flashed again, illuminating the ceiling of the ribbed structure, filling the rest of the interior with wavering specterlike shadows.

Mattie shivered and backed toward the opening. She needed to get home. The children would be frightened.

The minister should be safe enough in his wagon, she reasoned. Not even a madman would be out on a night like this. She could stop by the mercantile on her way home and ask Sara or Hiram to warn the reverend in the morning. Wishing she'd thought of the idea sooner, she reached for the tent flap.

A faint flickering of light behind her silhouetted her image, halted her movements. She turned and saw the soft glow of a lantern toward the front of the enclosure. Someone had to be here. Maybe they hadn't heard her.

"Brother Abraham. Is that you?" She peered toward the pulpit.

"Sister Turnbull, what a surprise," a harsh voice grated behind her.

Mattie whirled, her hand on her pounding heart. "Brother Abraham, I didn't realize you were there."

Dressed in black, the minister seemed one with the darkness. Like a shadow, with only the pale skin of his thin face and his eyes giving him life.

"I didn't intend to frighten you."

"You didn't." Still, to turn and suddenly find him blocking her exit had unnerved her, especially when, after seeing the light, she'd thought to find him at the front of the church.

He glided closer.

Uneasy, she stepped back and bumped into a bench. "I really wasn't expecting you to be here, with the storm and all."

"The storm?" He tilted his head, listening, as if aware of the tempest for the first time. "I'd hardly noticed."

Lightning cracked, lit the inside of the canvas, then plunged it into blackness. Thunder rumbled, increasing in volume until it exploded with a deafening roar.

Mattie jumped. How could he not notice that?

He stared at her, the distant lantern reflecting the gleam in his eyes.

A prickling sensation rose gooseflesh on her arms. Unreasonable fear tightened her throat. "I must be going. The children will be worried." She moved to step around him.

He reached out and grabbed her arm. "Why are you here?"

Her pulse pounding, she tried to think. Why had she come? *Jolene.* "I came to warn you."

His grip tightened. "Warn me?" he asked harshly. "Warn me about what?"

"I talked with Jolene . . ."

"Jolene?"

"From the Miner's Delight—she was beaten badly. She thought you might have seen the person who did it."

"That whore," he hissed. "She's dead."

"No." Mattie shook her head. "She isn't—but she has been badly injured."

"What did this vile creature say about me?"

"She said you needed to be warned. I guess she believed whoever beat her might come after you." As she listened to her words, Mattie thought how unreasonable they sounded. Even bizarre. Wrong. What if Jolene had been trying to tell her something else?

The preacher laughed, a terrible racking sound.

The strangeness of it sent a shiver rushing up her spine. "Now that you know, I really need to go." She forced a smile and attempted to shrug off his hand.

He bent close, his eyes glowing in the lantern light. "I tried to warn you, but did you listen?" He shook his head as if chastising a willful child. "I tried to give you another chance by asking you to lead the march against the saloon. But you refused. Now your time for repentance is over," he said, his voice rising in anger. "You must be punished for your sins."

"What are you talking about? I haven't sinned." The air seemed to have thickened, grown even hotter. Beads of perspiration dotted her brow, but Mattie shivered from cold. He was mad. "Please let me go. You're hurting me," she said, trying to reason.

His clawlike fingers dug into her flesh. "You'll never leave here."

Fear-born desperation gave her strength. She twisted out of his grasp and tore for the entrance.

He snatched her back by the hair.

She grasped in pain as he yanked her back to him.

"Jake Turnbull plies men with strong drink, robbing them of their money, their will to fight evil." His breath burned her cheek. "He leads them down Satan's crooked path."

He leaned closer, his eyes boring into hers. "Jake Turnbull is the devil's advocate. You are his wife. Tainted with his evil. His children are tainted."

"*The children?*"

"Even to the least of them. They are of his blood."

The vision of her children in this man's hands horrified her. "You can't blame Jake's sins on the children. They are innocent."

"They must be purified. It is the only way to save

them.'' His laughter raised the hairs on the back of her neck.

''You're insane!''

''That's what she said. The daughter of my loins. Once pure, innocent, now an abomination in my sight. She's beyond salvation. Next time, I will not fail.''

''Next time?'' She stared at him, seeing the fury, the hatred etching his face. ''You're talking about Jolene, aren't you?'' she asked, at last understanding what Jolene had been trying to tell her. ''You're the one who beat her!''

''Who else would have the right?''

Daughter of his loins. ''You're her father!'' That a father could do such a thing to his own child filled Mattie with rage. Her hand curved into a claw and she lunged for his face, her fingernails ripping his flesh.

He cried out and flung her away.

She stumbled against a bench. Then, whirling, she ran down the aisle.

Her dress wrapped around her legs. She fell, wrenching her knee. She pulled herself to her feet, limped toward the exit. He was coming after her!

Something struck her across the shoulders.

Pain dropped her to her knees.

She saw the upraised cane and flung herself to one side. It struck her arm. Frantically, she crawled between a row of benches, the cane striking wood all around her.

''I'm trying to save you.'' He screamed maniacal curses.

She scrambled beneath the benches, until she reached the outside edge of the aisle.

He was there, reaching for her.

''No!'' She dodged his outstretched hands.

Lightning flared. Blinding fingers of light raced down the rear tent spar. It struck the ground with a deafening explosion.

Mattie screamed.

Wood cracked and sizzled. Sulfur filled the air. The earth beneath her feet quaked.

The tent shivered and groaned. Flames licked up the fractured pole.

The madman stared at the sagging ceiling.

The tent billowed like a ship's sail caught in a stiff wind. When she thought it could go no higher, she heard another sound, more ominous. The crack of wood. Again. The center pole this time. It buckled, the rear canvas collapsing into the growing blaze. A lantern exploded, and flames burst forth. The fire was spreading, fast.

"Oh, God!" She whirled away.

He grabbed her skirt. "Witness the flames of hell."

Greedy fingers of fire raced toward them. The wind ripped loose more canvas. The front poles teetered.

"Let me go!"

He laughed, the sound shrill and macabre as he dragged her toward the choking smoke and searing heat.

She fought, kicked, but was no match for his mad strength.

"You'll not escape!" He drew back a fist.

"Jake! Help me!" Her head exploded in a burst of pain.

❦ THIRTY-ONE ❧

"She was here earlier, looking for you," Charlie said.

Jake shoved a lock of hair out of his eyes. Mattie had been there; the bartender had seen her. Where, then, was she now? Jake rushed up the stairs and checked each of the rooms, then he strode through the connecting hallway into the Miner's Delight. Ordinarily Mattie would never have considered going into such a place, of that he was certain. But in her present state of mind . . .

He opened the door and peered into Jolene's room. Her bed was empty. She can't be gone unless . . . Stricken by the thought she might be dead, he rushed to the doorway. "Jobe. Delilah," he called, his voice hoarse with emotion.

Immediately the two appeared at the foot of the stairs. "Mistah Jake?"

"Jolene. Her bed's empty. She isn't . . . ?"

"What? Empty? Cain't be—unless she fell out of it." Delilah shoved past him and entered the room. "She's sho nuff gone," she said, her dark eyes wide and frightened. She picked up something on the bed. "I don't 'member seein' this here before."

Jake snatched the handkerchief from her hand, then he brought it to his nose, inhaling the familiar scent. "It's Mattie's." His voice was unsteady. "Jolene must have gone with her. But how? Why?"

He ran down the stairs and out of the saloon. He checked

the livery to see if the wagon was still there.

It wasn't. He questioned the stable boy to see if he had seen either of the two women.

"I saw your rig tied out back," the boy drawled as if reluctant to let go of each word. "Then your missus drove off."

"Was Jolene with her?"

"She was alone. Near as I could tell."

Jake relaxed. "Maybe she went back to the ranch."

"Nope. She went that a way." The stable hand pointed up the street.

Confused, Jake walked up the boardwalk, wondering if Mattie stopped by the mercantile. A gust of wind jerked the hat from his head and sent it sailing against a storefront. He raced after it.

The hat skittered and danced up the street, rolling on, just out of reach.

Cursing, he chased the Stetson across a field. It came to a stop beneath a clump of sagebrush. Grabbing it, he slapped it back on his head.

On the rise, the gospel tent loomed, standing out from the darkness by a faint glow coming from inside. Another blast of wind hit. The tent moaned eerily, then it rose as if lifted by an invisible hand. Jake heard a snap as ropes broke and stakes ripped from the ground. Just when he thought it might take wing, the tent shuddered, then the center half of the structure sighed and sank, settling like an overgrown spider on the ground.

A light flickered and grew brighter. The tent was on fire!

With the wind shifting the way it was, the town would be next. In a gale like this, the whole place would be gone.

He ran to the mercantile and pounded on the door.

Hiram stuck his head out. "We're closed."

"Gospel tent's on fire," Jake shouted. "Sound the alarm."

"Mistah Jake! Mistah Jake!"

He whirled to see Jobe running toward him. "Did you find Jolene and Mattie?"

"We found Miss Jolene. She'd passed out and fell behind the draperies. We put her in bed and sent for the doctor."

"Did she say anything about Mattie?"

"Nothin' that made any sense."

Jake gripped the old man's shoulders. "What did she say? It could be important." Jake saw the whites of Jobe's eyes and knew he was scaring the man, but it couldn't be helped. Some inner sense told him he had to find Mattie.

"She said to stop Mattie. And somethin' about the tent."

"The tent?" The gospel tent! *"My God!"* The fire bell clanging in his ears, Jake whirled and sprinted back to the sagging canvas.

A muffled scream rose, then died on the air.

"Mattie!" Jake yanked at the sagging flap, then recoiled as a blast of smoke and heat hit him in the face.

He ran to the side, to a part of the structure that still stood. He took his knife from its scabbard and slashed a hole in the canvas. Then using the fabric to shield his head and face, he plunged into the inferno.

Billowing clouds of thick black smoke filled his lungs, making him cough. Heat seared his face. His eyes teared. "Mattie! Mattie, where are you?"

"Here," a voice cried.

"Oh, thank God!" Jake felt his way down the aisle. "Honey?"

A dark figure lurched through the smoke.

Not Mattie. Jake grabbed the preacher's arm. "My wife?"

The reverend pointed into white-hot flames. "She's there—go to her!" Then he burst into laughter, a sound so bizarre it sent chills up Jake's spine.

Jake plunged forward. But the smoke was too dense, he couldn't see.

Dropping to the floor where the fire was not as intense,

he crawled forward, making his way to the center aisle.
"Mattie!"

The roar of the fire was his only answer.

"Mattie!" he yelled again. A flash of pain slid across
his shoulder. Wincing, he twisted away.

"Feel the hand of God, sinner!"

"What in hell?" Jake saw the cane and threw himself to
one side.

Wood slammed into his head.

"Die, devil's son."

Jake reeled, dazed by the blow. Blood trickled down his
face. He felt dizzy, sick. He couldn't pass out. He couldn't.
He had to get her out. "Mattie," he called desperately.

Fire crackled. Flames licked across the backs of benches.
Maniacal laughter filled the air.

Jake fought the darkness. Smoke filled his lungs.

"Ja-ke. Jake?" a woman's voice called faintly.

Mattie. Renewed by the sound of her desperate call, he
struggled to his knees. The cane rose over his head. He
lunged at the preacher. The black figure tumbled backward
over a bench. Jake staggered down the aisle. "Mattie?"

"Here. Hurry!" The sound came from a section already
in flames.

Terror sent him to his knees. "Mattie, where are you?"

"Here," she sobbed. She was curled under a burning
bench. He pulled her out, slapping at her smoldering clothing. "Oh, Mattie, girl. I thought I'd lost you."

Fire dipped and whirled, roaring like some savage beast.
Any minute the rest of the structure would come tumbling
down. He had to get Mattie out.

"Stay close to the floor." He shoved a row of benches
backward making a pathway toward the hole he had cut.
Reaching the edge, a gust of fresh air rushed toward them.
"This way!"

A horrible scream trembled on the smoke-filled air.

Jake whirled toward the sound.

The minister stood in the midst of the flames, his hands

raised toward the heavens. His voice swelled, shouting curses upon the sinners.

Jake lifted Mattie into his arms, and plunged through the hole. Coughing, his lungs seared from the fire and smoke, he collapsed upon the ground outside.

"There they are!" someone shouted.

Cool water poured over Jake and Mattie, then several miners helped them to a nearby knoll.

"Are you two all right?" Hiram asked.

"We will be," Jake said as Mattie suffered a spasm of coughing.

Hiram nodded, then returned to fight the fire.

Jake drew in greedy mouthfuls of fresh air, his arms shaking as he held on to his wife. He'd come so close to losing her.

A loud *whoosh* and a rush of heat billowed as the tent collapsed completely. Blue flames leapt toward the sky.

Then raindrops, glorious, large and cold raindrops, began to fall, hissing upon the fire, settling the dust, scenting the air with rain-washed sage, wet smoke, and moist earth.

He brushed his lips across Mattie's brow as he savored the cool soothing feeling on his face, and sighed, "You're safe now."

Around them the townspeople ran, carrying water in an attempt to contain several wildfires scattered over the hillside.

The rain began to fall in earnest and Jake helped Mattie to her feet.

"Jake. Mattie?" Sara rushed toward them. "Thank God you're all right. Someone found your team running loose—"

"Where's Doc?" Jake interrupted. Mattie had burns that should be treated.

"He's at the Miner's Delight."

Jake swung his wife up into his arms and hurried toward town.

Taking refuge under an overhanging porch, Jake set Mattie on her feet and examined her in the lamplight. Her coughing had ceased but tremors still quivered through her body. "Thank God you're all right," he murmured. Shaken by how close he had come to losing her, he pulled her to him.

"Jolene tried to warn me," Mattie whispered on a cough. "But I didn't understand." Her voice broke. "He was her father, Jake. How could he beat her like that? He tried to kill her. He wanted to kill me. And you. And the children."

"The man was crazy, Mattie."

"It was my fault. This would never have happened if I hadn't brought him here."

"It's no one's fault, honey. No one's."

"But poor Jolene." She began to sob.

"Jolene will be all right." Right now, it was Mattie who worried him. Jake smoothed a singed lock of hair back from her face. "Now that you're safe, we'll all be all right."

❧ THIRTY-TWO ❧

A bright shaft of sunlight pierced a sliver of space between the lace curtains and played across Mattie's face. Disturbed by the glare, she raised a hand to shield her eyes and stared in surprise at the wrappings covering both of her arms. Bandages?

The fire.

A shudder ran through her, and she touched a sore spot on her temple. A faint squeak drew her attention to the doorway where the twins stood, their faces solemn. "Hello, there," she whispered.

Their eyes widened and their mouths lifted in broad grins. "Mama," they cried. Arms outstretched, they raced to her bedside.

Mama. She thought she'd never hear that word again. She drew their wiry little bodies close. Tears of thanksgiving filled her eyes.

"Are you all right now?" Lory asked anxiously.

"You've been sick for such a long time," Hal said.

"I have?" She couldn't remember. She gazed about, taking in the large brass bed, the frilly curtains, everything different and new. "Where am I?"

"In your new room. Papa fixed it up. Aunt Jolene helped."

"Aunt Jolene?"

"Hey," a voice hissed. "You kids get out of there."

"Jake?"

He stuck his head through the doorway, then he strode into the room.

"Can we tell everybody Mama's okay now?"

He grinned down at them. "Yeah! I reckon you can."

The pair bolted from the room.

Jake took a seat in the chair next to the bed. She had the feeling he had sat there many times before. He gazed down at her. "How are you feeling?"

"The children said I've been sick. I don't remember."

He cleared his throat, then he attempted a smile. "You had a touch of lung fever. The doctor said you inhaled too much smoke from the fire. We damn near lost you."

"I don't remember."

"We had to give you laudanum for the pain."

She held up her arms. "Burned?"

He nodded. "But they're healing up real good. Bock Gee's been putting some kind of salve on them. Says you probably won't even have any scars."

She noticed the jagged unevenness of his hair. The red spots dotting his forehead. "You were burned, too."

"Yeah. Not bad though." He gave her that crooked one-sided grin. "Besides, I'm so homely it wouldn't make a heck of a lot of difference."

Homely? She had never seen him more handsome. She was ready to tell him so, when a chorus of bright faces appeared in the doorway.

"Can we come in?" a freckle-faced young woman asked.

Puzzled, Mattie nodded.

Faith and Hope ran into the room. Joshua on sturdy little legs toddled after them. "Mama," the girls cried, taking up a position on either side of her. "Mamama," Joshua squealed.

"He can walk!" Mattie said.

"And talk. And get into everything," the strange woman said, coming into the room.

"Hello," Mattie said. "I don't believe I know you."

"You just don't recognize me. Jolene?" she prompted.

"Jolene?" Then she saw the faint scar running down the golden tanned cheekbone. Hardly noticeable unless you knew it was there. Jolene's hair, usually so perfect, hung in a riot of curls past her shoulders, confined only by a bright green bow. The dress covering her perfect figure was not silk, but calico. Jolene had never looked more beautiful.

The woman's face took on an impish grin. "How are you feeling?"

"Confused," she said. "What are you doing here?"

"I've been giving this big lug a hand with the kids," she said, draping an arm around Jake's shoulders.

He squeezed Jolene's hand. "Couldn't have gotten along without her."

Mattie stared from the titan-haired woman to the handsome blond man to the children. Like one big happy family. A pain, so sharp it took her breath, hit her middle.

"Mattie, are you all right?" Jake asked, his voice concerned.

"I think I'd like to rest now." She just wanted all of them to go.

"Sure, honey. Come on, kids. Everybody outside." He ushered the others ahead of him, then he stopped at the threshold. He frowned, his face a mixture of hurt and bewilderment, then he went out and closed the door.

Hot tears spilled down her cheeks. Jake didn't need her. None of them needed her. Not even the baby. Jolene had very effectively taken her place.

Later that afternoon, Mattie heard a soft tap on the door. "Go away," she said, her voice choked with misery.

The footsteps retreated.

A while after that, Lory and Hal stuck their heads into the room. "Mama, can we come in?"

"No. I have a headache." She couldn't bear to see them, loving them the way she did. It would be hard enough to leave them as it was. For she did intend to leave. Just as soon as she was able. No sense staying around and prolonging the agony. Jake and Jolene would be happy to see her gone, that much was apparent. She'd seen the warmth in their eyes when they gazed at each other.

She glanced at the gleaming brass bed, at last able to remember where she had seen it. In Jolene's bedroom. The bed linens, the curtains, the rugs, even the china pitcher and bowl. All Jolene's. Well, they had certainly wasted no time. Jolene's room was ready and waiting, and no doubt she'd be sharing it with Jake. Now all they needed was for Mattie to leave.

Mattie had considered the ranch her home, the children and Jake, her family. She'd had such hopes when Jake had shown her the new room. Then after the fire when he'd held her . . . But it was not to be.

She closed her eyes, envisioning Jake and Jolene together, making love, creating the child Mattie had hoped to have. Suddenly she wished she had perished in the blaze for the pain of Jake's betrayal was more than she could bear.

It was almost sunset when someone knocked on the door.

"Go away."

"I don't think so," Jolene said firmly, entering the room. "It's time you and me had a talk."

"I don't want to talk."

"Then listen." Jolene closed the door and locked it, then she crossed the room and sat down in the chair. "I know something is bothering you, and I think I have a good idea what it is."

"Nothing is bothering me. Nothing at all," Mattie said, turning her face to the wall.

"Oh, no? Then why are you behaving like a spoiled brat?"

Spoiled brat! She fixed Jolene with an indignant stare. "Am I supposed to be grateful that you waltzed in here and took over my husband and my children?"

Jolene began to laugh.

"What's so damned funny?"

"Oh, Mattie. If only you knew." The redhead wiped tears from her eyes. "While I love each and every one of the little rascals dearly, I can't wait for you to get well. As for Jake and me, I imagine he would have a thing or two to say about me taking your place."

"If you expect me to stay on and be your housekeeper, forget it," Mattie said furiously.

"Housekeeper? I have thought of you as many things, Mattie Turnbull, but never have I pictured you as anybody's housekeeper." Jolene's expression sobered. "I do love Jake very, very much, but not as a woman loves her man. Jake is like the brother I never had. He saved my life, risking his own, when I was fourteen. It's not a pleasant story, or one I've told before, but I think it's time you knew the truth."

The truth? Intrigued, Mattie listened.

"You know part of it already," Jolene began. "I wasn't always a whore, in fact I had a very strict upbringing." Jolene told how her father had driven her from her home; how she had been forced into prostitution. She told Mattie that Jake had rescued her from a Mexican brothel, and afterward how he had cared for her like his little sister.

She also related an ill-fated love affair with an outlaw who died at the end of a rope, and of their child, born too soon. Jolene continued to talk and the tale she told had both of them in tears before she was through.

"Jimmy wasn't a bad man. I wouldn't want you to think that about him. But he was born poor and seemed destined to stay that way. We had a small ranch, mostly dirt and rocks, but we had such hopes. We had a bad year and the bank took our land, our cattle, everything. That's why Jimmy turned to robbery. Not that the banker he stole from couldn't afford it. The man was miserly mean, kind of reminded me of Ben Satterfield. Anyway, after Jimmy died, I took the money he'd hidden and ran. Figured I'd earned it, although the law probably wouldn't think so. I showed up here and, well, you know the rest."

Mattie sat in stunned silence. Then in a faint voice she said, "It's a wonder you survived. I doubt that many women, including myself, could have lived through such an ordeal."

"Well, it wasn't all bad. There were happy times, too." Jolene sucked in a breath. "Anyhow that's all behind me. I'll be leaving soon. Kind of looking forward to it."

"You're leaving Sweetheart?"

Jolene nodded. "Now that I've buried my past I need to get on with my life."

"What will you do? How will you get by?"

Jolene grinned. "I'm rich. The smartest thing I ever did was grubstake those miners. Since they hit paydirt, I have more money than I know what to do with. But I intend to use it to accomplish some good." Her smile both sweet and sad, she gazed off in the distance. "First I intend to return to Kansas. I want to buy a headstone and put it on my mother's grave. Then, who knows? There are a lot of girls out there, some runaways, some whose men have abandoned them. I know what it's like to be frightened and alone. Maybe I can help them."

"What about the Miner's Delight?"

"That's right. You haven't heard. It's now called the Sweetheart Christian Missionary School."

"What?"

"You remember that mission you were always badgering back east? Well, they finally sent somebody. A young couple, still wet behind the ears, and she expecting anytime."

"They are here?"

"Yep, all three of them. The baby was born in the parlor of the Miner's Delight."

"Good grief."

"Exactly. After that I couldn't very well carry on a business, even if I was of a mind to. I'd keep seeing that precious baby." She chuckled. "Myrtle and Daisy were so moved by the event that they gave up the life and got married. The new minister did the honors. The girls are bent on being respectable; in fact, they will probably be occupying the front row in his church from now on. The rest of my girls took off for Leadville. And now that I've put my past to rest, I've decided to try for a new start.''

''That's wonderful,'' Mattie said in amazement. ''You mentioned a school?''

''I donated the building to the mission. I figured they could put all of those bedrooms to good use—with a few alterations of course.'' Jolene pointed to the bed. ''Since that wasn't exactly appropriate for a missionary school, I decided you might like it. If you don't . . .''

''It's lovely.'' Mattie ducked her head. ''If you could only imagine what I thought . . .''

''I can guess,'' Jolene said with a wry grin. ''Well, I think I've taken up enough of your time.''

Mattie fingered the quilt. ''Can I talk to Jake?''

''Sure, but before you do . . .'' She eyed Mattie critically.

''Oh, my. I must look a fright,'' Mattie said, touching her shorn locks, all at once self-conscious about her appearance.

''Actually it's quite becoming. Just needs a little fluffing here and there.'' Jolene quickly removed the tangles from Mattie's cropped hair, arranging soft curls around her face. ''There. Pretty as can be.''

''How can I ever thank you?''

''Just be good to him. In many ways Jake is like those children. He needs somebody to love and somebody to love him. I think you can be that person.''

''I certainly want to try,'' Mattie said sincerely.

''He took care of you, you know. Wouldn't allow anyone else to do it. He hardly left this room at all. I don't know what he would have done if you hadn't made it.''

''He took care of me?'' So she had been right about the chair. Love for him filled her. ''Thank you, Jolene.''

"Thank you, Mattie." Jolene winked, then she walked out the door.

Jake sat on the top rail of the corral, his shoulders hunched, his eyes focused on the ground. All this time he'd waited for Mattie to get well, thinking they could finally start a life together. Now that she was feeling better, she acted like she had no use for him. She didn't seem to like the kids much either. She wouldn't even let them in her room.

"Jake."

"Yeah." He twisted to see Jolene.

"Mattie wants to see you."

"It'd be the first time." He stayed where he was.

"Aren't you going to go talk to her?"

"Why? What's the use? She was ready to leave me before. Now that she's well, I don't see any sign that she's changed her mind."

"Of all the ornery, mule-headed, stubborn . . ." She heaved an exasperated sigh. "You two take the cake."

"You're some stubborn yourself, you know," he grumbled.

Jolene's eyes narrowed. "Are you going to come down from there . . ."

"All right, don't get your drawers in an uproar." He slid off the fence.

"Go comb your hair and wash your face," she ordered. "And talk to your wife."

"Yes, mama." He stalked off toward the house.

A while later he stood in front of Mattie's door. How could he let her leave him, loving her the way he did? How could he make her stay? He couldn't. Sighing, he opened the door.

Mattie saw Jake, his face scrubbed and his hair still wet from the comb. He hesitated in the doorway.

He reminded her of one of the twins, his face wistful but not at all expectant. *Why, he's scared*, she thought. Big, blustery, Jake Turnbull, whose gruff voice and manner made even the toughest miner turn tail, stood in her doorway like a bashful schoolboy. *He needs somebody to love and somebody to love him.* Mattie knew she had never loved him more.

"Can I come in?" he asked.

"I would like that."

"Mattie . . ."

"Jake, you must think me such a fool. I wouldn't blame you if you never spoke to me again after the way I behaved."

"You've been sick. I guess you have a right to feel peevish." He gazed at her a minute. "Where do we go from here, Mattie? I know you planned to leave me. I saw your bag. If you are still of a mind to leave, I would like to see you safely to wherever it is you want to go."

"Do you want me to go?" she asked softly.

He scowled. "No, but I won't make you stay if you don't want to."

"What if I do want to? What would you do then?"

His blue eyes took on a brilliant gleam. "I'd make sure you stayed out of trouble."

"Oh? And how would you go about that?" she asked, arching a brow.

"By never letting you get more than an arm's length away," he said huskily.

"That's pretty close." She gave him a teasing smile, then she held out her arms.

"Not nearly close enough." He leaned forward and wrapped her in his embrace.

Just when she was about to discover just how close he had in mind, the door crashed back against the hinges and the twins burst into the room. "Mama! Papa! Look what we found."

"I think we'd better teach them to knock," Jake groused.

"That might be a good idea," she whispered. "What is it you have found?" she asked the exuberant little boys.

"Solomon. And he's got babies." They thrust a sugar tin forward. Sure enough, there in the bottom, among a nest of wool from Jake's long johns and Mattie's yarn, a bright-eyed, one-eared mouse peered up at them. Beside her lay four tiny babies.

"I don't believe it. It is Solomon," Mattie said. "And he's—she's—a mother."

"Under the circumstances, I think a change of name might be in order," Jake said, grinning. "How about Salome?"

Lory thought about it for a minute. "He's still the same mouse. Why does he have to have a new name?" He looked at his brother.

"I like Solomon just fine."

"Well if he, uh, she don't mind . . ." Jake began.

Mattie giggled. "She looks content to me."

"Can we go show Aunt Jolene?"

"Well, I don't know how Jolene feels about mice, but I guess it's all right," Jake answered.

As soon as the twins and their mice disappeared from the room, Jake strode forward and locked the door. He returned to the bed and gave Mattie a wicked smile. "Now where were we when we were so rudely interrupted?"

She locked her fingers in his hair and pulled him toward her. "With five children you have to expect a few surprises every now and then."

He nuzzled her neck. "How about with six, or seven, or eight, or . . ."

Dear Reader,

I've just finished the last page of this book and already another hero and heroine are demanding that I tell their story.

To all of you who have written, I give you my heartfelt thanks, for your words of encouragement are what kept me going. I hope you have enjoyed *Heart's Folly*.

Sincerely,

Mary Lou Rich

You may write to me in care of:

The Berkley Publishing Group
200 Madison Ave., 10th floor
New York, NY 10016

Please include a stamped self-addressed envelope for an autographed bookmark and newsletter.

Our Town

...where love is always right around the corner!

All Books Available in July 1996

__Take Heart_ by Lisa Higdon
                    0-515-11898-2/$5.99
In Wilder, Wyoming...a penniless socialite
learns a lesson in frontier life—and love.

__Harbor Lights_ by Linda Kreisel
                    0-515-11899-0/$5.99
On Maryland's Silchester Island...the perfect
summer holiday sparks a perfect summer
fling.

__Humble Pie_ by Deborah Lawrence
                    0-515-11900-8/$5.99
In Moose Gulch, Montana...a waitress with a
secret meets a stranger with a heart.

*If you enjoyed this book,
take advantage
of this special offer.
Subscribe now and get a*

FREE
Historical
Romance

No Obligation (a $4.50 value)

Each month the editors of True Value select the four *very best* novels from America's leading publishers of romantic fiction. Preview them in your home *Free* for 10 days. With the first four books you receive, we'll send you a FREE book as our introductory gift. No Obligation!

If for any reason you decide not to keep them, just return them and owe nothing. If you like them as much as we think you will, you'll pay just $4.00 each and save at *least* $.50 each off the cover price. (Your savings are *guaranteed* to be at least $2.00 each month.) There is NO postage and handling – or other hidden charges. There are no minimum number of books to buy and you may cancel at any time.

Send in the Coupon Below

To get your FREE historical romance fill out the coupon below and mail it today. As soon as we receive it we'll send you your FREE Book along with your first month's selections.
